S.C.R.E

AN EDUCATIONAL FAIRYTALE

MW00886691

BY FRANK STEPNOWSKI

Outskirts Press, Inc.
Denver, Colorado

S.C.R.E.W.E.D.
An Educational Fairytale
All Rights Reserved.
Copyright © 2011 Frank Stepnowski
v2.0

Cover Photo © 2011 Frank Stepnowski. All rights reserved - used with permission.

Outskirts Press, Inc.
http://www.outskirtspress.com

ISBN: 978-1-4327-6848-5

Outskirts Press and the "OP" logo are trademarks belonging to Outskirts Press, Inc.

PRINTED IN THE UNITED STATES OF AMERICA

Table of Contents

Table of Contents continued

People all over the U.S.A loved
Why Are All the Good Teachers Crazy?

"This book saved my teaching career. Teaching can sometimes feel like an impossible task and it can often leave you feeling desolate and alone. Frank's book makes you realize that you are not the only teacher feeling around in the darkness."

-S. Abbot (Whale Cove, Canada)

"Only a teacher who really cares would risk it all to tell the truth. [This book] encouraged me to keep going despite the bureaucratic BS that comes with the profession. I'll keep getting my heart broken because after reading this book, I'm proud to be one of those good, crazy teachers!"

–K. Sobotka-Pokrywka (Philadelphia, Pennsylvania)

"Funny, heart warming, great insight and so well written. Don't let the title fool ya, there is much to be gained by anyone who reads this book."

– C. Grone (Atlanta, Georgia)

"I started reading this book and barely finished the intro before I was updating my Facebook status with how it was going to change my life and the way I look at education. To say that Frank gives us a fresh look at education would be a huge understatement."

–A. Heike (Peytona, West Virginia)

"The author has somehow maintained enough sanity to pen a "must read" for those of us who have become jaded by the everyday perils of "normal life." It's a 5 star read in a 1 star society. After reading this entertaining view on the underside of education, I now wonder if the circus is actually the greatest show on earth."

– S. Jones (West Chester, Pennsylvania)

"I am neither a teacher by profession, or an enthusiastic reader. But I read this book with lightning speed, enjoyed every minute of it. Frequently laugh-out-loud funny, with plenty of knowledge and wisdom for ALL demographics (NOT JUST TEACHERS!) and peppered with truly touching moments, this piece of literature is nothing short of fantastic."

– J. Secoda (San Francisco, California)

...and so did the people from New Jersey!

"As a teacher, I'm a tough critic and very cynical about books written about the teaching profession. I find most of them cute and heartwarming...but I rarely find them realistic in nature. [This book] was a breath of fresh air. I am grateful to read a book that tells the true trials and teachers go through everyday just to maintain some sort of order."

– M. Frey

"Anyone considering working in any level of education should sit down and read this. It will show you the ins and outs of the educational system in ways that no college professor or class could...this book is a mentor before you even walk into a school building."

– J. Sandman

"Finally, a look into what really goes into teaching the kids that not a lot of people want to teach. Frank tells it like it is."

– K. Czapor

"This book sheds light on our country's ineffective educational system and the apathetic individuals who have, over time, allowed it to become that way. This book is designed to infuriate readers about the way our schools are run and dare them to change it."

– K. Silver

"Behind all of the laugh-out-loud stories that Frank recounts in this book, there is one theme that remains as a consistent thread throughout, and that is that Frank loves teaching, loves the kids that he gets to teach and holds in the highest esteem his fellow 'crazy' teachers."

– J. Quinn

"I may sound prejudiced, but I do believe he deserves a whole lot more than 5 stars."

–M. Wilson (the author's mom)

"I haven't read it, but people tell me it is very funny."

– Dr. D. Stepnowski (the author's wife)

"The trouble with most of us is that we would rather be ruined by praise than saved by criticism."[1]

- Norman Vincent Peale

1. Hey students! This is called an **epigraph**; you know, a quote that precedes a book which is supposed to give you an idea about the theme of what you're about to read. Now, if you look at the cover – a screw embedded into an apple (a pretty common educational icon,) read the **synopsis** (summary) on the back of the book, and you read this epigraph, you should be able to use your **context clues** to get a pretty good idea what this book is about...

   Yep, salvation through criticism; well done, smarty pants. Now get reading.

Dedication

This book is dedicated to my dad;

Frank Stepnowski Sr.

a modern day Spartan who did his best

to turn a dense little boy

into an enlightened alpha male.

I wouldn't be half the man I am

if he wasn't the man he was.

S.C.R.E.W.E.D.

Step Comically Relates Exactly Why Education is Doomed.

"…and I'm feeling real shot down, and I'm getting mean."

–Alice Cooper (No More Mr. Nice Guy)

It was exactly 53 minutes into the school year and I knew the entire school year was screwed. We, the collective staff of Descaminado High School had spent 30 minutes drinking juice and eating bagels graciously provided by the PTA. (Actually, I always bring my own coffee and I never eat the free grub on days like this – call it my own private rebellion.) After a half hour of "How was your summer? You look great!" and "I can't believe we're back at this nuthouse," we were ushered, like lambs to the slaughter, into the band room for our first orientation meeting of the year. After 15 minutes of updates and mandates, the floor was opened to questions.

NOTE: any of you who have ever been to one of these dog and pony shows knows that when you are given the opportunity to ask direct, penetrating questions, designed to elicit thoughtful responses and purposeful change, you will receive, in retort, one of the many euphemisms for "oh, *do* shut the hell up so we can continue our glossy presentation on how this year is *supposed* to go." My personal favorite is "We'll take that under advisement." Translation: "Not gonna happen, thanks for playing, and we'll be keeping an eye on you, little Miss isn't-happy-with-the status quo."

At least this year, the powers that be were up front and honest. Our new principal, Mr. Marionette, hit the mute button on all of our concerns about state test scores, safety issues, and all things academic when he issued forth the definitive, albeit inglorious, words of the school board, who let it be known that, and I quote: ***"We don't want to hear the problems, we just want to hear the solutions."***

187 days, 7 hours and 7 minutes left in the school year, and we were already doomed. But you know what they say about people with nothing to lose. I was busy scribbling out a little algebra problem that I planned to send to the members of the board when Mr. Sideburnz (You remember him from the first book right, kiddies? My dark apprentice and expert in all things righteous, punk rock, and literary) peeked onto my paper and quipped, "Don't do it" in a tone of voice that said, "Damn, I was thinking the same thing."

You see, my darlings, I figured it was time that those that made the rules should have to endure those same rules. So I took the liberty of sending each member of the board this problem:

If Area = LxW , and the Length of a yard is 17 ft., what is the Area?

What?

Hey, I don't want to hear your *problems*, I just want the *solution.*

I figured if we could overlook things like the fact that inner city parents don't traditionally read to their kids, that some of the kids we taught simply do not care about school because they're busy earning money to keep the electric on at home, that 25% of our freshman girls were on their first or second pregnancy, that some of the kids being asked to take an 11th grade equivalency exam were only in this country for six months and didn't even SPEAK THE **LANGUAGE** YET, what are a few algebraic inconsistencies between friends?

The responses I got were less than enthusiastic.

Some even bordered on hostility.

Alas, wide are the shoulders borne to bear the load of reality.

The bosses were not happy that their idealism was exposed and, in typical "board of (insert anything here)" form, they tightened the screws on anybody beneath them on the hierarchy ladder. The aforementioned screwing, made manifest in various demands, deadlines and dire prophecies, prompted the following poem to be left in my staff mailbox:

"Twas the day before the students come back and it seems to me, Step hath already managed to piss off the powers that be."

Guilty as charged, Mr. Kaufmadinijad. What? You didn't think I recognized your handwriting? Please.

Now then, back to the matter at hand *yet again* (learn to deal with my easily distracted narrative voice now, folks, it'll make the rest of the reading much easier, trust me.) A quick review of the food chain of the average school system will reveal why education in the country is F.U.B.A.R.

Allow me, your humble servant, to summarize:

In the farthest reaches of the galaxy, far, FAR removed from the realities of inner cities and dilapidated schools, one parent families and gang activity, are the **BIG politicians**, they're more out of touch with what's going on in the classroom than Ozzy Osbourne is with the price of socks, (**NOTE** – *If you're gonna hand me the "black president" thing, stop. Seriously. He's a politician, folks; therefore, he is no longer a color, a gender, or a human, come to think of it. Bottom line, I grew up in the "hood," he didn't, so spare me the insinuation that he, or anybody on Capitol Hill, sympathizes with what goes on in real classrooms simply because they **look** like who I **teach**,"*) so they pass laws that demand the impossible and offer woefully inadequate funding to "support" the accomplishment of their pipe dreams. These unrealistic timelines and baselines annoy the **Senators**, who are busy trying to get re-elected (and "pay back") the small handful of people that funded their $100,000,000.00 campaign for their Senate position, so they water board the **Local politicians**, who chuck the responsibility of educating our youth like a hot potato into the unsuspecting laps of the **Superintendents**.

The **Superintendents**, far removed from their classroom tenure, (like generals who served in battle a long time ago but forget what it feels like to get shot at) nudge the boulder of unfathomable expectations down the hill and onto the **Principals**, who are already up to their necks trying not to get fired for a plethora of things they never thought they would be responsible for; hence, they "delegate" the deluge of dookie in the direction of the **Vice Principals** who (for no conceivable reason) want the job of the principal, who has aged a decade in his first three months, so they *gladly* accept the crappy funding, unrealistic expectations, and ever-changing accountability measures and constantly evolving state tests.

Yes, they gladly accept all of that, for about three seconds before dumping it all onto the unsuspecting **Supervisors**, who are crushed under the weight of a job nowhere near commensurate with their salary, spilling the whole mess onto the **Teachers**, who are then forced to inflict it (in small doses) to a **Student Population** that, at the high school level, probably couldn't read 40% of the words in this chapter.

Allow me to synopsize my synopsis: A leviathan (that's a really big thing) ball of crap travels downhill at frightening speed, ultimately splattering all over the student population that will ultimately bear the burden of not being able to do the impossible with the inadequate; and that burden will then become the burden [in the form of crime, jobless rates, economic collapse, mass illiteracy, global embarrassment, etc.] of the politicians that started the ball rolling in the first place.

Like I said people, screwed.

Foreword:

The voices would like a word with you.

"Voices inside my head; echoes of things that you said."

— The Police (Voices Inside My Head)

Hi everybody! Your humble author here; I'm sorry to bother you with this crap, but the publishers, in conjunction with my psychiatrist (not sure how *they* synced up) **NOTE TO SELF: do not leave the Blackberry lying around during primal scream sessions,** have decided that I should, in their words, "offer some proof that I am, indeed, crazy, so as to further 'validate' the title of my last book, *Why Are All the Good Teachers Crazy?*" Furthermore, they feel that (again, their words) "a brief exposure to my unstable personality and profane tendencies, combined with a little self-effacing humor" will "provide a more smooth transition into the novel and create, in its author, a vulnerable protagonist."

To which I replied (in my words) "What a load of horse puckey! Sounds like a transparent plot to advertise and sell more copies of the old book whilst simultaneously allowing me a chance to poke fun at myself in a cheap attempt to make the reader feel sorry for me, thus overlooking my unhealthy anger, scathing criticisms and foul language. *My* readers (I said, again this is *me* talking now) are far too intelligent and insightful to be tricked by such an obvious appeal to their vanity. I won't do it."

So my publishers pulled the plug on the book.

So I called Oprah.

She didn't answer.

So I called one or thirteen other publishing companies.

They didn't answer.

So I called my publisher back and said (in my words,) "after careful consideration, I think a brief exposure to my unstable personality and profane tendencies, combined with a little self-effacing humor might be just what this book needs! However, most people judge a book by reading the first few pages so there's no WAY this stuff is going first!"

"That's OK," they hissed, "put what you want first, *then* include this as the *Foreword*."

So here goes: I'm going to let a few of the more prominent voices in my head talk to y'all for a few minutes. They will have a short leash and I'll have my hand on the 'mute' button should they decide to try to take over... as they so often do.

"Ladies and gentlemen and... other?"

Yes?**Yes?** yES??

"The nice people from the place that sign daddy's checks think you should be allowed to talk to the nice people for a few minutes. Do you promise to behave?"

...

I said, do you promise to behave?

Yes.**Yes!** yES?!

Very well, have at it, then.

Well, it's about damn time he let us talk!

Easy! Too much too soon and he'll shut us down, take 'er slow for now.

And then?

Right... then we let the bastard have it.

i wANNA tALK

Relax, you. You'll get yer chance.

oH, oK – bUT I gOTTA lOT tO sAY.

Fabulous...

Listen, the big shot author (and right now I'm making those quotation mark thingies in the air) decided to let us, the... um, the...

Extensions of his personality

Thank you, "extensions of his personality" have our say right here in the beginning of the book so as to... how did he put it?

nOT sCReW uP tHIS bOOK LiKE wE dID tHE lAST oNE!

Not distract the reader in this particular text with myriad narrative voices.

tHAT aIN'T wHAT i sAID

Shut UP.

sORRY

If you don't mind.

Sorry.

sORRY

Right. So Mr. "Oh–I–wrote–a–book–I'm–so–freakin'–awesome" decided to write another one. Lucky you. Furthermore, he decided to let us, the righteous and reptilian impulses that serve as his muse, speak the truth about the pompous twat, and...

Ah, ah ah...

Right. Start small, build up, before he shuts us down.

Correctomundo.

So, what shall we tell you about Frank Stepnowski?

pSSSTTT! hE cALLS hIMSELF sTEP, rEMEMBER?... tHAT'S dUMB

Ah, YES! How could I forget! Frank Stepnowski has become, for better or worse, "Step" to most of the world outside his wife and kids.

Self-important much, "Step?"

Aaaaanyway, "Step" has issues.

No kidding. He's letting US talk, out loud. Get to what they don't know.

THEY dON'T kNOW hE aSKED fOR aN ALLIGATOR pUPPET fOR hIS 42nd bIRTHDAY!

Thank you. I'm sure the readers are riveted. The truth is, the narcissistic twit did ask for an alligator puppet for his birthday because he – get this – dreams of someday being on the Late Late Show with Craig Ferguson and talking about his book, and CraigyFerg uses an alligator puppet in some of his monologues. I know, I hear you. This kid has delusions of grandeur, right? That ain't the half of it. Listen, can I take the kid gloves off now?

Actually, I think I'll take it from here.

But…

But nothing.

Fine.

bUT I dIDN'T gET tO…

Shut up.

oK

This Frank Stepnowski, Step, whatever the heck he's calling himself today is a character all right. For a guy who reads ALL THE TIME you'd think he could write better. I kid you not, this kid has reading material (the kind with no pictures) stashed at every toilet, on every table, and in every nook and cranny of his existence. Dude reads more than he [CENSORED], and that's saying something, he…

This is your version of insightful?

Piss off. As I was saying, dude reads ten thousand pages of everything a month and this is only his second book. If you don't count all that angry poetry he wrote as a teenager, Man *that* shit was messed... (mute)

Apparently, our beloved creator has a limit to what he'll allow us to divulge. So that I don't get "muted," I'll get to business of getting down to business. Let's clear some things up about the author and this book you're about to subject yourself to for no apparent reason: Step, despite having a great family, great life, great job, and great abs...

tHAT lAST oNE iS a LiE

Ahem, he's listening.

oH

...despite ALL of the aforementioned coolness, Step is angry. A lot. In fact, he is in a near constant state of pissed off-ness. Hence this literary baboon turd you're holding. Apparently, "shit head Shakespeare" wasn't content being marginally funny and locally successful. Nay, he felt compelled to spray his venom about the educational system all over the toilet seat of the literary world. It seems he still thinks that anybody gives a sh... (mute)

oH gOODY gOODY! i gET tO sAY tHINGS! mR. sTEP iS nOT sO bAD. tRUE, hE cONDUCTS iNTERVIEWS wITH hIMELF iN fRONT oF tHE mIRROR aND hE sTILL sECRETLY wANTS tO bE rICH sO hIS wIFE wILL fINALLY rESPECT hIm aND hE oNLY wORKS oUT sO hARD aND gETS tATTOOS 'cAUSE he iS rEALLY iNSECURE aNd ... (mute)

tHAT dON'T mAKE hIM a bAD pERSON!!! (I said MUTE!)

OK. Sorry about that. I really thought letting the fellas have the floor might prove insightful; you know, start the book off with some pithy commentary before attacking everyone and anything with little regret.

Didn't work.

Everything they said was a pack of lies.

Except the "abs" thing.

And the alligator puppet.

I love my alligator puppet.

Don't you judge me; I'm young at heart, you bastards.

At any rate, it's time to get started weaving another tangled web (metaphor) of stories so I can sit like a spider (simile) in wait; then when the educational system flies into my trap(personification) "I can attack it with great and furious anger (allusion.)"

Christ, he's at it again.

Freakin' show off.

i tHOUGHT aLLUSION wAS a mAGIC tRICK

Excuse me for just a moment won't you?

Oh, crap, he heard us.

Well you were kind of loud...

i lIKE mAGIC tRICKS

Ladies and gentlemen and... other?

Yes?**Yes?** yES??

The audience is already confused, and I need to get the actual book started. I gave each of you a chance to offer some insight into me but you wasted your time taking shots at my eccentricities. Now, this person paid good money for this book so I have to get down to the business of impaling the educational system and/or making this very patient reader laugh.

Gonna do that all by yourself are you?

No angry inner voice?

Or surgically, albeit verbose, commentary?

oR sLIGHLY iNSANE rAMBLING??

And what about the REST of US??

Oh, I'll call on all of you from time to time. But for now...just me and you, gentle reader, just me and you.

THE 800 POUND GORILLA SQUATS OVER THE INDUSTRIAL-SIZED EDUCATIONAL FAN

"We just get by, however we can. We all gotta duck, when the shit hits the fan."

– Circle Jerks (When the Shit Hits the Fan)

The Day this Book was Born.

"I've had enough of bein' trodden on. My passive days are gonna be long gone. If you slap one cheek well, I ain't gonna turn the other."

– The Who (Had Enough)

Ladies and gentlemen, before our ride begins, please remember to keep your hands and feet inside the restraints and secure all valuables and small children. Anyone with a weak constitution, heart condition, or chronic fear of the unedited truth may want to evacuate the ride now, and step to the left toward the clearly marked exit signs. Please know in advance that this book, like most amusement rides, will suck almost as much as you love it.

O.K., I started the last book by telling you that I became a teacher because I thought most teachers sucked. I exorcised a lot of demons and told a bunch of funny stories that many people wanted committed to paper, and I got a chance to thank a plethora of folks that deserved to be thanked. I figured it would take a good long time before inspiration hit me that way again.

Yep, that's what I figured; until I asked an innocent question to one of my co-workers.

The first book had been selling pretty well thanks to word of mouth and the supreme dedication of a few great people and the selfless acts of countless others, and it was even starting to get some attention in papers, radio, and other outlets. However, every time one of my industrious students or supportive peers submitted an article on the book to the local Descaminado township newspaper, it was tossed into the waste pile.

"Hey Mr. Amaretto," I asked one of my forthright and righteous colleagues, "the talking heads in this place are constantly telling us to push the positive stuff. So why won't they promote a published author in the English department of their High School?"

He looked at me like I had made a suggestion that was about a mile past ludicrous, "No way, Step" he replied, "there's too much heavy stuff in that book. The profanity, the violent stuff; they'll never promote that."

I was floored and, for a rare occasion, speechless. I just shook my head, retrieved my copies from [the divine and always helpful secretary] Joy C., and walked back to my room. To say I was pissed would be an exercise in obscene understatement.

Soon, my prep period ended and I finished another day of educating the youth of America. The *minute* the last student of the day left the room I actually said, out loud, to no one in particular:

"I'll tell you what my book *DIDN'T* have in it! It *didn't* have teachers getting reprimanded for not being able to establish "academic baselines" for kids who lived at different locations every night, didn't speak English at home, or made more money dealing drugs in one week than their teachers did in a month. It *didn't* have a few hundred kids who live in a different (and much worse) city going to another school illegally under fake addresses diluting an already troubled school with gang and drug activity and apathy that lowered already poor state test scores! It *didn't* have a school that allowed kids to graduate despite tons of unexcused absences, failures and write-ups, and it most certainly *didn't* have a student who, after being refused admittance to the alternative school after recently being released from incarceration found and (after grabbing the attention of a teacher and other witnesses) brutally murdered a neighbor's dog and was then caught, with heroin in his pocket, by police – only to be re-admitted a few days later!"

I could go on at length, believe me. No, my first book didn't have any of that. My first book didn't have a lot of things in it – because at least the people at Moorzakunt Academy, my previous place of employ, knew what they were, a group of tragically flawed people trying hard to teach a group of bad kids.

Clearly, the powers-that-be in the Descaminado school district, the ones that were "embarrassed" by the "heavy stuff" in my first book were traveling up that river in Egypt.

You know, De Nial.

I don't know much, gentle reader, but I know this for certain: if you don't *admit* your problems, you'll never fix 'em. In fact, they will probably get worse because crap can very quickly become the status quo; and *that* got me to wondering...

I wonder how many other school districts are so busy covering their asses that their heads have gotten jammed up in them? I wonder how many other parents, teachers, administrators, students and tax paying citizens are FED UP with people claiming to be "in it for the kids" when all they're really interested in is protecting their weak, pathetic, non-accountable posteriors?

Yeah, I got to wondering.

Then I got angry.

You wouldn't like me when I'm angry.

Then I started writing... again.

No, my first book didn't have quite a few things in it,

but *this* one will.

If that statement entices you, congratulations – you are my *target demographic!*

If that statement scares you a little bit, then you are my **target**.

This book is a bit different than the last one. *Why Are All the Good Teachers Crazy?* was a "fictional" (nudge nudge wink wink) recollection of things that happened to me as I made my way through the turbulent waters of the teaching profession. S.C.R.E.W.E.D is more of a cathartic response to the post-traumatic stress disorder that any caring person involved in education suffers from; it's also a dark fantasy about what kind of school would be necessary to fix the layers upon layers upon layers of bureaucratic bullshit that has [accidentally or very calculatedly] made it nearly impossible to teach kids effectively in our current educational system.

Some of my muses came from whispers heard in teacher's lounges. Some came from "alcoholically liberated" declarations at happy hours. Some were born [unfortunately] from very real situations that I witnessed in the hallowed halls of academia. Some came from straight talking, good-hearted but frustrated teachers, administrators, and parents; but most of them came from the inky black shadows (memories?) in the corners of my mind. So, as always, if you want to point the finger at someone, point it at me but, as always, be prepared to have that finger broken and shoved up your ass.

Everybody strapped in?

Good.

Everybody comfortable?

At least for the moment?

Good.

Let's begin then.

Enjoy the ride.

Step

I Ain't a Village.

"It takes a village to raise a child. It takes an army to march a mile, yeah."

– Black Stone Cherry (You)

Hillary Clinton said: "it takes a village to raise a child" and, believe or not, I agree with her. What Hot Stuff Hillary failed to mention (because she doesn't live *anywhere near* the villages where my students live) is that A TON our students *are* raised by their villages.

And those villages are fuuuuuucked up.

I'll try to forego repeating the litany of problems that you already know affect our student population: single (if that) parent homes, teenage pregnancy, gang affiliation, drug problems [for the kids, their parents, or both,] etc., all combined with a rapidly increasing social belief that to be intelligent and respectful is somehow "wrong" and "lame."

What I will do is tell you three stories.

The first one I heard waiting in a barbershop, the second while shopping with my daughter and the third is from my own personal war chest of agony. I tell you these three stories, not because they're particularly different or any more extreme than the thousands of other stories I could tell you, (in fact, they're not nearly as bad as some of the ones I've heard,) but because I heard, or re-lived, them all within a 48 hour time period, in three vastly different areas, which leads me to believe that things are tough all over.

While I believe that these stories may be eye opening to a good chunk of the population that don't fully realize what teachers are up against, the infinitely depressing reality is that many of you will read these stories and say "I can top that."

Like I said, the villages [that are raising our kids] are not exactly the "therapeutic settings" needed to manifest healthy, intelligent, well-adjusted kids with good self-esteem.

Especially when those kids are, literally, eating shit.

Yes, you heard me correctly.

I was waiting for my man Joseph to work his magic on my sons at Sulimay's barbershop in Fishtown (best haircut ever, 10 bucks) and I got to talking with a young guy who overheard that I had written a book about the crazy stuff that happened to me as a teacher, and he told me that his wife was an elementary school teacher in Philly and that she didn't know how much longer she could keep doing it. I told him that I sympathized, and after talking for a while he told me about a recent event that had really disturbed his young wife; seems that she had a nine year-old boy in one of her classes that came to school sick that week. The boy asked to go to the nurse, and upon being granted permission, was gone for almost the entire period. Naturally, the young woman called to verify that the boy had, indeed, been in the nurse's office the entire time. He was, and he was sent back to class shortly thereafter. When the teacher asked if he was ok, he replied that he was fine and "that it was just something that he ate." Shortly after, child services appeared at her door, requesting that the young boy go with them. When the young lady inquired what was going on, and pointed out that the boy had said he was just sick from eating something, the social worker asked, "Did he tell you *what* he ate?" I'll spare you the graphic details, but the boy's mother was a drug addict, (no dad at home, I know…shocking) and when the boy complained of being hungry, his psychopathic 15 and 13 year old brothers held him down and force fed him feces. One can only wonder why that poor child doesn't care about his math homework.

The pathetic part of that story was that, before the young man telling me the story was finished, my youngest son Frankie (who was 11 at the time) whispered in my ear, "the boy ate poop, didn't he?" because he had heard me relate a similar story a few years before when I worked at my former school. That story should never have been told once, let alone twice. But hey, powers-that-be in the educational system, let's focus on achieving "Adequate

Yearly Progress" on the state test scores, right?

Idiots.

Fast forward to the next evening, and my daughter and I were shopping for a Christmas present for mom, so while Sam roamed the aisles looking for something I can pay for but that she can take credit for, (smart kid, that daughter of mine,) I ran into a guy I know whose son (we'll call him James) teaches elementary school in New York. Since he, too, was doing the "wait for the child to spend his money" routine, we got to talking, he asked me how the book was doing and I, in turn, asked how his son was doing. Turns out he had just spoken to his son on the phone, and his son told him about something that happened that very day (which was, for the record, two days before Christmas.)

Being the day before Christmas break, the classrooms in James' elementary school were doing the "Christmas party" thing. One of the little girls (we'll call her Tori) in James' homeroom couldn't seem to stay awake, and didn't want to eat any of the cookies, cupcakes, etc. at the party. When James got down on his knees and asked Tori if she felt alright, she responded, very drowsily, said that she was "just tired from looking for mom." Further inquiry led James to find out that Tori and her grandma spent more than a few mornings a week, before school, searching the abandoned houses in their neighborhood for Tori's mom, (Again, no dad. I sense a theme developing, don't you?)a crack addict who continually traded the welfare and child support check, if there *was* one that month, on drugs. So this little girl was looking for her mom in a crack house, before school, two day before Christmas. But hey, powers-that-be in the educational system, let's focus on "collecting quantifiable data" so as to properly measure student achievement.

Douchebags.

That night, we had a few people over the house, one of which was a bloke I taught with at my former place of employment (let's call him Emmit) and, of course, I told him about the stories I just told you; whereupon he mentioned a name from my past in the following manner:

"Talking about that kind of stuff, what ever happened to Randall?"

"Damn," I replied, "I almost forgot about Randall."

"Yeah," he admitted, "I was surprised his story didn't make it into your first book."

Oh well, better late than never.

Randall Flagg (named changed, of course, to protect…well, everybody) was one of the walking wounded at Moorzakunt Academy, an approved private school specializing in the care and education of children with a myriad of emotional, educational, and psychological crosses to bear. Randall was a bit younger than the guys I was used to having in my class. If you'll remember, (or if you're new to my ramblings,) I dealt predominantly with male students, ages 16 to 20, that were, to put it mildly, the ones that NEVER played nicely with others. Enter Mr. Flagg, age 14, but so "completely incorrigible, so vile," and "so beyond the reach of the educational system" (not my words) that he was promptly plopped into my room because "if Step and his boys can't control the little shit, nobody can."

Thanks a lot, administration and counselors. I'm working miracles here with the "criminal element" and you decide to reward me by dropping this little detonator into a room of ticking time bombs. Say it with me, folks: "no good deed goes unpunished." Before I go off on THAT rant, let's get back to Randall's story, which I will summarize for your convenience:

I launched a pre-emptive strike on Randy before he ever set foot in the actual room in the form of a quick "listen, if you get your shit together and start acting somewhat sensibly, people will say 'oh, *he* just needed a strong male role model,' (because, go ahead, say it… right! **No dad!**) and *my* reputation will grow by leaps and bounds. So you see, we can help each other here, and *you are in complete control* of your situation, so you decide how you want to handle this."

Randall Flagg liked that scenario, and it was all high fives and good vibrations until about three or four months later when he came in on a Monday morning and promptly announced that "he wasn't doing shit" and that I had "best leave him the f—k alone."

"Good morning, Randy." I quipped

"Don't play with me Step," he mumbled, "or I'ma go the f—k off."

"Go head off then nigga!" snarled Tyree and Ray, in no mood for Randy's drama on a Monday morning, "so we can f—k yo little ass up."

Well, *that* did it.

Randall William Flagg lost it. He turned over his desk, spat at Ray and, on his way out of the room, deliberately flipped over the picture of my late son Cain that I kept on my desk. It was that act, deemed nothing short of suicidal by my maladjusted but very loyal teens, which saved him from certain doom. Even I knew that for him to violate the one item deemed sacrosanct by everyone that knew me was a five-star cry for help.

So I tried to help him.

I tried to talk to him.

He punched me in the face.

Then he cried,

A lot.

That was my first experience with a kid that really, truly, *wanted* to be locked up, beat up, or given up for dead. Randall wanted to be anywhere but where he was. I'll bet a lot of you can guess why. When I drove him home that day (long story, don't ask) we pushed open what passed for a front door and I saw why Randy was imploding.

Suffice it to say, Randy finally got his wish, and his self-destructive behavior led him to be placed in a residential facility, where he continued to act out until he ultimately wound up behind bars. His mom, the empathetic matriarch who had sabotaged her son's academic and social progress by demanding that he "get his ass out there and sell [drugs]" so they could keep the lights on, was upset only that her source of income was now beyond her control. She was left with her house, which contained nothing but an old beach chair sitting in the middle of an empty, rat-infested house. The image of Randy's copy of

I Am Legend (a book we were reading in my class) and his notebook sitting under a bare light bulb on the bare floor near a blanket and a pillow still makes me want to simultaneously vomit and commit homicide to this day.

Alas, such are but three stories; and there are a million stories in the naked city, and countless more than that nationwide. However, knowing full well what lurks in the underbelly of our student population, the politicians and the school boards continue to preach a system of education that handcuffs teachers and creates a black hole of information that makes it nigh impossible to teach these kids what they need to know in the way they need to be taught.

It takes a village to raise a child.

I ain't a village.

And I suspect that, even if I were, there are a lot of people that would burn me down, because they simply do not *want* many schools to succeed, because they do not *want* a population of educated young people that will evolve into educated, empathetic adults; **because stupid people are easy to control**.

And with these thoughts in my head, and more than a few Bombay Sapphire and tonics in my bloodstream, I fell asleep after the company left and…

He's not really going to say it, is he?

Yes, he is.

I HAD A DREAM! A dream that someday, in the not too distant future, the elephant-sized shit will hit the industrial-sized fan, and the educational system in this country will perform the function that it was designed to do.

It will collapse.

Rising from the rubble will be a new type of school, a type of school based on harsh reality. Born of a sense of insightful desperation and willing to function as the instrument of righteous cruelty needed to whip our fractured youth back into shape.

But who would lead this readin' and writin' revolution?

I said, who would lead this revolution…

Well who the heck did you think it was gonna be?

Sarah Palin?

The nut jobs from Acorn??

Spongebob Squarepants?!?

Don't look at me like that, and don't you judge me, DON'T YOU JUDGE ME!

After all, it's only a dream…

One man's trash is another man's treasure

"Take it from me, parents just don't understand!"
    –DJ Jazzy Jeff and the Fresh Prince (Parents Just Don't Understand)

Just another beautiful October day in Descaminado High School. I was busy team teaching with Sheryl Arbora, a fresh faced, hyper-motivated addition to the English department at D.H.S We were unleashing the allegorical levels of Sophocles' *Antigone* on a class full of 17 year-olds that were trying harder to act interested in Sophocles than I was trying not to look at Ms. Arbora.(Super hotties are not uncommon in the English departments of America.) In the middle of our Greekly tragical extravaganza, a news update was broadcast into our classrooms. It seems that the president had passed something known as The Absentee Parent Act of 2012, and things were never going to be the same again. We immediately got the internet running through the Smartboard (sorry for all the teachy-techno-talk. Bottom line: we started broadcasting the reactions to the new law into the classroom via a big computer monitor.)

Seemed like a good idea at the time.

NOTE: I'll be honest. I voted for John McCain in the 2008 election. I thought the media-manufactured "Maverick" war hero would do a better job of pretending to run the country than the as-yet-untested-walking-race-card-rock-star. That having been said, when President Obama passed the A.P.A. during the last year of his first term, I sent an E-mail offering to mow his lawn and trim the hedges, maybe do some nice topiary in the shape of a conservative donkey, or a bipartisan elephant, or Bill O'Reilly. *That* would've jolted the commander-in-chief awake every morning.

Truth is, I dig O'Reilly; his reaction to my T.E.A.M. approach to scholastic reform was enthusiastic to say the least. I even said I was willing to go on his Fox News T.V. show provided Megyn Kelley did the interview. I'd let her grill me like a Memorial Day hot dog, (phallic pun intended.) My news anchor frankfurter fantasies aside, President B.H.O dropped the metaphorical bomb that essentially launched my first "alternative methodology" school.

But I digress.

When the president passed the A.P.A of 2012; hereafter jokingly referred to in teachers' lounges as the "Obama gonna hamma baby mamma" bill, people started scrambling for educational placements that would do what schools had always done.

Raise their kids for them.

Only this time, they actually got involved in the scholastic process because they faced the very real possibility of going to jail if they didn't. I know, fucking awesome, right?

The Absentee Parent Act was a 1,073 page document that said, and I'm paraphrasing here, " every 'baby daddy' and 'welfare mom' out there who are ignoring their kids, or using them purely to cash an SSI check, had better get their collective asses in gear and start actually raising their children (preferably better than they, themselves, were raised) or they would receive a free course in responsibility via the state penitentiary, where they could learn to schedule classes on the value of proper parenting in between a full schedule of senseless violence and anal violation. "Lest those six figure income parenting conglomerates think *they* were beyond the law, the A.P.A stated: (and, again, I'm paraphrasing,) "you self-righteous cocksuckers that think your gross annual income gives you the right to let your arrogant little offspring raise themselves are horribly misguided, and you had better start working the little princess and the little prick into your iPhone calendars, because if Brittany and Hunter continue to throw away perfectly good educations in your absence, they'll be visiting your bloody white collars in the land of rape and honey."

There's more, but I think you get the point. The law was put into effect at midnight, Friday, September 13, 2012 amid much fanfare and, as you might expect, nobody changed their behavior in the slightest way.

Until *October* 13, 2012; hereafter referred to in hushed tones in mini vans and supermarket lines as "the day Big Brother stopped watching and started shitting on the fan.

"Ms. Arbora, a room of suddenly attentive seniors, and I sat riveted to the in-class broadcast, watching scene after scene of parents being taken into custody for ignoring their parental duties. There was a plethora of screaming, crying, attempted bribing, and at least one televised episode of pant soiling.

I think I spoke for all of the teachers when I finally shouted: "HO-ly long overdue Batman! This is the greatest day in the history of education!" I would have said more, but the moment that forever changes my life intervened, in the form of one woman who was televised being dragged from her Hummer hybrid with 26" rims. As the camera closed in on her frantic eyes, streaked black with tears and L'oreal eye shadow, she screamed loudly and clearly into the TV:

"They want me to raise my kids, but what the hell do I know about how to raise these little bastards?!? You can't trust the churches, they're full of pedophiles, the military doesn't want them because they can't even read, and THE SCHOOL SYSTEM CAN'T CONTROL THESE KIDS, LET ALONE TEACH THEM, so what the hell is a parent like me supposed to..."

Click

The TV went off, and the light bulb over my head went on.

"I don't like the way you're smiling," observed Onyx.

"You're not thinking about what I think you're thinking about?" inquired Katherin.

"What happened to the TV?" wondered the newly awakened Jose.

The rest of the commentary from room 113 was lost to me, as I was in the middle of an educational epiphany:

"The schools, the way they are now - can't control these kids, let alone teach them."
I thought.

"So what the hell are parents, desperate parents, supposed to do?" I thought.

"What is *up* with the TV?" moaned Jose.

I snapped out of my daydream of world domination and into action. I promptly walked down the hall, around the corner, and into Mr. Marionette's office.

"I quit!"

Mr. Marionette muted the TV he had been watching and turned to me, his hands folded to conceal a wry smile dancing upon his lips.

"Somehow," he responded, "I knew you would."

"I totally dig this job, I've spent the best years of my life here, and you were totally cool to give me this teaching gig, but..."

"But you have something you need to do," he finished for me.

"Yes."

"Somehow," he smiled, "I knew you would."

I turned to leave, filled with the original ideas that would soon manifest themselves in the first T.E.A.M. (**T**rust in our **E**xtreme **A**lternative **M**ethodology) school when Mr. M. fired his parting shot:

"Hey Step?"

"Yes, sir?"

"For all of us...go all the way, or don't bother."

"Yes, *sir.*"

It was then that I left the classroom and moved into the big office that I never get a chance to sit in for very long anyway. I was about to start a new chapter in American education; a chapter, it turns out, that a whole hell of a lot of people were waiting to read. I was about to become the P.R.I.N.C.I.P.A.L. (**P**erson **R**esponsible for **I**mplementing the **N**on-**C**ompliance **I**nitiative for **P**unishment **A**lternative **L**earning) of a new kind of school. The kind of school that could, with ruthless efficiency and tough love empathy, reverse the downward spiral that is education in America. Like the doctor says: "this may sting a bit, but you'll be all better when we're done."

Interested?

If not, I completely understand.

But *just in case* you are, welcome to the T.E.A.M.

BRIDGE BUILDING BEGINS
WITH BRAVE WORDS
AND
BLOODY KNUCKLES

"Discipline is the bridge between goals and accomplishment."

– Jim Rohn

Hey non-English teachers! An exposition is a literary technique wherein the author (in this case, played by yours truly) provides the reader (in this case played, and very well I might add, by you) some background information to inform the readers about the plot, theme, etc. Basically, it's me telling you some stuff now that will keep you from saying: "What the hell is that? Did I miss something?" later.

Exposition:
Change You Don't Have to Believe In.

Fast forward a few years (from 2012 to 2015 to be specific.) A few things have changed. Actually, a lot of things have changed but I'll get you up to speed on the ones that y'all need to know for purposes of clarity. The world did *not* end in twenty twelve. Of course, the pile of Mayan calendar bullshit hadn't even attracted flies before the profits of doom (No, I didn't spell it wrong; think about it) dropped the "we're all gonna die in 2020 and the signs can be seen in the hidden messages of the Alien vs. Predator movies" theory.

Idiots; but I digress…

1. We finally got around to electing Oprah Gail Winfrey President of the United States, relieving her from the pressure of actually running the country from behind the scenes while simultaneously creating the illusion of maintaining her media empire.

2. Scientists announced that they had perfected the cryogenic freezing process and that for 4 easy payments of a whole lot of currency you could become a well preserved popsicle that could be re-animated at a later date as per your request. Geeks everywhere rejoiced (we knew George Lucas had inside information on government projects!) and rich folk whined (can't we have aaaanything just for ourseeeelves?)

3. Jim Morrison emerged, very fat and very well read, from Nimes, France and Tupac came out of hiding from prairie province of Saskatchewan, less tattooed but more forgiving. Nobody gave a damn.

4. The fallout from the *A.P.A. of 2012* was, to put it mildly, significant. Absentee parents finally, under threat of painful retribution, remembered that they cared about their kids but (simultaneously) recalled the fact that they didn't have a clue what to do about that. So, armed with liquid cash they made working while the kiddies ran rampant, they turned to the people that had been raising their kids for generations – the schools. Of course, most of the schools were stuck like great, lumbering Wooly Mammoths of incompetence in the tar pits of bureaucracy.[1]

NOTE: The unemployment rate dropped like a stone after the whole *lex talionis* law was passed and murderers started getting put to death, crooked CEOs were fed to the people they robbed, and illegal immigrants that committed crimes were immediately deported, etc. but that's a whole other book

Which led to…

5. The first T.E.A.M. School got up and running. I tried, I really did, to get it going right after the *A.P.A.* dropped, but thanks to the fact that I was a white, middle class, middle-aged male that was actually born in this country and paid my taxes every year, I was mired in a legal holding pattern for several years until I could get any funding, permits, etc. to get up and running. I love the smell of irony in the morning!

6. President Winfrey, having suffered the slings and arrows of starting a school herself (Leadership Academy scandals of 2007 and 2009 anyone?) called me and expressed a sincere, altruistic desire to see the T.E.A.M. schools succeed, and offered her support in whatever capacity I deemed necessary.

7. There was a bunch of other stuff, but I'll save some of the tasty nuggets for later. (Got to give you some reason to keep reading, right?) Besides, the Jim Morrison/Tupac holographic video transmission (*LA Woman* with Tupac rapping *California Love* over the chorus) debuts in five minutes and I need to see this. OK…so I gave a little bit of a damn.

1. And THAT, kiddies, is how you construct a kick-ass metaphor!

Disci-p-l-i-n-e,

Find Out What It Means to Me!

"All I'm askin' is for a little respect when you get home"

– Aretha Franklin (Respect)

May 20, 2015.

Wow. My dream was about to become a reality. The doors of Cortezz Academy Alternative School, which would shortly become the New Jersey entity of the T.E.A.M. school movement, would open in 103 days. The world was watching and, being the world, waiting to for us to fail miserably.

Crap. My dream was about to become a reality. We already had a waiting list, a basic curriculum, and a profusion of highly motivated teachers and staff ready to do their jobs the way they had always envisioned doing them. I was elated. My sphincter was tighter than a crab's ass (and that's watertight, son.)

What is my priority? What is the one thing that will immediately separate us from the schools that have, by my calculations, failed in the past? Well, the mission statement says that …no, fuck that, enough rhetoric, you never get a second chance to make a first impression. What will define us, here in the embryonic stages of our development, before we have time to learn from our mistakes?

"Go back, asshole," said a loving voice from inside my head. You knew exactly what you needed to change when you were in the trenches. What? Too much time filling out paperwork and going to meetings make you forget? Then go back, boy, and get angry again.

Thank you, said I to nobody in particular, I shall. I went back to visit Descaminado High School, the last place I taught before setting off on my occupational odyssey. I walked the halls, looking for a sign that would tell me what would be the signature of my school of the future. What needed to change the most, right off the bat, for education to truly…

"Man, step off. Bitch-ass mofucka, I'm a grown-ass man."

I turned the corner to see a slightly disheveled young teacher that looked weary (from dealing with such nonsense when he should've been teaching) trying to get a simple answer from a young man who was clearly being noncompliant.

Turns out the teacher, whose name was Mr. Smartino, simply asked the student, whose name was Mr. Cliffs, for a hall pass. Mr. Cliffs, who was out of uniform, talking on a cell phone (not allowed,) and in the hallway without a pass, ignored Mr. Smartino. Mr. Cliffs then proceeded to get threatening, rude, and profane when Mr. Smartino had the audacity to do his job by asking Mr. Cliffs for a pass.

Mr. Cliffs, God bless him, solved the philosophical question I had ventured into these halls to answer. This did not, however, change the fact that Mr. Cliffs was about to take part in a little experiment; which he volunteered for when he started cursing at Mr. Smartino, and that he solidified his involvement in when he looked at me and sneered: "The fuck you lookin' at, old man?"

I smiled, for so many reasons.

Then I began talking to Mr. Cliffs, in the velvet-tongued way the fox asked the Gingerbread man to move closer to his mouth, as I moved toward him slowly, but with clear purpose: "You know, many are the young wolves who have had their throats torn out thinking that the "old" alpha male was ready to relinquish his position."

Mr. Smartino saw what was coming, and stepped back.

Mr. Cliffs, Allah bless him, did not.

*"Da **fuck** that supposed to mean? I know this, you best back up offa me before I pop off. I'ma do what I **want** 'cause I'm a grown assed man up in this piece, and…"*

Translation: "What, sir, are you saying exactly? In lieu of an explanation, I'll tell you what I think I know, that you would be advised to stop walking toward me, as I am about to lose my temper and (being a "man") may have to damage you physically in some way to manifest my frustration."

So, before we get to what went down between Mr. Cliffs and I, allow me to drop some knowledge on you. I always love it when I'm forced to confront a teenage boy who, for any number of reasons, needs to be made aware that his behavior is unacceptable in civil society. I particularly love it when said teenager gets belligerent; mainly because nobody ever tried talking to him and explaining this sort of stuff. (Read: no dad)

This is what we call, in the education profession, a "teachable moment."

Anyway, this inevitably leads to the child posturing and threatening, which invariably leads to me pointing out *in a completely professional manner and with politically correct vernacular*, that I am most certainly NOT the person to be engaged in such a manner. This usually leads to one of my favorite lines:

"I'm a grown assed man." (I always feel the urge to inquire as to whether the child's actual buttocks are grown to a set parameter, or if perhaps that's not what he means. I never do get around to it.)

So, for the benefit of any and all of the males that I have ever encountered, will encounter, or any of you at all, for that matter, I offer the following nugget of wisdom:

Real men do not have to *tell* people that they are men.

If you have to *tell* me that you're a "grown assed man," you're right.

Minus the "grown,"

minus the "-ed,"

and minus the "man,"

Bill Gates doesn't have to tell anyone he's rich,

Bruce Lee didn't have to tell anyone he was tough,

And I don't have to tell you I'm right.

And now back to our story…

Where were we? Ah yes,

*Da **fuck** that supposed to mean? I know this, you best back up offa me before I pop off. I'ma do what I **want** 'cause I'm a grown assed man up in this piece, and…"*

BRANG!!

That's the sound a 6'1",185 lb. miscreant makes when slammed unceremoniously into a locker by a 6' 3", 270 lb. apex predator that's not ready to relinquish his position at the top of the food chain. Said restrain*ee* (upon realizing that his strongest efforts to break free lead to excruciating pain at the cost of very little effort from said restrain*er*) quiets down in expeditious fashion, which is good, because the restrain*er* is just warmin' up.

"And **nothing**, *little* boy. Oh, you were *finished*? Good. You don't know me, and you do… not… want… to. Clear?"

"Man, you ain't allowed to…"

BRANG!!

"*As* I was saying, you are breaking at least five rules that I can think of off the top of my head, which means you're probably used to breaking rules, *and getting away with it.* But I don't play by the rules here, either, 'cause I don't work here, so there's nothing stopping me from taking your grown-assed spine and snapping it like a fucking *toothpick*. And I think we both know that nobody would *miss* you. Am I right, *little* boy?"

Mr. Smartino smiled.

Mr. Cliffs, Zeus bless him, soiled himself just a tiny bit, a fact that would've gone unnoticed had he not had an asparagus omelette for breakfast. It was at this point that Officers Gotchaler and Officer DeChiefs (the on-campus police officers of Descaminado High School) arrived, having been called by Miss Lexliner, who took umbrage when anyone but her made the students' lives miserable; small wonder that she was adored by many.

"Sir," commanded officer Gotchaler, hand on his baton but not looking too anxious to use it, "please step away from the asshole."

"Tom," interjected officer DeChiefs, "Smartino says that James here was being totally belligerent and non-compliant when Mr..."

"Stepnowski." I assisted.

"...when Mr. Stepnowski intervened."

Gotchaler responded, correctly, "That still don't give him the right to assault him."

"Even though *you've* always wanted to," I implied.

Officer Gotchaler eyed me, temper simmering just below boil. "James, get to class."

"What?!? Dis nigga gonna put his hands on me and..."

"Now." Demanded Gotchaler, "*Before* I remember why we're all out here in the first place."

Mr. Cliffs, Ra bless him, knew when to zip it and fled to the safety of a poorly managed classroom run by a teacher that wasn't particularly interested in his return.

"Now, Mr...Stepnowski, is it?" inquired Officer DeChiefs, "We have a few questions for you."

"I have one before you begin." I countered. "You guys want a job?"

I'll spare you the details, but Tom Gotchaler and Jean DeChiefs became the two-headed Cerebus that guarded the gates of my first T.E.A.M. School. They also became prime shareholders, savvy bastards that they were. Apparently, dealing with the student population on a visceral level every day led them to believe that extreme alternative schools where altruistic ass kickers replaced politically correct pussies might just turn profit. We were just laughing about that the other day over Coronas at the shooting range on Tom's yacht.

Question: What would be the immediate, obvious thing that set *my* high school apart from the ones that were currently lumbering along like manatees trying to run the Death Valley 10K? (A brutal, but real, race - look it up!)

Answer: Discipline.

Immediate,

righteous,

I-don't-give-a-fuck-what-you-think,

you-wouldn't-*be*-in-this-school-if-you-didn't-need-this,

and besides, your legal guardians signed off on it,

DISCIPLINE.

One hundred and two days and counting. Suddenly, I can't wait.

There's no left eye in T.E.A.M.

"I am the result what's better left unspoken Violence begins to mend what was broken"
– Lamb of God (Omerta)

April 1, 2016

"Can't a nigga go the bathroom without a grenade going off?! This school gets on my damn nerves!" This was about the third time Jacques Tatum got caught in the hallway during one of my "lateness checks," and it never ceased to be entertaining.

"Jacques," I replied in a voice that concealed my obvious delight, "One, don't use the 'N' word, even with the "a" on the end. Two, it's not a grenade; it's a riot control *device* that hurls little plastic balls in a variety of directions at an incredibly fast speed. Three, your parents understood and approved the methods I employ at this school before they paid to send you here."

"You always say that shit," mumbled Stevie Jones, barely audible, as his hand revisited a scar on his forehead left by an earlier don't-run-in-the-hallways-because-surprise-we're-trying-out-fishing-wire-today "incident."

"That's because that *shit*," I echoed in the relaxed tone of someone who had given this speech before, "happens to be true. Every one of the people who cared enough about you to send you here signed contracts saying that they agreed with how we do things; and how we do things, occasionally, hurts."

"I was taking a …"

"Save it, Jacques, you were in the bathroom too long which led to your wandering the halls, which led to your unfortunate bruising. Steve, if you weren't running in those same halls, your forehead wouldn't have a line across it. Lisa, if you hadn't…

"I know, I know," Lisa whispered, in a voice that sounded like she was crumpling up a napkin from her lunch tray, "if I hadn't tried to steal that walkie-talkie, I wouldn't have this scar over my left eye."

Well *that* quieted them down.

About fucking time.

When I first received approval for the loan that would eventually become the down payment for what would eventually become the Cortezz Academy Alternative School that would eventually become the first in a chain of T.E.A.M. (Trust in our Extreme Alternative Methodology) schools, I never dreamed that people would bend over backwards to get their kids into a school designed to, as it says in the brochure: "employ a variety of alternative methodologies designed to immediately rectify poor academic performance and anti-social behavior."

Who am I kidding? Of *course* I dreamed that this idea would take off like a rocket. After dealing with asshole Superintendents, chicken-shit administrators, guiltless, clueless, enabling parents, and lazy, arrogant, violent, stupid, non-accountable students for over 30 years as a teacher, I had a pretty good idea what it would take to really change our educational system for the better. I'm not talking about the kind of "change" president B.H.O. promised back in 2011 before he got caught up in that little "educational funding controversy," leaving us with No Child Left Behind (The Director's Cut Edition.)

Nor did I mean the "change" that president Schwarzenegger authored during his abruptly ended tenure. (Killed by a sub-machine gun – irony, anyone?) And I certainly didn't mean the kind of "change" that self-appointed monosyllabic monarch King Alberto Gorey tried to usher in, along with the monarchy, when he dumped the 'No Kids Can't Read' initiative on an uninterested public that wondered, "isn't that the global warming douchebag whose wife is dating the singer from Megadeth" before changing the channel to American Idol.

No, my savvy reader, I was going to bring real ch-ch-ch changes to the academic world. I was going to send a shock to the system. I was going to drop the hammer on all the students, parents, administrators, and politicians who thought that the educational status quo was sufficient. In the now immortalized words of my first customer, Pope Peter II (upon dragging in his less-than-compliant nephew, Santino:)

"About fucking time."

The ideas that eventually manifested themselves into the subterranean educational revolution that eventually became the capitalist coup of the century started as daydreams.

I would be standing at some bullshit staff meeting or in-service training, (I *had* to stand because if I sat I would've been out like a light in minutes,) and I'd be thinking:

"Wouldn't it be great if, instead of long-winded meeting filled with thinly veiled references to certain non-compliant staff members, the powers-that-be would just call the offenders on the carpet [in private] and put their asses on notice that their job security was in serious jeopardy?

Wouldn't it be great if, instead of discussing, over and over again, the same five to ten percent of the student body that were CONTINUALLY non-compliant, disrespectful, and *useless*, we could say to them: "you're entitled to an education *some*where, but (since you're a detriment to the overwhelming majority of kids that actually *want* to learn) it ain't here, and don't let the door hit you where the good Lord split you?

Wouldn't it be great if, instead of a million convoluted (and thus impossible to enforce) rules, the entire system relied on the ancient wisdom of *an eye for an eye?*

Wouldn't it be great if things like *time served* and *tenure* couldn't save the fat, uninspired twats that stopped working on their craft and starting simply coasting (at the expense of the district and the learning of their students?)

And wouldn't it be great if only the inspired, hard-working people that really CARED about their students kept their jobs, because administrators stopped measuring them based on "quantifiable data" like *time served* and *test scores* because they're no longer afraid of losing their jobs to politicians who only understand 'quantifiable data' like *time served* and *test scores?*"

Wouldn't that be great?

I thought so. So I became the P.R.I.N.C.I.P.A.L. of my own school. A place where improved social skills, a sense of empowerment and (gasp) above average academic achievement led to the reduction of low self-esteem, which led to the reduction of anti-social behaviors, which led to... well, you get the point.

Turns out there were a *lot* of people who were fed up with the lowered standards, tolerated violence, and half-assed teachers that saturated traditional schools; turns out, as well, that they were willing to part with a lot of their hard earned money to send their kids to a facility that set high expectations, **demanded** behavioral compliance, and weeded out complacent teachers like radiation on cancer. And how did we do this?

With strict discipline, raised expectations, simplicity of curriculum, solidarity among the staff, and love.

And, of course, the occasional riot grenade in the hallway.

To quote Secretary of State X's great great grandfather, "by any means necessary."

There's always room for Hardjello.

"So go ahead and act tough, like you're John Wayne's son; but things can change fast… I could kick your ass"

— Justin Moore (I Could Kick Your Ass)

Needless to say, in a scholastic setting such as the one we choose to maintain at our T.E.A.M. locations, there will always be those non-compliant young whippersnappers that think, (largely due to their previous experiences of being *allowed* to get away with everything short of murder in their old schools) that they could do the same here in the hallowed halls of my new reality.

They can't.

This, of course, doesn't stop 'em from giving it the old I'll-never-go-to-college try.

Which is why, when I started the T.E.A.M. schools, I recruited a certain breed of teachers from the ranks of those I had previously worked with.

Enter one Peter Hardjello. Despite the weird last name, Peter the great was strong, smart, and extremely volatile in an *I-care-about-you-enough-to-beat-the-shit-out-of-you-to-teach-you-a-valuable-life-lesson* sort of way.

"Do you have a pass young man?"

A simple enough inquiry.

"Pete was on hall duty, and there but for the grace of God went a student, (let's call him Charles) who happened to be out of uniform, ignoring him, to his locker, which is not allowed between periods. That would be strikes one, two, *and* three."

So here he was, young Mr. Hardjello, making the terrible faux pas of actually *doing his job* and asking a kid for a pass. Pete stepped up to the young perpetrator like the sheepdog approaches the sheep. The problem? Sometimes the sheep don't *know* they're the sheep.

"Man, back the fuck outta my face," suggested Charles, *"I'm gettin' my shit for gym."* (NOTE TO PROSPECTIVE EMPLOYEES – you can spot such sheep pretending to be wolves easily: pants hanging off ass, large hooded sweatshirt or T-shirt, cell phone out and a dull look in the eyes that comes from willingly throwing away an education.)

"I'm not in your face…yet," chimed Mr. Hardjello, "and I simply asked you for a…"

"Man nobody asked you to follow me to my locker motherf---"

Have you noticed that dialogue at my T.E.A.M. schools often goes uncompleted?

"Young man, I am simply trying to…"

"Tsk! Bitch, I'ma warn you, you best back off afore I pop off on your big ass! Now back up offa me!"

At this point Charles thought it would be prudent to push Mr. Harjello so as to emphasize his point. Mr. Hardjello, whose deltoids resemble small cannonballs, thusly became the iceberg to Charles' seriously misguided Titanic; employing his unique brand of what I shall call, for lack of better verbiage, behavior modification.

The silence that followed the aforementioned "behavior modification" was deafening.

At least until I arrived, doing one of my daily hall sweeps.

"Morning Peter, nice of you to clean the floor." I remarked, smirking.

"Good morning, Mr. Step," he sang, "just dragging, er, *taking* this troubled young man to the re-education room."

"I assume you cashed in one of your cards for this. How many do you have left?" I inquired.

"Uh, I think I have one right here. Oh wait, I might have my last one for the month right in this…"

"Carry on Peter," I sighed, "you can borrow one of Mr. Duncan's cards, he never uses them, God bless him. I honestly don't know how he does it."

And so continued another day at… what's that?

Oh, you want to know about the cards.

Silly me, I assume too much; the cards, yes, one of our better ideas.

Read on, child.

It Takes a lot of Heart to Club a Spade on the Diamond.

"You got to know when to hold 'em, know when to fold 'em"

– Kenny Rogers (The Gambler)

So you want to know about the cards? Well, I appreciate your inherent curiosity (and the fact that you dropped hard-earned coin on this "book") so I'll tell you the whole story. Actually, I'll tell you even if you didn't spend your pesos on this book, 'cause I love you in a non-touching kind of way. (Unless your name is Scarlett Johansson and you happen to be reading this book, in which case I love you in a very definite touching as much as you want kind of way.)

But I digress...

The whole concept of the cards started with a 4'11" social studies teacher named Victoria Gonzalez, who was known very affectionately as Smalla Abdul.

It all started when one of our politically incorrect new admissions, a 17-year-old Vietnamese boy known as Than Spade, told Ms. Gonzalez to, "kiss my ass, bitch, etc." before bumping into her – all because she was foolish enough to ask him to stop talking on his cell phone in class. Mr. Spade was subsequently escorted to the re-education room, and he now understands three things very well:

1. A bitch is a female canine and not a term used to describe a female social studies teacher.

2. A cell phone is a wonderfully diverse piece of technology that doesn't need to be used in the classroom.

3. The human knee is a hinge joint that was designed to only bend *one* way.

Later that day at one of the bi-weekly happy hours that I funded,[1] Smalla Abdul accosted me with all the fury of an intoxicated Chihuahua.

"You shhhould give ush cards! Like get outta jail free cardsh! Kid pishes you off, you get to crack him! One hit per card."

"That's an interesting idea, Smalla. I'll think about…"

"Think shmink!! You should DO it! That would put the fear of God into 'em."

"I said I'll think about.."

"It WOULD!! Fear of God, one hit per card, little ffffuckers." And off she went.

Mr. Hardjello and Mr. Brian Capz, approached me with *cat-that-ate-the-canary* smiles on their faces.

"What was that all about, boss?"

"Ah, Peter and Brian," I purred, rubbing my hands together with relish, "two rocks upon which I've built my church. THAT was a diminutive history teacher giving me a grrrrreat idea."

The following Monday found my entire staff bitching and moaning about an impromptu staff meeting. You see, even though they were all teaching in their dream job, the bitching and moaning about staff meetings never ends.

The complaining was replaced by high fives and cheering when I formally instituted the newly minted "Gonzalez addendum" to the disciplinary code: Two cards a month per teacher, one clean hit (above the waist) per card, no eye gouging, fish-hooking, etc. Any unused cards could be redeemed at the end of the month for $200 each.

I think somebody actually started 'the wave' in the auditorium.

1. Note to my fellow administrators: a few Coronas w/lime (at your expense) a month go a loooooong way toward healing minor emotional cuts.[2]

2. Oh my Gawd! He's encouraging student abuse *and* staff inebriation?!? What kind of monster is this man?!? One who understands the words WORK OF FICTION.

Tuesday at 12:00 I described in detail, much to the chagrin of our already posttraumatic student body, the new rule. I moved some funds around and started the month with $4,000 dollars in the reimbursement fund and two slightly modified playing cards per teacher.

I ended the month with $4000 dollars in the reimbursement fund and a *significantly* less confrontational student body.

Not that the system wasn't prone to occasional acts of over zealousness.

Smalla Abdul, on a particularly beautiful day for baseball, marched into the center of baseball practice with an 8 of clubs and a Queen of hearts and unleashed a vicious 1-2 combination on our Vietnamese third baseman. I've also heard it whispered that Coach Capz slid Smalla his 3 of clubs so she could finish the job.

Who says sports doesn't build character and camaraderie?

Captain America.

"I thank God for my life, and for the stars and stripes, let freedom forever fly, let it ring. Salute the ones who die, the ones that give their lives, so we don't have to sacrifice, All the things we love."

— Zac Brown Band (Chicken Fried)

I am a patriotic guy. I love my country. I support the troops that train, fight and die for me and my family to have the life we enjoy. Freedom is not free, I understand this. I have friends in the Marines, the Army, and the Navy SEALs, and believe you me, when I think I'm working hard, I need only think of them and that shuts me right up. I know far too many families that have lost children, spouses, and the loved ones in the line of duty, and I remember every single one of them. While I take issue with some of the policies and decisions our government make (and what rational person wouldn't?) that doesn't stop me from professing my love for the U.S.A. to the point that some of my more snarky friends have taken to calling me "Captain America."

So it come as no surprise that when Darrrell Negron, refused to stand for the Pledge of Allegiance because *"this country is bullshit and I don't give a shit 'bout no dead soldiers."*

I bitch slapped him.

It was our first year at the original T.E.A.M. School, and I was still putting some time in the classroom while we fine-tuned the curriculum and raced to meet demands for enrollment that were expanding faster than the waistline of an Italian girl after the wedding reception.

> • **NOTE: Now just *wait a minute*... if you read my first book, I made it <u>perfectly clear</u> that I'm a fan of the full figured gals, (still waiting for a call Latifah!) so put away your pitchforks and torches ladies.**

- **CAVEAT:** After this chapter was completed, it was revealed that Queen Latifah came out as a lesbian; therefore <u>all</u> non-photo-shopped women with curves may now apply.

- **CORRECTION:** My wife, the statuesque Dr. Dawn has asked, (via full Powerade Zero bottle to the head,) that I clarify: I am kidding. *BONK!*... and blissfully happily married.

Darrrell, whose name I am NOT misspelling, if that's any indication of the shallow gene pool this troglodyte emerged from, was one of the members of our inaugural class and he was, how can I put this delicately? An ignorant, racist, misogynistic, violent piece of shit.

I first encountered this charmer when he was introduced to Ms. Zeeno, our mild mannered, terribly polite librarian. She asked if there was anything in particular that Darrrell liked to read.

Darrrel replied, and I quote, *"you best back da fuck up offa me, you white ass bitch. I ain't readin' no books and I ain't doin' no..."* His charming retort was cut short as Mr. Hardjello stepped in between Darrrell and me, in effect preventing me from cutting our enrollment down by one. Pete, who was known to break a few living things on occasion, had the cooler head at this time and thus prevailed. He unfolded a piece of paper, hovered dangerously close to Darrrell and reminded him that his only known guardian, his mother (big shock there, right?) had authorized, in writing, notarized, in duplicate, the use of ANY... MEANS... NECESSARY to maintain a safe academic atmosphere in this, his new academic home. The three main words were punctuated by pokes to the chest that were subtle enough to be non-damaging but obvious enough to say **please, ignorant little child, do something foolish so I might honor this contract of which we speak with the primitive joy of a grizzly bear on a wayward salmon.**

By now, a crowd of enforcement had gathered, including officer Gotchaler and officer DeChiefs, so young Mr. Negron allowed himself to be escorted from the library with a parting shot at me:

"Youz a bitch ass mufucka who thinks he gonna do something!"

"And the best part of **you** ran down your mother's leg."

The fact that that retort came, with frightening clarity, from the aforementioned Ms. Zeeno hit the mute button on our proceedings. Mr. Hardjello and I took our leave into the hallway. I moseyed up to the officers and Darrrell and whispered in the victim's ear:

"I might be a bitch ass mufucka, but I'm also your English teacher. (I still taught a few classes myself.) See you tomorrow at 7:15 a.m. in room 113, buttercup." I blew him a kiss and went my merry way before he had a chance to respond and dig himself into a deeper hole.

7:15 a.m. and Darrrell and the rest of my first period English class sauntered into the room as the soothing resonance of a D chord faded in the distance. That "riot control device" we set off in the hallway last week sure did the trick, no tardy little children today. The morning announcements began and I had to watch myself, against a blue and black backdrop repeating the commandments that each student and staff member of T.E.A.M. Schools would adhere to, along with any other pertinent information. No "birthday shout-outs" or "team spirit" shit. Sorry. We've got a lot of work to do cleaning up other people's messes; thus, all killer, no filler.

NOTE TO SELF: might want to re-think black and blue as the school's colors; furthermore, looking a bit creepy and politician-y on the pre-recorded morning announcements – may want to consider a suit in earth tones, maybe a flower on the desk.

Once the morning announcements commence, the classes stand for the Pledge of Allegiance. While I didn't fully understand the significance of this ritual when I was in school, I do now; not because of something I learned in class, but because of something that an older gentleman that served overseas told me in a conversation in my late teens. I'll leave the quiet dignity of that conversation private, if you don't mind. However, I learned, as many of us do, that Pledging Allegiance to our Flag doesn't mean you condone everything your country does, but it does mean that you respect the sacrifices made to keep this country free and that you appreciate the freedoms you have.

Even if one of those freedoms is to be a five-star asshole.

Which brings us back to Darrrell.

All of my teachers are expected, in respectful and authentic terms, to explain some version of what I just said to their homeroom students, thus facilitating a basic understanding of why they should (and will) stand for the Pledge of Allegiance. For my part, I employed a strategy that I have used for years in my classroom. I hang pictures of soldiers, some dirty, some bloody, some dead, around the flag. I tell my students that if you don't understand why you should respect the flag as an icon yet, at least show respect for those people that suffer in silence for you every day. 99% of the time that works like a charm, and it often opens up dialogue that helps me stimulate the repressed patriotism lurking just below the defensive postures of many of our "damaged goods" teenagers.

Yep, works 99% of the time.

Which brings us, for real this time, back to Darrrell.

Darrrell refused to stand for the Pledge of Allegiance because and I quote, verbatim: *"this country is bullshit and I don't give a shit 'bout no dead soldiAAh-hahhhCRASH!"*

When Mr. Negron disrespected a woman in front of me that was strike one, two, and two and a half. When he expressed his lack of respect for all things American…

Strike three. You're out.

Well, not *totally* out…not yet.

I had, with enough force to get the point across but not nearly enough to bruise or break anything, put Darrrell on his ass, at which time I thought it might be pertinent to elaborate on the precariousness of his current situation, in terms as delicate and literate as I had at my current disposal:

"Stay down, SHUT up and listen, you skinny little *turd.* You're in this school because you never learned how to behave in civilized society. That changes TODAY. I'm sorry your dad ran away and didn't do his job." At this point, D.N. started to get up, but I said "don't" in a manner that even his narrow ass understood as a threat to his physical well-being *for life*. "I'm sorry your mom doesn't seem to be able to control the child that she obviously loves, and I'm sorry that you've reduced me to this type of behavior. Nonetheless, I have an entire school of people relying on me to create an environment of safety and learning, and if you plan to disrupt that every day then please know that I will fucking ***hospitalize you*** long before you get the chance."

Remember those cameras everywhere? They work. So it should come as no surprise that officer DeChiefs arrived in a timely fashion with one of our new security members, Mr. Treusch, a former Marine with a heart of gold, a head for Asian philosophy, and a body like the gorilla bouncer from *Who Framed Roger Rabbit* – all in all, one of my better hires.

Darrrell was rrrestrrrained, with minimal rrresistance, and taken to a YuCKy room. Having been through this type of nonsense about a million and one times, the students and I quickly resumed class; since it was early in the year we were about to…huh? What's a what? Oh…sorry, YuCKy room, right. Again, I forget, us being friends and all, to explain all the new wrinkles unique to T.EA.M. schools.

YuCKy rooms are the evolution of what used to be called "Beta Rooms" at my first job at Moorzakunt Academy. Basically, it was a place where an out-of-control student was taken, allegedly, to calm down, reflect on his/her inappropriate behavior, and speak to a counselor. Hmmmph… hmmmt… sorry, I don't mean to laugh but, ppphhhtt, hmmmph… sorry. Let's review: angry student, physically restrained, to a room with no surveillance, and forced to pour his heart out to some fucking twit that doesn't know, or care to know, the kid. I'll let you fill in the blanks with how that usually went. I got a look at the slightly more evolved manifestation of this farce in the form of ISS (in-school suspension) during my second tour of teaching duty, at Descaminado High School. During ISS, students [who had repeatedly violated the school's code of conduct] were expected to *do work all day, quietly, that they collected from their teachers* while a plethora of teachers on "duty" periods supervised them one period a piece. I'll give the logic of that approach a minute to sink in. Students, who obviously don't give a fuck about the rules, expected to collect make up work, then take the initiative to do it on their own, while being supervised by a bunch of teachers watching the clock so they can get the fuck out of there as soon as their time is up; pure genius, right? What could *possibly* go wrong? Well, as my dad was fond of saying: "Don't bitch unless you've got a solution and the ability to make it happen." Such was the genesis of the YuCKy rooms.

YuCKy is a pretty lame acronym for "You're in Control, Kid." The YuCKy rooms were places where, given *one* chance to responsibly atone for whatever action got them there, the kids could ask for whatever staff member(s) they felt a kinship or trust with, and they could engage in [what we hope was] some meaningful dialogue about the offense in question. Much more often than not (or the YuCKy rooms would have been ChuCKed) these dialogues resulted in some self-awareness, a tighter bond between younger person and peer, and sincere, non-pressured apologies. Mr. Sideburnz came up with the brilliantly childlike acronym, understanding two vital principles of dealing with volatile kids.

Uno – If the kid feels like he's in control of the situation [even if he most certainly ain't,] he will be much less likely to resort to less civilized means of expressing his frustration.

Dos – It's really hard to stay angry when you have to say funny words like "yucky."

I'm not sure how Sideburnz discovered these principles, being young, single and prone to Hooters girls orgies and Jagermeister-related cupcake tattoos on his buttocks. (1/3 true. Wanna know which third? Buy some Jager, put on your wonder bra and go looking. You, too, ladies!

I, however, discovered the "funny words keep you from being angry" principle when my son Mason, as an infant, seemed to revel in shitting and pissing on me during diaper changes, whereupon my slightly older daughter Sam would, without fail, laugh and say "icky-poo!" Hard to stay mad after "icky poo," folks; even now I smile, and swear I smell old milk.

But enough reminiscing, back to our class. We were about to pick up where we left off in Aldous Huxley's classic *Brave New World* when I noticed 17 year old Christian LaFleur looking at me with that look that a tiger has been known to give the zookeeper with the steak.

"Something you'd like to add, Mr. LaFleur?"

Same look, only now, upon closer inspection, did I notice just the hint of tears welling up in young master LaFleur's eyes.

"Something you'd like to add, Mr. LaFleur?"

"Thank you."

"For?"

"My brother Bobby was a Spec. Ops guy in Operation Desert Storm and..."

He had to stop for a minute, so I let the weight of his words hang there for just a few seconds, then: "I'm sorry, son, I really, really am."

"S'okay," he replied, composing himself, "but I was about two seconds away from ending that little..."

"Got it" I cut him off, before he verbally incriminated himself, "glad you didn't have to do anything you'd regret. Can we move on?"

The general reaction of the crowd seemed in approval of that idea and hey, I'm all about the will of the people so...

Epilogue

I tried, more than a few times, to talk to Darrrell about, well, anything. I put in an inordinate amount of time trying to find a staff member, a student, a coach, that established some sort of connection with him. In hindsight, I had a better chance of finding a Brazilian boy that didn't know what a soccer ball was. Darrrell made no attempt whatsoever to ingratiate himself to anything with a pulse, including our four legged friends (Darrrell was later cited for cruelty to animals in an episode that I, for the benefit of dog lovers everywhere, will abstain from relating at this time.) or those without a home to call their own. One weekend, approximately two months after joining the ranks of our student body, our little cherub was involved in a gang initiation that involved *beating a homeless man to death*. Lacking whatever emotional darkness it takes to actually participate in the murder, he chose instead to (according to witnesses) laugh at and taunt the homeless victim, and later act as a witness against the perpetrators. Oh, yeah, Mr. Negron was making friends and influencing people on both sides of the law. He's currently hiding out in witness protection somewhere until the gang that I shan't name but who favor blue-ish tones finds him.

So, you ask, what is the lesson hidden here? Actually, the lesson isn't really hidden at all; it's just been so deeply repressed that we refuse to see it.

Some people simply cannot be saved.

There, I said it.

I look forward to your letters and Emails.

Some people, and make no mistake about it they are rare, are simply beyond wanting or deserving redemption, at least on this Earth. Furthermore, I think we have a hard time identifying the Darrrells of the word because we spend WAY too much time worrying about political correctness and the emotionally sunburned feelings of a nation of people with victimization complexes. We simply refuse to confront people, even when they're completely inappropriate or non-compliant, simply because we're afraid of having to get to know them a bit better, hurting their feelings, or dealing with their lawyers.

Fuck 'em.

Darwin? Survival of the fittest? Works for me, and it sure as hell (according to last year's T.EA.M. financial reports) seems to work for a large percentage of our population here in the old U S of A. If you think about it, starting a chain of schools that hold people accountable for their actions, take the time to emphasize personal relationships, and demand compliance to a set of rules designed to get everybody working might,

just might,

have been instrumental in returning us to the *shut your mouth, work together and get it done* mentality that CREATED this country.

Captain America, indeed.

Our children should sit on Satan

"Ye are of your father the devil, and the lusts of your father ye will do."

John 8:44

Sometimes, albeit rarely, the drudgery of having to indulge parents who think they know what's best for their children long after they've paid perfectly good money for you to reverse the error of their ways leads to an amusing anecdote. It doesn't happen often, but an unpleasant event can lead to a nice little surprise, kind of like when you flush the toilet after a particularly tedious session of putting the kids in the pool and the toilet paper gets caught up in the watery vortex and tickles your business on the way down. I love that.

Oh, sure, that's just *me*, right?

Liars.

I was just about to run out to Dunkin' Donuts and grab enough coffee to fill a small kiddie pool for myself and the secretaries when I made the ill-advised decision to respond to "just one more phone call" before I went on my quest for a copious cadre' of caffeine.

I know, I know…what the *HELL* was I thinking?

I pushed the answering service button and was greeted with the oh-so-soothing sound of an angry parent telling me how his daughter was being unfairly treated by one of my teachers. (Just for fun, pinch your nose a little and repeat the following testimony to why stupid people shouldn't breed in that tin can voice that the answering service provides:)

"Uh… hello, Mr. Stephanowkis… hello… I think I got the machine… what? No, I'm telling him now. I SAID I'm telling him… uh, hello, Mr. Stepanooski, this is Aqua Marinara's father and I helped her with that homework, you see…"

NOTE to reader: I have no honkin' clue what homework he's talking about and I only know who Aqua Marinara is (off the top of my head) because she's constantly in trouble, usually for cheating.

"...so I really don't compreHEEEEND how she coulda plasticized. I mean, I helped her with the vocabularic elements of her... I'm talking to him now! Yes! I'm telling him that I helped her! Sorry, Mr. Stepanovich, as I was saying, I don't see how Aqua could have plasti, pager, what? Oh, PLAGiarized. She couldn't have done that, I mean, I helped her..."

NOTE to reader: If you're completely baffled right now, give it a minute and I'll translate. If you're not confused, good for you! A teaching career is in your future, should you ever decide to take a massive pay cut and experience the joy of migraines. But let's get back to Mr. Marinara's diatribe, shall we?

On second thought, let's cut to the chase. Aqua's daddy thought his daughter was being unfairly accused of plagiarism because he helped her with her analysis of Edgar Allan Poe's *Masque of the Red Death*. The first thing I did was call in Aqua's English teacher, the seemingly ubiquitous Mr. Honeycomb who, I was certain, has done all due diligence regarding this matter, especially when he showed me Aqua's paper, and then he pulled up an internet site dedicated to the analysis of a certain melancholy Romantic author. Does the word *verbatim* mean anything to you? After a few laughs I dismissed Mr. Honeycomb and thanked him for his time.

Note to <u>administrators</u>: this is how these kinds of meetings should be conducted: Are you right? Are you sure? Can you prove it? You can? Thanks, I'll take it from here.

Note to <u>teachers</u>: Have your shit together so the aforementioned meetings go as I just described.

And so I rang up the Marinara residence to defend my teacher, illuminate the parent, and prepare the student for the forthcoming repercussions.

Oh, that it went that smoothly, but that wouldn't make for a very funny story now would it? Mr. Marinara implied that perhaps, because *Poe was his favorite in college* that perhaps he, *dare he say, wrote better than Poe* and that's why I was confused.

"Did you just imply that you're a better writer than Edgar Allan Poe, sir?"

"No, I don't think that's what I said."

"Yes, it is."

"What I meant was..."

At this point, MISsus Marinara took over, having functioned up to this point like the Greek chorus, chiming in from the rear of the stage. She demanded a meeting, as I clearly didn't understand the importance of stigmatatizing (her word, folks) children.

Any of y'all ever had one of these "parental concern" conundrums that went from bad to worse, but led to a story that you would inevitably re-tell at happy hour, family parties, etc.?

Yeah, something like that.

I had already given the Marinara parental unit too much of my valuable time. Their daughter had cheated, blatantly, and was caught; furthermore, she was trying desperately to get her parents to back off because she KNEW she was busted and didn't want them to compound her impending doom. I tire quickly of virtual Egyptian parents who sail down de Nial and try to turn their kids into little non-accountabilisauruses in the process. People like them are the reasons I opened my own school.

Suffice it to say, I was sharpening my fangs when *dos Marinaras* arrived.

Nonetheless, professionalism has its price, so I sat them down, offered them beverages, maybe a scone? "No, not a snow cone, a scone, it's a – never mind – what can I do for you today?"

MISsus opened up with a handwritten, clearly practiced oration that made MISter beam with admiration, Aqua wince with embarrassment, and yours truly clench his ass cheeks to keep from spontaneously combusting into hysterics.

Note to <u>the reader</u>: If this was a true story, I might have secretly secured the first page of said letter, knowing that I would use it later in a book. This is pure fiction, however, because none of the parents out there could *possibly* author such a letter as the one that follows:

Our children are delicate flours. We must treat then as such, and accept except their mistakes. Educators sit in there comfortable chairs, but our children should sit on satan and shine like the sun. False accusations can hurt as much as fists, and we must be carful not to jump before looking both ways before we cross the street...

Must I continue?

No?

I thought not. Truth be told, I interrupted once we got to the "false accusations" part.

I do admit, though, I have always contemplated calling Ms. Marinara back and alerting her to the fact that while she meant to imply that the children of tomorrow should park their delicate posteriors on SATIN, or another reasonably royal material, she had, in fact, suggested that we plop our youth ass first onto the no doubt pre-heated lap of the Fallen One. Maybe one of these days after a few tequilas...

Anyway, I cut her off after the "false accusations" part, set her straight that her daughter cheated, her husband may have helped her but that Aqua chose to ignore his "better than Poe" assistance, choosing instead to cut and paste right from a third party source the minute her parents went to bed. She got caught, she would be punished, the end. I left out the part that Aqua's worst punishment was going to be sending her back home with the two dipshits that conceived her, but hey, professionalism is my middle name.

Total time spent on this problem (including prerequisite paperwork): 3 hours

Total time that should have been spent on this problem: 10 minutes

Learning/teaching/valuable time lost: 2 hours and 50 minutes

Number of times this happens every day in schools countrywide: You don't want to know.

Cost to the taxpayers: You *really* don't want to know.

I believe there's a lesson in there somewhere.

In the meantime, let's just let our kids sit on Satan and see how it goes from there. I mean, it can't be any worse than throwing 'em up on Santa Claus at the mall at Christmas, or making them sit on Aunt Becky's lap at Thanksgiving, or having them sitting around waiting for Superman.

T.O.Y to R.I.F. in 72 HRS

"My road of good intentions led where such roads always lead. No good deed goes unpunished!"

— Idina Menzel (No Good Deed Goes Unpunished)

"What are those?" inquired the entirely too perky Ms. Radley.

"Those, my dear," I replied, "are the new cameras. No more *it wasn't me or I wasn't part of that*. Now we can see, in glorious high definition, every square foot of each of our T.E.A.M. facilities. Two people can monitor the… uh, monitors; saving time and money and punishing the wicked in expedient, biblically righteous fashion.

"Wow," Radley replied, in a way that made you think chocolate wouldn't melt in her mouth, "President Winfrey doesn't fuck around."

O.K., maybe the chocolate wouldn't be so safe. "No, indeed, Madame President is quite happy with the speed with which we are rectifying the educational mistakes of her predecessors, and with her happiness comes…"

"A shitload of grants and technology." she chirped.

Yes, the chocolate would be in definite jeopardy on the tongue of Ms. bubblier-than-thou. "Correct as usual, Ms. Radley. Now ask me what those generator looking thingies at the end of each hall are."

"Oooh, Mr. Step," she purred, with all the fake sexual attraction of a Las Vegas escort, "what do thooooose things do?" (Eyelashes batted for dramatic effect.)

The look I gave her said *your job is already secure as a result of your character and teaching prowess but thanks so much for the ego boost.* "Those things transmit, with the touch of a button, our hallowed halls live, in streaming Technicolor, to the T.E.A.M. network, so parents can…"

"Watch their little cherubs from their T.V.s and computers and phones."

"Correct again, little Miss clearly-not-attracted-enough-to-stop-interrupting-me."

"Sorry, boss," she fake apologized.

"Your incessant perkiness affords you a great deal of leniency, Ms. R."

"To say nothing of my perfect attendance, ever rising state test scores, and community outreach programs," she reminded me with incessant perkiness.

Duly chastised, I couldn't help but smile. It was that sort of *fuck-you-I-don't-need-tenure-to-protect-me-I'll-just-be-so-awesome-you-wouldn't-dare-fire-me* attitude that attracted me to teachers like Radley. "You'd be amazed how many parents take a vested interest in the academic careers of their children when they can monitor them at will; and, as an added benefit…"

"You have the eye in the sky on the teaching staff 24/7 as well," chimed in the newly arrived Mr. Joshua Psicopata.

"Not that I have anything to be concerned about with *this* fine staff," I countered. (Eyebrow raised for dramatic effect.)

"Of course not," he smiled, "but it's nice to have, right, Big Brother?"

"Oh, it's always nice to know that your staff is doing what they're supposed to do, *and be where they're supposed to be…* LITtle brother."

"Now that you mention it, I was just on my way to my conversational Spanish class (something new we were trying at T.E.A.M.) and I just thought it would be imprudent not say hello to the boss and the lovely Ms. Radley. Hello, boss. Hello, Ms. Radley. Must run – children to teach, you know!" and with that young Mr. Psicopata was off to save the youth of America from not being able to tell what their landscapers were secretly whispering about them.

Actually, it was my wife Dawn (who had recently vacated her medical position to oversee the finances of our exponentially exploding chain of alternative to the alternative schools) that suggested hiring the dynamic young Mr. Psicopata. You see, he had recently been laid off 72 hours after being named Teacher of the Year at his old school and…

What's that? Oh, you don't really want to hear that story, do you?

You do? Well, far be it for me to ignore the needs of my audience.

It all started on a rainy day in late May. *

My dark apprentice, Mr. Sideburnz, told me that he had nominated his BFF (best freakin' friend) Josh Psicopata for recognition by the Philadelphia Phillies baseball organization that, in goodhearted fashion, recognized 10 teachers from the tri state area, once a year, for excellence in the field.

I've been told that other MLB teams perform similar acts of altruism but, having been born and raised in the mean streets of the *City of brotherly what the fuck are **you** lookin' at*, I was particularly intrigued. Not so much in the pageantry, but I figured any teacher on Sideburnz's radar should be filling out an application for my school. Unfortunately for me, Josh Psicopata was very loyal to the New Jersey high school that hired him, and he loved his students too much to leave. Compounding matters, he [deservedly] won the 'Teacher of the Year' honor and was, with all due pomp and circumstance, honored in front of 47,000 rabid Phillies fans and one homoerotic Phanatic. Alas, once your name is on the jumbotron AND your peers speak about you to a packed house AND your image is in all the local papers AND you're featured in a local newscast AND you're cheered upon returning to your school AND a Youtube video of you winning the award goes viral…well, your job is as safe as the porn stashed at the Vatican.

Oh, you'd *think* that wouldn't you?

*Students! You DID catch the <u>assonance</u> (repetition of vowel sounds for poetic effect) there, didn't you? You did! Excellent, my little kittens, you shall have some pie!

Sadly for the students of Alistair Heduparass High School, Mr. Psicopata taught there during the tenure of governor *"let's cut spending on everything even remotely related to education but not on my buffet budget"* Tom Tommie. Thanks to this hoppity-horse looking academic Armageddon in a suit, young Joshua found himself in possession of a *"hey, we've gotta let you go due to a reduction in funding"* letter in his mailbox 72 hours after being recognized for his excellence.

T.O.Y to R.I.F. in 3 days.

I simply cannot make this shit up, folks.

But of course, I did, 'cause this is a *work of fiction.*

Thank you, governor hoppity horse[1]. Thank you, Heduparass High. Welcome to the revolution, Mr. Psicopata! Josh signed his contract in angry red Sharpie. I found that strangely poetic.

Lost in reminiscence, I almost forgot I have a school to run – a teensy oversight corrected quickly as the G chord sounded and our student population hit the halls for our strictly timed change of classes. We, at the T.E.A.M. schools ensured an orderly transition from room to room with…what's that? Oh, the G chord? Sorry, it's just that sometimes I feel like we're f(r)iends and I forget you haven't been here during the development stages of the school. Allow me to get you up to speed.

I decided, a long time ago, let's call it 3rd grade, that I did not like being ushered from room to room at the sound of a bell. Bells are for stock market openings, prizefights, and awesome AC/DC songs, but they are most certainly NOT the sound of revelry I wanted to snap me from my scholastic reverie.

What sound, then, would I have if *I ran the world* to announce that I was time to move from one learning environment to another? The answer seemed

1. Hoppity horse – simply awesome toy from the 70's; basically a big, round bouncy ball with a horse "head" with "ears" that you could grab and hold onto during particularly vigorous bouncing.[2]

2. Remarkably similar to my favorite sexual position, but I digress…

obnoxiously simple: Power chord, played through a Gibson Les Paul running through a Marshall amplifier, loud enough to cause a visceral reaction without blowing your head off. A sound that said, "Hello Cleveland! We're here to rock your faces off, now learn some Historeeeeeeeeyyyahhh!" So, since I do run the world –or at least my little portion of it now – every change of class is preceded by a different chord: A, E, G, D, F etc. Amplified and justified. **INSPIRATION THROUGH AMPLIFICATION!**

What?

Hey, you stick your neck out on an extreme alternative school of your creation and you put whatever sound you want to change classes. My world, my sound, and it was time for fourth period so *BOWMMMMMMNNNNNNN!*

Whoops! A minor (in drop D tuning;) that means it's actually *fifth* period, and time for lunch in the cafeteria.

Where does the time go?

"Good afternoon, Katherin, you look lovely today. Hello, Jorge', thank you very much. Ladies, walk while we talk, thank you. Miss Galati, would you like me to own that iPhone? No? Thank you, dear. Thank you, Marcus, and good luck today. I'll see you guys in lunch in a few…"

Excuse me, reader, but officer Gotchaler has just informed me that a few uninitiated students are planning a food fight. This should be hilarious. I'll catch up with you later.

Huh? Oh, you want to come along. I'm sorry, how rude of me. Come right along, but, for your own safety, stay just outside the cafeteria until the festivities, if they do unfold, are over. While we walk, officer Gotchaler is going to show you the "technology" we used to catch our would-be french fry flingers and lemonade launchers.

NOTE: It occurs to me as I edit this that *French fry flingers* and *lemonade launchers* both sound like euphemisms for deviant sexual types. You were thinking that too? What a relief!

And here he is!

"Harry."

"Mr. Step. Officer Gotchaler."

"What's new, Harry?"

"Branzdorph, Castagna and Otawatam…Otowatamillie…Tim are planning to start a food fight at exactly 1:00."

"And to what do we owe the honor of this information, Harry?"

"I don't want to be around for the repercussions" he answered honestly, absentmindedly fingering the scar just above his left eye.

"Still pissed about being called Harry Potter, then, are we?" He glared at me enough to know that I was right. I glared back enough to let him know that he had done the right thing and, because of that, the scars wouldn't be on *him* this time.

You want a side of "ouch" with that platter of stupid?

"Don't do me dirt or you're gonna get hurt."

— Sammy Davis Jr. (Keep Your Eye on the Sparrow)

Lunch time; you remember it. You sat with whatever group of people could stand your eccentricities for 40 minutes and you stuffed the peanut butter and jelly that was never quite right, (but you never got your lazy ass out of bed to **make** it right, did you?) and snacks into your mouth in between insults, crude jokes, and *"I think he/she likes me."* If you were one of the privileged (or if mom was running late) you were afforded the opportunity to sample the culinary artistry of your particular academic asylum.

"Ah, the tater tots were parTICularly crispy today, were they not Jeeves? I say, sir, I found the strawberry milk to be of a parTICularly fine vintage today..."

Yes, the cafeteria is the hotbed of activity in most High Schools, and ours was no exception. However, here you don't get to sit where you want, for a variety of reasons, not the least of which is that most of the voluntary segregation going on in this country occurs in the realm of bland tacos and day old tapioca. In the T.E.A.M. dining room(always liked the sounds of *dining room* better than *cafeteria* – more Hogwarts, less Cell Block D, know what I mean?) you sat where we told you to sit, you forged new alliances and learned empathy and understanding for those that had the nerve to be different from you. No goths with goths, jocks with jocks, nerds with nerds, outcasts with outcasts, manatee loving cross-dressers with manatee loving cross-dressers in this dining area. This was to be an altruistic asylum of appetizing applesauce.

Oh, and no food fights.

This is not to say that they didn't try; however, I've always been of the opinion that any kid willing to waste perfectly good food in an attempt to:

A) ruin somebody else's perfectly good clothes/face

B) ruin/deface perfectly good property

C) disrupt a perfectly peaceful environment,

is a kid that needs to learn:

A) the value of edible food in a world of hunger

B) the amount of work necessary to maintain clean surroundings

C) the wrath of an angry mob when kept from their pizza because of *you.*

So it was with particular interest that I and our ninja-like security staff watched as young misters Branzdorph, Castagna, and Otawatemileyen readied their edible artillery for [what they thought] was going to be a pineapple and pepperoni projectile party. I have to confess, they put some thought into their pre-emptive strike menu: strawberry milk for umbrella coverage and saturation effect, grapes for shotgun-like dispersion, followed by pudding for that often sought after "chocolate napalm" effect. All this rounded out nicely by Otawata... Otowatamillie... ahem, Tim's handful of oranges (for those select targets that held a special place in the hearts of their enemies and required a long range ballistic citrus that would inflict significant damage.) Those juicy would-be grenades were to be thrown by Richard "the rocket" Castagna, pitcher for our baseball team and slow learner. (He was on the field when Smalla Abdul socked the shit out of his third baseman *and got away with it,* so you'd think he knew corporal punishment was, indeed, and option.)

Before the unholy trinity could mentally text "WTF" to one another, Officer Gotchaler and his partner, big Jean DeChiefs "appeared," flanking the table of would be perpetrators (imagine that!) and the soothing voice of yours truly was heard over the speakers as I walked slowly, for dramatic effect, toward the next contestants on everybody's FAVorITe GAMEshowwww: *"Hhhhhhooooow the FUCK could we be this STUPID?"* (insert applause here.)

Puddings, produce and pride were all being rapidly stuffed in unspeakable areas as the trilogy of twits became increasingly aware that they were on display (to the entire cafeteria population.) The mob does love a good show – the Romans proved that – as do the pay-per-view numbers for the last WWE spectacle.

"Boys" I purred, careful not to refer to them as young men (because young men don't waste food by throwing it now do they?) "*what* exactly are you doing?"

    "Nothin'," lied Tim, *"just gettin' ready for lunch, dawg."*

The anticipatory howls of the mob tipped Tim off in expedient fashion that his answer was, to put it mildly, incorrect. Just in case, I took the liberty to lean in closely (no microphone needed for this one) and gently inquire: "**What** did you call me, boy?"

    "I meant Mr. Step" corrected Tim, with all due penitence and what appeared to be the genesis of a tear or two. *"We were just getting ready to eat our…"*

        We were gonna start a food fight," confessed Richard Castagna with all the speed of an Abu Ghraib prisoner hooked to a battery. Leave it to the Italian to turn in the group in hopes of immunity.

NOTE: I look forward to your letters about my stereotyping of the Italian race. The REAL Richie Castagna is my [Italian] brother-in-law AND my lawyer (and a damn good one at that.) You'll be getting counter-sued by him; how's *that* for irony, "paisan"?

"I'm well aware of that Richard, as are the officers here and the other administrators and the legions of fans, including your parents, watching. Wave to the cameras, boys, you're about to be famous."

Branzdorph actually waved, prompting positively evil looks from his co-conspirators and causing Officer DeChiefs to stifle a cough that looked suspiciously like laughter.

"You have several options, gentlemen; three, to be biblically exact. Would you like to hear them? Of course you would. Option one, one week of volunteer service with the local food bank, which should be just enough to help our homeless brothers and sisters around this holiday season, at the same time reminding you how fortunate you are to have surplus food with which to consider food fights. Option two, two weeks of helping the ladies in the kitchen: fryer grease, cleaning chemicals, open ovens and angry Greek women, what could go wrong? Option three, we finish lunch and act like this never happened."

> "*Seriously?*" pined the clueless conspirators, having never experienced this particular dog and pony show.

"YEAH!" chimed in several hundred students, who had witnessed this routine before, some of which were on the *receiving* end, "LIKE NOTHING HAPPENED!"

> "Until tomorrow," smirked officer Gutcahler, "when *everybody* loses 10 minutes of lunch time for your little stunt."

> > "And the next day, and the next day, and the next day," assisted officer John, "until they just…can't…take …it anymore."

NOTE to self: Those two work very well together, must remember to keep that tag team intact.

"And so I ask you, only once, boys – your choice?"

> "Option one" they all mumbled, unhappy to have volunteered for food bank service (they'll get over it, and they'll feel better about themselves when they're done, trust me) but happy to have avoided what *might* have been any number of potentially hazardous mishaps.

"Of course" I smiled. "Enjoy your lunch, men. Oh, and Tim?"

> "*Yes, sir?*"

"You've got pudding coming out of your back pocket."

> "*Shit.*"

"Really? I thought it was chocolate pudding."

"No, I meant... yes, sir. Sir?"

"Yes, Tim, you may be excused to clean yourself up. Unless you'd like to go with him, Branzdorph, and take your spoon.

"That's disgusting!" he announced, taking the bait.

"Really?' I sprang the trap, and yet I heard that you and Bertha Coklaminsky..."

"Okay OKAY!" he protested, abject fear in his eyes.

But that's another story for another book.

You say "naked in the science lab" like it's a bad thing.

"She blinded me with science!"

— Thomas Dolby (She Blinded Me with Science.)

Obviously, one of the themes of my T.E.A.M. Schools is that punishments, when meted out, should fit the crime and have a *purpose*, which is always to educate in such a way as to prevent the repetition of such behavior. That having been said, due diligence is the best way to prevent the type of [student and teacher] behaviors that cripple our more traditional educational institutions. I can hear the legions of spineless jellyfish that call themselves administrators crying, all jellyfish-like: (insert your own whiny jelly fishy voice here) "weeeeellll, that's eeeaasyyy for yyouuuu to say, Step. Yyouuuu have unlimited finaaaaaancial reeeeeesources!"

"Quite correct, my overly-voweled friends. However, I have faced down the wrath of President Winfrey, the ire of Secretary of Education Carlin, and the seagull-like 'mine, mine, all mine!' mentality of Secretary of Defense Hanks (I don't believe it, either. Apparently, Oprah loved him in *Saving Private Ryan*.) to GET those unlimited finaaaaaancial reeeeeesources, so suck me sideways.

But I digress.

One of the things we work very, very hard at (no pun intended) is preventing any sort of sexual activity between our students on school grounds. We have deep, penetrating discussions (no pun intended) in the hopes of keeping any such messy, illicit activity from sneaking in our back door (no pun intended.) Full frontal (no pun intended) honesty and vigorous oral (no pun intended) ~~discharge~~ discourse allow us to take the creative positions (no pun intended) needed to prevent sexual harassment, inappropriate touching, and any misogynistic behavior.

Of course, when you have 47 schools spread apart (oh yeah, we were growing, more on that later) over the United States, with a student population that is ever growing, widening, and turning purple with the strain of skyward increase; mistakes are bound to happen.

It all started when…what? Oh that last pun was *totally* intended.

It all started when our new science teacher at our West Virginia school, Bettie Bunsen, insisted that the chem. lab be spotless and sterilized before each class was allowed to leave. Don't get me wrong, I think she was brilliant in her demand that the little miscreants take ownership in their surroundings, and I applaud Principal Estep for her support in what came to be known heretofore as the "cleanliness conundrum." Nonetheless…

It all *really* started when April Horneetode cast her first glance at Heil Duwacheesez, a young lad from the Netherlands that never could seem to grasp the most basic concepts of his new American schools. (Like don't call the vice principal a "cum chugger" before throwing a desk at her for example.) Young master Duwacheescz was given the obligatory "*Welcome to Hell*" speech from some of West Virginia's finest. (Hard to believe that the same state that gave birth to adorable little Brad Paisley spewed forth these scary looking bastards. Kudos to Principal June Estep for letting them out of their cages long enough to keep order in her school.) At any rate, who should be on her way to her science class but April "maybe I shouldn't have attacked that undercover female cop with a pencil for her Lady Gaga tickets" Horneetode. She was to have remarked, as I was later told, *"I'd let that boy land shark[1] me in the middle of the gym during warm-ups."* Charming.

Obviously, such flash attractions are nothing new in the hormonally driven hallways of high school America. Why I can fondly recall my teaching days at Moorzakunt Academy and Descaminado High School where certain stairwells, hallways and bathrooms were known dens of iniquity and had nicknames

1. What, you ask, is "land sharking?" Sorry, but I simply can't be privy to that sort of sexual deviancy. Go ask the most sexually adventurous person you know to tell you.[2]

2. If somebody should come up to you and ask "what's land sharking?" and you resemble, in any way, Scarlett Johansson, that's Frank Stepnowski… on Facebook… why not log on now?

that proved it. Yes, I remember all too well the "booty barn" (boys' bathroom outside room 4 at M.A.,) the "freak zone" (stairwell just before the girls' locker room at D.H.S.) and, of course, the "spank that ass and call me Big Poppa wing" (right outside the main office at D.H.S.)

O.K., I made that last one up, but if you taught at D.H.S., you know it ain't *too* far from the truth.

Against this rising tide of teen lust we armed ourselves, at the T.E.A.M. schools with state of the art surveillance technology, state of the art hall monitoring systems and, when all else failed, state of the art snitches. **(Yeah yeah, I hear all you little wannabe thugs "snitches get stiches, blah blah blah." Not in my schools. Know what keeps the wolves from the door in *my* school? A bigger, wiser wolf (with presidential approval for corporal punishment) in the front office.)** *Recognize,* bitches!

Of course, all of the aforementioned buffers pale in comparison to the force of nature that is a psychotic teenage girl with a slight acne condition and purple hair that wants Dutch franks and beans on the menu. Being a creature of positively bipolar nature (read: teenage girl) April wanted sloppy Netherlandian nookie from a kid she had never even spoke to, but in a place of pristine cleanliness, so as to avoid disease. While the irony of that last image sinks in, I refer you back to Ms. Bunsen and her sparkling science labs.

You do see where this is going, don't you?

I do wish, gentle reader, that I had (at the time) your powers of foresight.

I was conducting one of my bi-annual tours of our individual state facilities, and while Principal Estep and I were enjoying some sweet tea, pecan pie and paperwork, we were interrupted by a most interesting interruption.

One of Ms. Estep's surveillance devices, a promising young lad with a slight speech impediment, name of François Poopavitch, burst in with an announcement.[1]

---

1. We forego certain bullshit protocols at T.E.A.M schools, such as waiting outside an administrator's office with a piece of information vital to maintaining control of the school. Lest you think that leads to a lot of "false" alarms, it doesn't. Just ask the first kid that ever tried – John "lefty" Kane. Shame about that hand, real shame.

"Principal Essschchhtep, Mr. Sssschhhtep…hey, did you know your namessscchhh scchhhound almossschht the ssscchhame?"

June, to her credit, managed to maintain dignity even as she spoke through clenched teeth and gracefully wiped the spittle that had rained forth from young Francis' ssschhhpeech.

"You were *saying*, François?"

"April Horneetode and Heil Duwascchhhhcheescchhez were jussschhht found naked in the sccchhhiensscche lab!"

That particular announcement, combined with the vigor with which it was delivered, created no small amount of salival precipitation; so June and I though it prudent to escape the tsunami of tspit and get to where the real problem was coming from. (no pun intended.)

Principal, and mother of two, June Estep was a force of nature when she burst through the door into the science lab. Gesturing to the obviously upset Ms. Bunsen that she would see to her hygiene concerns momentarily, she first ripped into Heil, who already looked pathetic: sunken pale chest, quivering hairy legs and [what I'm sure were shriveled] naughty bits covered, thank the Lord, by a West Virginia T.E.A.M. School soccer towel.

"You… you… DARE… in *my* school?" June frothed, "When I am finished with you…"

Heil interrupted, with a look of complete innocence that only a true idiot could pull off. *"I was just dooeenk vat she sed for me to do. Dis ees a clean place, ya?"*

April, for her part, waited about half a second before throwing her Holland love sponge under the bus: *"He tried to rape me; I don't even know his name."*

The look of hurt in Heil's eyes was too much for even me to take so, with a simple glance, I sought permission from Principal Estep to intervene. She seemed preoccupied in deciding what form of medieval torture to drop on the nearly naked Netherlandian, so she was more than willing to let me have a word with skankus maximus.

Seeing an opportunity that might never happen again, I:

1. Addressed April, the misguided young lady

2. Asked Principal June Estep for permission and

3.Let April know that I knew she was fibbing.

"Now April. May I, June? *You* lie!"

Get it? April, May, June, July? July…You Lie?

Guess you had to be there, it was fucking hilarious, even the dopey Dutch boy laughed, but he stopped on a dime when June eyeballed his barely covered family jewels and the closest acidic chemical with malicious intent.

"Huh?" was the monosyllabic response from our purple-haired heroine.

"Ahem, well," I continued, "you're bullshitting, and there will be…"

"No, he tried to rape…"

"You are **BULL. SHIT. TING** young lady! And there **WILL** be repercussions! Repercussions that will get significantly more **SEVERE** if you interrupt me one more time!"

"Yes, sir."

So as to maintain Principal Estep's authority and possibly salvage some sort of repertoire with this young lady, I leaned in close enough to smell the unique odor of clove cigarettes, Bubblicious watermelon and body odor.

"Lucky for you I intervened when I did, young lady – Ms. Estep hasn't even started thinking about the uses for some of this lab equipment…yet."

"She is *now*," chimed in 'bad cop' Estep, right on cue.

"Why don't we get these two sloppy monuments of low self-esteem dressed, get their parents in here, and administer the appropriate punishment?"

"Or I could just put *these* to use" snarled June, who clamped a particularly vicious-looking pair of what appeared to be forceps shut with a flourish.

The last thing I saw was an entirely too pale buttocks and another posterior (covered only by what appeared to be *Twilight* underwear) motoring toward their eventual penance and recovery.

Epilogue

Lest you think my vision for the T.E.A.M. Schools is one of visceral and/or violent response to every situation, think again. April received some counseling (no, not the normal bullshit; some real, genuine conversation with people she respected and that she knew cared about her) about her promiscuity and that she was better than that for so many reasons. I even sent her a letter once I was back home telling her that if she was my daughter, I would be heartbroken, but just as elated if she chose to grow to respect herself. Better late than never, and she was still a very young girl.

Heil Duwacheesez managed, with a bit of help from our extreme alternative methods and the corn-fed behemoths that Principal Estep kept in her employ, to become quite the student, eventually gravitating toward a career in… wait for it… teaching chemistry.

Must have been dee cleanliness of dee labs, ya?

Got a letter from April Horneetode one day, whose real name was…

Whoops! I forgot, this is all fiction, complete fiction, based on no sort of reality whatsoever…

Anyway, if I *ever did* have a heart to heart with a girl *like* April who got caught in a *similar* compromising situation, *it would be nice* if she sent me a picture one day of her holding her newborn daughter, with a simple note that said:

"She'll respect herself from day one."

Thank God *that* never happened, because I'd probably cry… a little.

But I am far too callous and vindictive for such things.

A random rant near the middle of an otherwise perfectly good book.

"I've got a .38 special, up on the shelf; if I start actin' stupid I'll shoot myself."
— Warren Zevon (I'll Sleep When I'm Dead.)

Sorry about this, but I haven't been able to concentrate and if I don't get this out of my head and onto a page I'm never going to get this book written. Of course, you would have never known had I not mentioned it, but I thought that some of you might appreciate this unedited, visceral rant written in a moment of rare, raw emotional overload [furthermore, *some* of you *need* to hear this.]

I just had a brief discussion with a person that may or may not, for legal reasons, be my mother-in-law. I love her, mainly because she's real, and doesn't spare feelings in her quest for a world devoid of bullshit. The topic of our discussion isn't important, what is important is her assertion that (as a teacher) because I **get home** at 2:30 that I am **done** at 2:30. I feel that many people, outside the teaching profession, share her perception. I simply said to her that the term "done" is open to interpretation. To which she replied, "No, not really, if you were stuck there for another 5 or 6 hours you'd know what I mean."

To which I reply:

That's the biggest load of fucking bullshit I've ever heard. Just because you're **at** your job doesn't mean you're **doing** your job, as she well knows being surrounded by fucking morons that steal money just by walking in the door. Furthermore, any teacher that has kids (as I do: ages 15, 14, 12 and 11) knows that oftentimes, my job gets harder **after** I get home, as I try to juggle:

- the fucking *mountain* of paperwork that accompanies 100+ students (which I guess doesn't *count* because I'm not doing it at a *desk* under the fucking *roof* of the place that underpays me,) along with

- the practice/game/time schedules of multiple kids in multiple sports and activities – you know, those things the "critics" go to, once in a blue moon, on the weekends, along with

- all of the shit I do to make up for you people that are "working so hard" during that extra few hours at your place of work. New flash: the house doesn't clean itself.

Teaching is one of those professions that (if you give a shit about doing your job right, which I do) you don't leave when you leave work. I do more work at home most of the time than I do at school. It's kind of like playing professional football – you spend *countless* hours preparing behind the scenes so you can just *react* and *perform* during game time because, *during* game time, there are a veritable army of people trying their level best to knock your fucking head off and keep you from doing your job.

Of course, that doesn't *count* because you don't see that part on TV, right?

BullllllllSHIT.

Listen, I know goddamned well that there are teachers that need to be pulled and thrown away like weeds because they're strangling the "good plants" in our staff and tainting the name of the profession, but I also know that, in every profession, there are people putting in all kinds of hours "at the office" and doing absolutely dick and getting paid overtime for doing it. I have worked, and continue to work, with people from both groups, you know who you are and fuck *you*. However, I also know plenty of people (like my wife, and my mother-in-law) that log tons of unpaid hours on their job sites because they were born to do what's best for the *team*. I also know a lot of teachers (like me) that, if we were lawyers and could bill for the time we're "contemplating" our "cases" would be billionaires.

Bottom line, I respect the reality that being "on the clock" does not automatically equal "on the job;" conversely, please understand that just because I am *home* at 2:30 doesn't mean, by any stretch, that I am *done* at 2:30. Furthermore, if you do feel that way, keep it to yourself.

I'M BAD
I'M NATIONWIDE

"More tears are shed over answered prayers than unanswered ones"

– Mother Teresa

Hey fast learners! An **exposition** is *still* a literary technique wherein the author (that would be me) provide the reader (thankfully, still played by you) some background information to inform the readers about the plot, theme, etc. Since we're going to do some "time jumps" in this book, in this case from the year 2015 to somewhere around 2018, I thought it would be prudent to include some stuff to get you up to speed. Isn't that convenient? I thought so.

P.S. Not to worry, "time travel reading" is perfectly safe; side effects may but probably won't include: death, headache, indigestion, back pain, change of gender, muscle aches, flushing, stuffy or runny nose, an erection lasting more than 73 ½ hours, difficulty sleeping, and/or a sudden desire to eat all of the giraffes in a box of animal crackers. Let's get to some expositioning, shall we?

Exposition: Size matters.

Welcome to sometime around the year 2018. Despite some attacks from groups ranging from The Weather Underground to Agenda for Children to Save the Manatees (not sure what *their* beef was,) the T.E.A.M. concept seems to have resonated with America the beautiful, so much so that one school turned into two, two turned into four, and four turned into 47, one affiliate per almost each star on Old Glory, so things have, to put it mildly, intensified. To put it not so mildly, the 800 lb. gorilla's shit has hit the industrial-sized fan. Perhaps I should have followed Mother Theresa's advice (and I'm paraphrasing here) to "be careful what you wish for, lest it get too big for your chicken-fried fingers to hold onto it, fat boy." Sorry M. Tizzle, but I really thought that, since we were doing so well (student performance off the charts, staff morale through the ceiling, approval ratings nationwide approaching 80%) that we were obligated to share the secret formula with the rest of a parent and student population begging to be freed from the shackles of contemporary education. Furthermore, the aforementioned parental units were willing to pay the ever-increasing tuition to drink from the fountain, so with all respect to the haters – go big or go home, bitches.

Of course, mo' money mo' problems, and the big dogs got involved. I was forced to enter the Armani-suited dog fighting ring known as politics. You simply can't affect the educational landscape [the way the T.E.A.M. schools did] and not get pulled into the vortex. President Winfrey became a major player in the rise of the T.E.A.M. schools, but she was quick to call me on things when she saw them running astray, and she was quick to throw me to the wolves when they came howling, knowing that I would find a polite, erudite way to tell them to go screw themselves. While I did everything I could to keep my eye on every facet of the T.E.A.M. organization that was, in my mind, just a bigger version of the dream I started with, it became harder and harder to *guarantee* the level of excellence that I demanded of myself, my staff, and (most importantly) our students.

I never sought the spotlight, but it was on me now, BIG time; and I knew one thing for certain, while I was *in* that spotlight, I was going to drag a few other people out of their caves and into the burning rays of the light. People like the assholes that supported the way we test kids into one-dimensional robots, people like the irresponsible provocateurs that promoted playing the race card, (or any card, for that matter, when we disciplined someone,) people like the legions of "educators" that ran from accountability because they'd rather hide in fear than fight for what's right, and people like the 'absentee parents' that got this ball rolling in the first place.

Oh yeah, the T.E.A.M. School ideal (and its originator) got labeled the antagonistic iceberg.

But we sure scared the fuckers on the Titanic.

Wherein President Winfrey gives me permission to defrost a comedian.

"[The government] doesn't want a population capable of critical thinking... they want obedient workers."

— George Carlin

Christmas Eve, and as I sit and sip my Christmas Eve coffee, spiked ever so slightly with my Christmas Eve *Patron' Café* tequila (Thanks, Brian and Jill!) I reflect fondly upon those first few days, when the first T.E.A.M. School opened, long before the Scholastic Help International Team was formed; hereafter referred to in glowing terms on Capitol Hill as the S.H.I.T Storm.

I had a vision; I would have said I had a dream but I already used that joke and somebody already gave that speech. The funny thing is, Martin Luther King and I had a similar goal in mind – equality. Our modus operandi, however, was to be slightly different, while Dr. King wanted to be an equal opportunity *employer*, I sought educational equality at its most primitive level. That is to say, smash the spoiled, arrogant, ignorant, non-accountable, overly enabled, low attention spanned youth of our country into submission, then slowly and strictly build them back up while reminding them to appreciate the quality education that their country so richly afforded them.

A sort of equal opportunity *destroyer*, if you will.

You would have thought that I would have run into all sorts of problems, what with my extreme approach to discipline and all. Surprisingly, I only faced one problem on the first day we started taking applications: How on Earth was I going to accommodate OVER ONE HUDRED THOUSAND PEOPLE that wanted to get their kids into my schools?

Answer: Set the tuition high enough to cause an aneurysm in any non-serious applicant.

Result: Even more applicants.

"Why didn't I think of this earlier?" I thought to myself, "I'm a genius."

"Why didn't you think of this earlier?" [my wife] Dawn accosted me. *"You're an asshole."*

Dawn had recently given up her job as a nurse practitioner for a prestigious inner city hospital that I can't mention for legal reasons (but it rhymes with Semple Mooniversity of Killadelphia) so that she could manage the input and placement of new students in my fledgling T.E.A.M. school. At first I wasn't thrilled at the prospect of losing her six-figure income, especially since there was always the worry that my "vision" would get blurry in a hurry. Now, with the reality of going international almost overnight, combined with the fact that President Winfrey was on speed dial, I was happier than ever to have Dawn running the scenes behind the scenes. After all, her subtlety and relaxed approach to deadlines would be indispensable.

"Gradkowski!! I'd better have those medical clearances for the 30 new students at the Detroit facilities in my right hand in an hour or I will rip your dick off with the left!"

That's my girl.

As the T.E.A.M. approach to education became the weapon of choice for 47 out of 50 states (Florida, California and Delaware holding out like the expensive green properties in Monopoly that nobody wants anyway) it became imperative to involve me in the educational framework of our great nation; a fact that must have pleased President Winfrey to no end, as evidenced in the following conversation, which was my first and last in the actual oval office, where the coffee was lukewarm but the carpet is really, really nice.

> *The big cheese*: *"Stepnowski, I cannot believe an iconoclastic rabble rouser like you is going to have a say in national educational policy."*

The humble servant: "Oprah, Oprah, Oprah, I am but a humble servant who wishes to…"

> *The head honcho*: *"Shut UP. And call me Madame President. Friends call me Oprah."*

The wounded soul: "Ouchie."

> *The Alpha female: "Appoint a suitable Secretary of Education, and get it done yesterday!"*

The visionary asshole: "Yes madam president, and may I say that you are looking…"

> *The Commander-in-Coach: "Get out. Now."*

The spanked ass: "Yes, ma'am."

For a guy who was about to forever change the face of education, you'd think I would get a bit more respect, or at the very least some *hot* coffee. Alas, outside the plushly carpeted inner sanctum of Senorita Presidente', I was a pretty big deal. Big enough to start barking orders around so I could follow the orders that had been barked at me.

"Gradkowski! Get George Carlin on the phone!" I commanded.

> *"He's been dead since late 2008, Mr. Step." Gradkowski reminded me.*

So I reminded him. "That's only 4 years, and money is no object."

> *"Oh, I'll get right on that after I'm done…"*

"You will do it *now*, Gradkowski"

> *"Uh, I'm late getting these medical clearances to Dawn."*

"Oh…better get to that before she rips your dick off. Tell Hoover to call."

> *"Right away Mr. Step."*

Luckily for me, old George Carlin had enough foresight to be cryogenically frozen, and his estate managers were under strict orders to thaw him out only in the event that, and I quote, "the human race actually does something worthy of anything but a kick in the nuts and a fiery fucking apocalypse."

Call me crazy, I thought this fit the bill.

"You're fuckin' crazy," said George, looking none the worse for wear after four years of the Han Solo treatment.

"Hey, things have changed a lot in the last four years," I argued. "We elected a partially African-American president, and he started holding parents accountable for raising their kids."

"Get the fuck outta here; you wake me up for that?"

"They assassinated an Austrian president, Secretary Pickens created alternative fuel sources that essentially stopped our dependence on foreign oil, we cured blindness, and Guns N' Roses put out a new album."

"Fuck outta here, I was resting, kid."

"A third Bush tried to restore the monarchy on American soil."

"Get the fuck outta – what?"

"You heard me."

"That's too much potential material to turn down."

"No way George," I demanded. "If you take the Secretary of Education job, then THAT'S your priority. Stand-up comedy becomes your occasional hobby. That's the deal, or you go back to being an observationally humorous creamsicle."

"You drive a hard bargain, Step, but you seem like a nice kid."

"And you're a stubborn old Otter Pop.* Now here's our mission statement."

"Mission statements are for…"

"I know you're feelings on this, Mr. Carlin, I practically memorized every stand-up routine you ever did, now if you'll please read this."

He read it.

"I'll take the job."

*Otter Pop - a brand of frozen snacks sold in the U.S.by Jel Sert. I recommend Sir Isaac Lime

"Of course you will."

"Boy, am I gonna stick it to these limp dick, chickenshit, asshole motherfuckers," he laughed.

The rest, as they say, is history – or at least the material for a bunch more chapters in this book. It was a good start, and every journey begins with a single Step (pun totally intended.)

What's that? You want to hear the mission statement? Oh it's a beauty; gave President Winfrey a migraine and made Vice President Carter (no relation to Jimmy, youngest son of Jay-Z) toss his cookies. Tell you what, you go ahead and keep reading and I'll read it to you myself later. Off you go; I've got to find a surgeon that can repair Kowalski's one-eyed wonder worm.

Author's Note:

One of what (I'm sure will be many) regrets in writing this book is that I never got a chance to send a copy to Mr. Carlin himself. George Carlin was, without a doubt, the comedic voice of reason that "spoke to me" most profoundly throughout my life; he got smarter, meaner, and more erudite as he got older – only in my wildest dreams does my narrative voice follow a similar pattern of evolution. Maybe we're both wrong, George; maybe there is a heaven and (insert laugh here) we'll both get there and you can read this someday. In the meantime, I'll speak for you, just this once, on behalf of the people that won't like this book: "Fuck 'em if they can't take a joke."

We see everything in terms of black and white, except black and white.

"I'm not the only one, that's why I'm not bitter 'cause everybody is a nigga to a nigga."

– Ice T (Straight Up Nigga)

"Oh shit," I hear you mumble to yourself, "he's not going *there*, is he?"

Yeah, he is. I taught kids of every shape, size, socioeconomic status and temperament for 20 years before beginning my T.E.A.M. Schools which, to date, have added nearly another decade to my service to the community. Therefore, I say this with neither sarcasm nor insincerity: I honestly don't think I remember how to be racist.

I say *remember* because, in my angry youth, I disliked a lot of people and, in my ignorance, I immediately assumed (because many adults who I *thought* were wiser than me told me so) that people were "bad" because they were richer than me, darker than me, lived in a different part of the world than me, believed in a different god than me, etc. etc., ad nauseum. It took me a few years, but I figured out that most of the people who I thought were worldly wise were, instead, narrow-minded douchebags that chose to vilify anything outside their VERY small realm of understanding. I distinctly remember my moment of clarity: I heard choirs of angels singing and the resplendent light of enlightenment shone down upon me from an opening in the heavens.

Ok, that's not *exactly* how it went down. It actually happened in the middle of a chicken salad sandwich.

I was wolfing down what I'm sure was my second or third chicken salad sandwich, patiently enduring the last 10 minutes of the Saturday afternoon news, anxiously awaiting a Bruce Lee movie marathon. Something the

Channel 6 broadcaster said just pushed me over the edge and I turned to my dad and said "These people are just completely full of crap." Whereupon my dad, soft spoken chap that he was replied, "No shit, Sherlock, I've been telling you that for a few years now, but you're THICK."

NOTE: When my dad called me "thick," (and he often did,) the angry adjective was always accompanied by a forefinger-to-the-head tapping motion that seemed to imply that the density of my cranium made intelligent commentary feel like an unwelcome visitor.

I confess, I have used that motion on my children and my stepchildren (students) alike. I also confessed that I came to adopt my father's view of the world and its human inhabitants. Goes somethin' like this:

1. *Nobody* gets your respect without earning it, 'cause everybody puts their pants on just like you, one leg at a time.

2. On the other hand, you treat *everybody* [at first] as though they're worthy of being looked in the eye and listened to.

3. I fought for people to have the right to *say* whatever they want about you, but

4. I also gave you the ability to *do* something about it.

5. When dealing with people, *keep* your promises, *finish* what you start, take the time to do things right the *first time*, and <u>always</u> *be accountable* for your actions.

"What about... you know?" I asked him on the day of the chicken salad debacle.

"What about what?" he asked, frustrated with my thickness.

"You know...professors, the president, people that..."

"Money, big houses, or some piece of paper doesn't make a man better than another one," he snarled, "but you'll realize that more and more as you get older, and..."

"What about the niggers, spicks and the white trash that live around us?"

At first I thought the look he gave me was because I interrupted him. I was anxious, and since he was in a mood to talk, and he was treating me like an adult and talking straight, I jumped the gun and tried to push the conversation ahead, trying to sound "edgy" and "mature" in the process. To this day, I flinch just thinking about what an asshole I must have sounded like.

NOTE: I have had students "jump the gun" on me countless times for the same reason, and I always, *always*, remember that day and take it as a sign of eagerness, not disrespect.

My dad looked at me with the pain of a father that thinks, on some deeper level, that he has failed his child in some fundamental way. As a father of four, I know that feeling all too well.

> *"Frankie,"* he began, *"people are people. They…"*

(he paused, holding it together)

"Dad? Y'alright?"

> *"Treat people the way they treat you, Frankie, all people. All people, the way they treat you."*

It's been well over three decades since that conversation and, although the exact verbiage is lost to me, the fact that my dad (a man who *drove himself to the hospital after having his kneecap severed* in a work accident) was **hurt** because he thought his son had a narrow mind and a big mouth remains hard wired into my decision making.

You simply don't forget that kind of shit, folks.

Don't get me wrong, my dad's a hell of a lot closer to Walt Kowalski in *Gran Torino* than he is Dumbledore in the *Harry Potter* movies (and damn proud of it) but he's man enough to know that bullshit comes in every shape, size and color, and to expect any different is simply naïve. I have come to know the same; hence, I treat everybody [initially] as worthy of my love and attention, but if you fuck that up once, shame on *you*. Twice? Shame on me. I've taken that attitude into the classroom, the boardroom, and even into the oval office when Oprah called me on the carpet in early 2021. Allegations were being made (and aren't they always?) by anonymous sources (and aren't they always?) that certain practices being employed in my T.E.A.M. Schools were, by definition, racist. Apparently, there were too many black and Hispanic kids in my remedial reading classes.

I was summoned to the big house to meet with president Winfrey, Secretary of Education Carlin, a few of our, *cough, cough... BULLshit... cough* distinguished Senators, and Sal Sharpieton. I know what you're thinking: Sharpieton? Still alive? How? Simple answer, 5 words: Only the good die young.

Oh no he **DIDn't**!

I made the drive to 1600 Pennsylvania Avenue on my own. I guess I could have hired a driver or called a cab, but I kind of like the time during the drive to collect my thoughts and thicken my skin for the forthcoming flogging. I suspect some of you do the same, am I right? As I pulled into view of the home of Oprahs Maximus Presidentus, I sang along with the *Talking Heads*, who were blasting forth from my custom Bose sound system (the one luxury I allowed myself being the head honcho of T.E.A.M.)

> *"Burned all our notebooks. Whoo!*
> *What good are notebooks?*
> *They won't help me survive.*
> *My chest is aching, burns like a furnace,*
> *The burning keeps me alive."*

Truer words were never spoken.

The usual precautions were taken, protocols were observed, and I was finally led into a very warm, well-furnished conference room filled with cold, well-armed people. I decided to take the offensive:

"Hola mi amigos! The piñata's here, everybody got their sticks?"

That got me a wry smile from Oprah, a poorly concealed thumbs up from George Carlin, and assorted shocked countenances from our *cough, cough... DOUCHEbag... cough* distinguished Senators. Sal Sharpieton looked like he took a bite of a diarrhea and oyster Po boy, which earned a big ol' fucking smile from *me*.

NOTE: For purposes of clarity, I shall synopsize the extensive conversation that took place that day, with the speakers identified in play form.

Least I could do, right?

You're welcome.

The Cast of Characters

President Oprah Winfrey (hereafter referred to as **POW**) – media mogul, worldwide altruist, alpha female, currently serving her 2nd term as president of the United States, a position she earned in nearly unanimous fashion after president Schwarzenegger's notoriously short, and bitterly contested, time in the White House ended in an ironic mishap during the AK-47 accuracy competition at the *Arnold Classic Bodybuilding and Bombs Weekend.* Vice President [and first lady – don't ask] Shriver, unbeknownst to her, had agreed to a pre-nup that required she be tied, lovingly, to Ah-nahld's ship as it was set aflame in classic Viking funeral style.

Secretary of Education George Carlin(hereafter referred to as **GC**) – comedic genius, public speaker extraordinaire, lightning rod of controversy, embittered old Irish bastard whom I had the great privilege of un-cryogenically freezing in the hopes that I would have an ally on the inside as I put my foot up the ass of an educational system he had so often chastised.

The Distinguished senators from Interesting, Caring, Kid-friendly states (hereafter referred to as **DICKs**) a veritable rodent's nest of career politicians who would never *dream* of spending more time paying back their primary fundraisers than looking after the best interest of their chosen constituency.

Sal Sharpieton(hereafter referred to as ---
Hi, this is author's legal counsel, hereafter referred to as those nice people in the expensive suits that keep him non-bankrupt. We though it prudent to interject here, seeing as how Rev Sharpieton is, as of the writing of this book, very much alive and therefore capable of suing a career teacher with four kids and an ironic sense of humor. Therefore, Sal Sharpieton will hereafter be referred to as **Rev. Sal**)

Frank Stepnowski (hereafter referred to as **ME**) – alliterative author, part-time narcissist, passionate protagonist, leader of the educational revolution, currently defending myself against unfounded (aren't they always?) accusations that certain aspects of my T.E.A.M. Schools are, by definition, racist.

The conversation

POW: *"OK Frank, you're familiar with the allegations, so let's get right down to it; your response?"*

> **Rev. Sal**: "Be*fore* we begin, I'd like to be made completely aware of the spe*ci*fic charges so I can prepare a *thor*ough response on behalf of my…"

ME: "One, you weren't the one asked to respond. Two…"

> **Rev. Sal**: "In order for me to…"

ME: "TWO! If you wanted to be up to speed on the proceedings, you should have read the briefs like everyone else at the table, th…"

> **Rev. Sal**: "In *or*der to…"

> **GC**: *"THREE, shut the FUCK up and let the people who actually know what the fuck they're TALKING about carry the conversation! Jeez Louise!"*

POW: *"Gentlemen, that's eNOUGH. Mr. Carlin, you will watch your language in this forum. Mr. Sharpieton, you will have the opportunity for questions at the proper time. Mr. Stepnowski, your response please."* (Whereupon she cast a pleasant glance in the direction of everyone that said *"the next person that interrupts these proceedings will be fed to my genetically engineered Oprah otters, which will slowly chew you to death."*)*

---

* For the record, I don't know if Oprah has genetically engineered wil life that do her bidding, but wouldn't it be cool if she did? Winfrey wombats, attack!

ME: "First of all, Madame President, I make every attempt to personally visit all of the facilities that carry my mission statement. You are well aware of how difficult it is to maintain the ideal level of control over schools that bear your name…"

POW: "*Careful…*"

ME: "Especially after that unfortunate incident at your Leadership Academy for girls back in 2007…"

POW: (maintaining her dignity but clearly fuming) "***Point taken. Continue, please.***"

ME: (convinced I could hear the approaching chatter of ostentatious otters) "So while I can't verify the exact goings-on at every one of my facilities, I stake my reputation on the knowledge that none of the procedures or behaviors at my schools are even remotely racist."

> **Rev. Sal**: "Your repu*ta*tion? Your repu*ta*tion is that of a man who sees *vio*lence as a suitable method of con*troll*ing young men and women."

ME: "Corporal punishment was not something I invented, Sal, (he *hates* it when you don't call him Reverend) and many of our greatest leaders in industry and philanthropy managed to survive it. And, if I can be honest, I don't put a lot of stock in the words of a man whose career longevity owes itself to a doctrine that encourages racial division."

> **GC**: "*Freakin A right! If we're gonna close down every place that strong-arms people into compliance, we can start with the Catholic Ch…*"

POW: "***That's quite enough, gentlemen,***" professed our prolific president, with just the slightest implication that the HARPO cyber-hippos were lurking hungrily nearby.

> Meanwhile, the **DICKs** woke up long enough to mumble: "mumble, mumble, trying to sound important and concerned, mumble, mumble."

ME: "Madame President, with all due respect. I've read, and re-read, all of the accusations in this document, and they're all vague, thinly veiled implications that just because certain demographics aren't scoring higher in certain subjects in a few of my schools, then those institutions are, by definition, racist. If you want to get technical, racism is the belief that race determines how we act or what we do, and that certain racial profiles are inherently superior or inferior, which we all know is…"

POW *"Bullshit."*

ME: "Exactly, and I really don't want to get technical, because semantics are an exercise in confusion. Permission requested to cut through the aforementioned bullshit and get right down to the heart of the matter?"

POW: *"I wish you would."*

> **GC:** *"Imagine that."*

> > > **DICKs:** "mumble mumble this sounds as though this might affect us in some way so I guess we should pay attention mumble mumble."

> > **Rev. Sal:** "ZZZzzzzzzz."

POW:(with a wink and a nod) *"Must've been time for the Reverend's afternoon nap, probably for the best; continue, please, and choose your words carefully."*

> **GC:** *"Yeah, kid. All joking aside, you defrosted me to help you redefine the status quo in education, and the President has been more than supportive.* (Quietly) *"I'm as shocked as you are…"*

POW: *"George…"*

> **GC:** *"…so if you're gonna say something now, make it COUNT."*

ME: "Fine. We never went anywhere but backwards trying to ram political correctness down the throats of a society that has, if anything, become more anesthetized to words and empty threats. We created Head Start programs and then lost the same kids as soon as they entered the real system. We let decades of students fall behind, ironically, during the years of No Child Left Behind; and we turned a blind eye to patterns and reoccurring trends under the lie that we didn't want to hurt the feelings of kids that could handle the truth because we were worried that their narrow-minded, lawsuit-happy parents and lawyers would sue us for noticing that there tended to be more black kids in the lower reading classes…"

Rev. Sal: "Huummpphh, wha? Whadhesay? I …YAWN… I ob*ject*."

ME: "Go back to sleep, *Reverend*, literally and metaphorically."

POW: (Intensely focused) *"Go on."*

ME: "So instead of simply accepting what we know are fundamental truths, verified by the kids themselves…"

POW: *"Such as?"*

ME: "…such as the fact that inner city parents traditionally do not read to their kids and that, in those households, which are often single parent homes, organizational skills are not taught. Or what about the fact that a lot of our Hispanic students are the only ones in their household that speak English fluently? Or what about…"

POW: *"Are you insinuating that the white students all come from good homes and…"*

ME: "Don't play devil's advocate with me, Oprah, you know damn well that I see everything in black and white *except* black and white."

POW: (softening noticeably) *"Yes, we talked at length about this when you first decided to take your T.E.A.M. Schools nationwide."*

DICKs: "well we mumble mumble weren't party to those mumble mumble… discussion, and…"

ME: (exasperated) "NO, you weren't! Because you're never there when the heavy lifting needs to be done, are you? You just wait until someone says something that *only you* find offensive and then you push your own divisive agendas, overlooking the fact that you're retarding the educational process in the name of keeping your fat, lazy, tunnel-visioned asses in the spotlight and on the podium. I will NOT be witch hunted by you lazy BASTARDS while I am busting my BALLS to rectify the educational gridlock that YOU helped create, simply because there are a few more black kids in my remedial writing classes this year. Guess what? There are a few more Hispanic kids in my remedial reading classes too! Guess why? Because they're the only ones in their households that el speako the fucking language-o! And you know the best part of this whole bullshit argument?"

POW: (quietly, powerfully) *"I'm listening, and this is your closing argument."*

ME: "The fact that the kids *don't care* about what class they're in. They just want to learn! They just want to know that somebody knows their faults, doesn't care, and just wants to help! THEY can handle the truth; it's only people whose longevity is predicated upon keeping people divided that can't handle the harsh realities that our teachers must face every day. You remind me of the lawyers that tried to make my parents hate each other more during their divorce so they could keep the money rolling in, and you make me fucking sick. Apologies for the language, Madame President, but I have quite enough legitimate character flaws to answer for without defending myself against manufactured ones."

POW: *"Thank you! Mr.…."*

ME: (pushing it) In*closing*, I will not allow the virus that is political correctness to corrupt my mission to truly love, teach and assist in the character development of the kids that have been placed in my care."

POW:(playful, but in charge) *"Thank you? Mr.…."*

ME: (*really* pushing it now, so speaking quickly) "atagreatpersonalcostto theirguardians!"

POW: (reminding me who's in charge with an oh-so-subtle verbal bitch slap) *"THANK you, Mr. Step, that WILL be all. Gentlemen, I trust we all agree that the T.E.A.M. Schools are vindicated, but…"*

Rev. Sal and the DICKs: "but…"

POW: (reminding them who's in charge with a not-so-subtle verbal bitch slap) *"But NOTHING. Frank, we will continue to monitor your progress, and it has been considerable, and for that you are to be commended, but always be vigilant that your colossal ego does not take precedent over the mission statement that you and I discussed in this very office a few short years ago."*

ME: (TAKIN' it…to the limit…one more tiiiiiimmme) "What? Worried I'll run against you if you try for a third term?"

POW:(noticeably unthreatened but obviously entertained) *"Good day, Mr. Stepnowski."*

GC: (slapping Rev. Sal and some of the DICKs on the backs) *"I'll tell you what, fellas, this fuckin' thing might just work after all! Don't'cha think?"*

George shot me a wink as I let myself out, letting me know that he was thoroughly enjoying himself, which gave me a warm fuzzy feeling inside that was soon erased as a very large black man in a very expensive black suit blocked my way, towering over me, and announced himself (in a voice that made Mike Tyson sound like John Wayne) as Tyrone Nurse, the new head of the Secret Service. Now, gentle reader, I'm about 6' 3", 260 lbs. or more depending on whether cream puffs are in season, so when I say large enough to tower over me I mean VERY FREAKIN' LARGE.

I opened my arms and exposed my center line in a gesture of vulnerability, maintaining eye contact in a gesture of respect but locking my back leg in a barely perceptible move that only a guy like him would notice. The entire move took two seconds and asked "Shall we dance or shall we dialogue?"

"I heard your entire conversation with the president." He admitted.

"I'm sure you did," I loosened a bit, "can never be too careful with the boss, right?"

" Whatyou're doing is right, and what you said is right. We will never advance as a people unless we stop playing the race card and take ownership of our lives, the good and the bad."

"Interesting assessment coming from the black, and…"

"Gay"

"…gay head of the Secret Service, who exclusively protects the black, female president of the United States."

"Long way to go yet." He countered.

"Well, if you heard any of my other conversations with the President, and any of my press conferences, then you'll know that *that* problem isn't my fault because I'm white, and I'm *tired* of hearing that it is. To be honest I, and all of the teachers I've worked with, of *all* races and genders, have done more in the classroom to erase the ignorance that fuels the problems that are plaguing this country, than any of the assholes pointing the fingers at us."

"I agree."

"And furthermore, wait…what?"

"I agree. Thank you sir, keep fighting the good fight." And with that Tyrone the gay black giant in the beautiful black suit stood aside and gestured to the exit that I was to take today.

I stopped, shook his hand. "Carry on soldier."

"Say hello to my nephew when you get back to the Washington facility."

I froze. "Nurse. Nurse? Wait a…DeMarcus Nurse is your nephew?"

He nodded.

"Bit of an asshole, that one."

He nodded, lowering his sunglasses and raising his eyebrows as if to say "**no shit**," without actually *saying* "no shit."

"I'll be *sure* to mention our conversation; enjoy the rest of your day, Tyrone."

> *"Oh, I will."* He smiled, knowing that he had just given DeMarcus back a little of the grief he had no doubt caused Tyrone and his family over the years.

And so endeth another day in the life. As I jumped on I-95 on my way back home, I checked my watch. Still plenty of time to double back, pop in for a surprise visit to the Washington facility (principal Vicki Gonzalez is always happy to see me, having been a former student of mine) and perhaps a chat with DeMarcus Nurse.

Definitely a chat with DeMarcus Nurse.

In the mother of all private ironies, I switched from Talking Heads to some old school rap,

Blasting *Express Yourself* by *NWA*, I rapped along as I headed back into Washington,

"I'm expressing with my full capabilities
And now I'm living in correctional facilities."

Not if my teachers and I can help it, DeMarcus. Not if we can help it.

What? Did you just shake your head when I said "I rapped along?" (insert faux angry Anglo hand gesture here) Oh no you DIDn't! I'll have you know that my flow is *ridiculous* and, with the possible exception of that Marshall Mathers kid, I may be the finest white rapper to emerge from the U.S of A.

Ok that's a complete lie, I just made that up and I don't know why. Sounded alright, the beat was tight and the flow was pretty fly. I really can't rap at all, so I'ma just leave y'all and know when to say goodbye.

A Race with the Four Horsemen

"I rise and shine like the sun on the one; we dance together, we overcome. A wake up call to wake up all."

– Kool Moe Dee (Rise N' Shine)

Shortly after getting home from my day visit to Washington (and a lovely lunch with principal Gonzalez and DeMarcus Nurse,) I pulled into the driveway longing for a few minutes of peace and quiet before –

INCOMING CALL FROM PRESIDENT WINFREY.

So much for that idea. "Good evening, Madame President."

"You can relax Frank, we're off the clock."

"If you don't mind me saying, ma'am, but you ain't ever off the clock."

"Ah, too true, Frank, too true. Listen, I'd like to follow up for a few minutes regarding today's meeting before I pretend to get some sleep."

"Sure thing, O, but give me few minutes to get in the house, set up the video chat on the laptop, say 20 minutes, and…"

"Do what you have to do. That'll give me time to grab a glass of wine, slip into my video chat lingerie and bunny slippers."

"Really?"

"No, not real—."

"Because if you wanted to, I would *not* be opposed…"

"Twenty minutes, Frank."

"You got it, boss."

Mere moments later I was in my video chat lingerie (kidding) and Gene Simmons dragon boot slippers (not kidding) and talking face to face with the Commander in Chief.

"Hello, Madame President. Nice robe."

"Thank you."

"I was expecting something in violet; you know how much I love The Color Purple."

"You're an ass."

"Duly noted; now, about today's meeting?"

"Yes. As you know, I called you in on the anonymous..."

"And aren't they always?"

"Frank..."

"Yes ma'am, zipping my lip, ma'am."

> *"I called you in on the anonymous reports of alleged racist practices in your T.E.A.M. Schools which, no surprise, were unfounded. However, those accusations show that we still have a way to go in terms of the public perception of what our kids know and how we treat them."*

"No argument there, Madame President."

> *"And that got me to thinking. We have the opportunity to do something really special with the T.E.A.M. Schools, something that may ultimately affect how we "do education"[1] in this country, for better or worse. I know you, and I know your people, so the issue of race relations is not an issue..."*

---

1. Funny thing, Oprah made those little 'quote thingies' with her fingers when I said "do education" even though she was in the West Wing and only I could see her. This does not, in any way, make her weird.

"It will always be an issue, boss, but I am honored to hear that from you, and I will pass that sentiment on to my teachers and staff. Please continue"

> *"I will. I think that we need to rethink how we approach educational testing. Clearly, the high stakes testing approach has failed miserably, and I would like to use your schools as a pilot program for a different way of measuring student performance, and I want your input on how we should do it, although I have some ideas. Of course, in conjunction with that, we need to engage in further dialogue as to how you and your administrators will remain accountable."*

"Engage in further dialogue? You're starting to sound like a politician, President Winfrey."

> *"It's late. Forgive me, Mister Stepnowski."*

(Laughing) "I know what you mean, boss, and you're right. So that's two of the horsemen."

> *"Come again?"*

"Biblical reference, The Four Horsemen of the Apocalypse?"

> *"Continue…"*

"Well, the way I see it, two of the four horsemen of the Educollapsealypse are educational testing and race relations, which you addressed. But I think parental involvement and accountability need to be addressed as well. The parent thing I've got covered, but I need your support if I'm going to be able to start simplifying this mess of a system that wastes money on hiring people just to figure out the rules that we pass to rectify the policies that we passed last week."

> *"That's a mouthful at nearly midnight, Frank, could you…"*

"Simplify? Gladly.

- Race relations,
- Accountability,
- Parental involvement, and
- Educational testing.

These are the underlying issues that must be addressed at the T.E.A.M. Schools if we are to be better, and more effective, than the schools currently stuck in the educational quagmire that we created here."

"You do realize that, in that order, you just came up with the acronym RAPE?"

"No, but that's why you're running the country and I'm just a schmuck with an idea. I've gotta say, though, those issues have been raping our students for generations. I'll take care of the P (parental involvement), you take care of the E (ed. testing), and we'll split the difference on the A (accountability); how's that sound?"

"And what about the R (race relations?)"

"A black female president and a white male entrepreneur talking, depriving ourselves of well-deserved sleep, in our fuzzy slippers, in the wee hours of the morning, about how to better serve future generations of students. That's a pretty good place to start, boss. Agreed?"

"Agreed. And how did you know I have fuzzy slippers on?"

"'Cause my wife gave them to you at that educational fundraiser thingie last year and you *loved* them."

Madame President Oprah Gail Winfrey smiled the smile that only those burdened with tremendous responsibility and that care about that responsibility can smile.

"Good night, Frank."

"It certainly is, Madame President. Good Night"

O.K., gentle reader, you'll hear my take on the race issue in a minute. Then, you need to hear how we deal with the four horsemen of the educational apocalypse.

WARNING: The following pages will contain entirely too much common sense (translation: controversial material) to ever be fully implemented, so don't get your hopes up, or your panties in a bunch, when you read them.

CAVEAT to the warning: In the words of Gracchus: "Rome is the *mob*." So if enough people *want* it…

EPILOGUE: Where I stand on the issue of racism in schools.

Unfortunately, I have had to deal with the issue of race entirely too much, in situations where it had absolutely no bearing on the job I was trying to do; teach children.

Ironically, the reason I had to deal with this issue so much was because I chose to stay in teaching jobs where the overwhelming amount of students I taught were considered minorities.

Fortunately, I already spoke my mind regarding "playing the race card" in my last book; feel free to check it out.

Interestingly, since the aforementioned book was published in October of 2009, I have been fortunate enough to have had many people send me books (written by people FAR smarter than I) that echo certain aspects of what I said. I refer you to Thomas Sowell, Dinesh D'Souza, Frederick Lynch, Bishop Desmond Tutu, Richard Rothstein and so many more; interesting reading all.

My opinion is that people are being kept at odds with one another because the first part of "divide and conquer" is **divide**. I'm not interested in division. I subscribe to Ken Blanchard's assertion that "None of us is as smart as all of us." I really do, and I'm pissed the fuck off that my kids (and by kids I mean my biological kids and my students) are growing up in a world where they'll be forced into wasting time defending themselves from indoctrination and divisive rhetoric when they should be educating themselves and helping others.

Now, lest you think I'm Saint Francis of Notasissy, I'll tell you what I think in plain words so you can quote me later. You can just tear the page out of the book, unless you're reading this on a Kindle or E-book, then you'll just have to copy them.

Note to Students, take note of my fluid and varied use of transition words:

To begin, I think that calling someone a racist has become equivalent to calling someone a witch in the late 1600s. Racist is an ambiguous term, often used by ignorant people that either can't verbalize a more sophisticated argument or that don't want to admit the *real* reason they don't like the accused. Furthermore, accusations of racism often require no tangible evidence but can yield tragic consequences toward the accused.

In addition, I think that anyone who defends themselves too vigorously against such an accusation may have something to hide, or a job to keep that requires they get on their knees for political correctness, if you know what I mean. In 20+ years of teaching, I have been accused of racism a few times, usually because I had the audacity to fail a student because he/she didn't rise to my high expectations of them.

While we're at it, I think the idea that black people can't be racist is bullshit, and usually kept alive by middle aged (or older) idiots that, in believing this, don't realize that they are marginalizing the same people they are attempting to support.

Furthermore, I think that any person that allows themself to be identified by a single term: black, white, gay, handicapped, poor, Republican, Californian, Crip, Step, cop, Catholic, conservative, diabetic (etc. etc. etc. on and on and on until I puke) has already marginalized themselves and ensured their own limitations, so they don't need my help to "hold them back."

However, I think that there is reason for hope. I have had frank discussions with thousands of my students (of all races, genders, ages and levels of education) over the years and, if anything, they've been conditioned to distrust EVERYONE until a person earns their trust and maintains it through proper conduct; and I think that's a hell of a lot more pragmatic than going into any situation with the idea that *this* person will treat me better than *that* person.

Finally, I think that these are the opinions of one man and, as my dad used to say, "Opinions are like assholes, everyone's got one."

That having been said, where I stand on the issue of racism in schools? It exists, but it better not raise its head in one of my T.E.A.M. Schools, or I'll cut it off. Accuse a teacher of racism because he or she is pushing you to perform better and won't relent? Get the fuck out. Imply that a student can't do the work because he or she is [insert label]? Get the fuck out. Suggest that my T.E.A.M. Schools are racist because we don't play the political correctness game? Get the fuck out.

Don't like my way of doing things?

QUESTION: How many of you actually just said "Get the fuck out" out loud or to yourself? That is *awesome*.

What you need to BE to teach for ME (and what I've learned to do in support of you)

"Illumination comes so hard. Makes me see but it leaves its scars. At times I wish that I didn't know what I know now."

– Henry Rollins

I could go on for quite some time about what separates good teachers from bad, but most of that stuff was covered in my last book; so, as to avoid redundancy, I'm going to focus on what you need to stand for before you stand in front of a T.E.A.M. School classroom.

I recently went to see the comedian/Late Night Talk show host/American treasure Craig Ferguson do his stand up, and he said that when he was growing up in Scotland, "it seemed like the only two requirements for being a teacher were hating kids and being a blackout drunk." My approach to hiring teachers is similar in its simplicity. *Why* do you teach? *What* do you do to continually improve yourself as a teacher? You had better give the right answers to those questions or I won't even consider giving you an application.

You'll notice that I didn't ask if you love kids, because you don't have to love kids to be a teacher. I know many of you will take issue with that statement and you are well within your rights to do so, but I'll tell you this, I've had my ass saved financially, legally and medically by accountants, lawyers, and doctors that didn't give a rat's ass about me beyond whether my check cleared. Furthermore, I've learned a tremendous amount from teachers that I am fairly certain cursed my parents for having me. (Hi, Mr. Mendez!) So you don't have to love kids to teach at T.E.A.M., but you'd better be ready to *teach* them like they're the ones about to operate on your grandma. Who knows? Someday they *might* be.

And once you start teaching for me, you had better plan on *improving* your craft continuously during your time here or you will be put out on your ass with the same speed and absence of mercy reserved for any student who refuses to comply with our simple rules. We're all in this boat together, everybody paddles as best they can or we sink; therefore, we all paddle like our asses are on fire or you get thrown the fuck out of the boat. End of story.

Don't like it? Don't apply.

Fortunately, the T.E.A.M. Schools were given a bit of leniency regarding professional development, given that we operate as an independent entity outside the public school sector (thank you, President Winfrey.) However, my expectations are a bit more stringent, as my teachers are expected, in lieu of lesson plans, to submit reports of what they're doing to improve their teaching prowess, whether it be formal education or simply building their knowledge base in their chosen subject area. I keep my finger on the pulse of all of my teachers, and I take their input and advice very seriously; as I have learned from experience that the people in the trenches often have the most practical advice on how to fight the war. Know how I do that? I free up a lot of time by being direct with people. You'd be amazed how much time you save when, if you have a problem with someone, you speak to them, in private, with the clear distinction that while you are their boss, you care about them. I neither saw nor felt that through most of my teaching career. My principals report directly to me, in person, once a month, via video conference or in-person visit. It saves a lot of paper, prevents misinterpretation, and lets us look into each other's eyes, a lost art in communication. Most of the administrators I dealt with were cowardly people in the business of keeping their jobs even if (and in some cases, *especially* if) it meant throwing their teachers under the bus. Let me give you two examples of the kind of "leadership" that taught me exactly what not to do once I assumed the burden of leadership as P.R.I.N.C.I.P.A.L. of the T.E.A.M. Schools.

But first, I need you to look in my eyes. Good.

These stories are *completely* fictional.

Got that? LOOK at me, please. *Completely* fictional, got that?

Good.

Story #1 – Pissed in Gym

The geniuses on the school board of Baka High School, a high school from the very large, very diversely populated Takegawa school district, decided that, due to budgetary constraints, the Supervisors should cover two subjects, their main subject and an accessory subject. Example: Mrs. Alfredo, the Supervisor of the English and World Language teachers *for the entire Takegawa school district* would also have to cover the Art teachers as well. Now, Mrs. Alfredo is a smart woman, and she digs Monet so she loves the 19th century French Impressionists without even knowing it, but that doesn't mean she's qualified to assess Art teachers or their performance; but hey, she'll *try*, and she'll *support them* while she expands her knowledge base. The same could not be said for one Mr. Beef Stroganoff, one of the most universally loathed Science Supervisors on the 3rd rock from the sun, thanks largely to his robotic demeanor and the fact that he always aspired to "lead" so he bypassed any time in front of the classroom in favor of the bullshit theory on which he gorged himself on his way to a Ph.D. The same brain trust that has Ms. Alfredo cramming study of Art Theory into her 90 hr. work week also decided that Stroganoff should supervise the Phys. Ed. teachers in addition to the Science teachers.

A pasty, aloof, pigeon-chested Chemistry whiz that demands to be called DOCtor because he has a Ph.D., (You'll see this again in the next story, so pay attention, a theme is developing!) wants to see detailed lesson plans for this week's lesson on tennis and wants to see dodge ball banned because it "reinforces bullying." Oh yeah, the gym teachers are gonna *love* this guy. Now, DOCtor Stroganoff could've ingratiated himself with his new charges by simply admitting that he wasn't a Phys. Ed. expert, but that he would work in conjunction with the teachers to help them deal with their increasingly "difficult" student population.

Yep, he *could* have done that.

Instead, he decided to "help" the gym teachers by randomly showing up and "teaching" one of their classes for 20 minutes, then (based on the *wealth* of knowledge he acquired about the intricacies of that particular class during a *one day, 20 minute* interruption) chatting about what that teacher is doing wrong. The word you're looking for, ladies and gentlemen, is JACKASS. This asshole doesn't bother to schedule his visits, interrupts instruction, and then wants to hold an impromptu assessment session, based on nothing of value about something he knows nothing about, while class is still going on!

But it gets better. Doctor Stroke it off decides to pop in on one of Mr. Hetfield's more hostile gym classes on a rainy Monday in May. Teachers of the World (and people with common sense) what's wrong with this picture?

1. Raining, so the class is crammed in a hot gym.

2. Monday, in May, so the class is less than enthusiastic to begin with.

3. Unannounced interruption to a class full of easily distracted students,

4. by a stranger in a suit that hasn't established ANY kind of repertoire with these kids yet expects them to give him their full attention.

Say it with me: Jackass.

But it gets better. While captain clueless is "teaching," a student (let's call him Micah Muhammad Myers) walks over to the corner of the gym, drops his well exposed boxers down to his non-uniform compliant jeans and *pisses in the corner of the gym.* How many of you are shocked by this? Hmmmm... How many of you are not? Hmmmm...pretty much equal. What a shame. Beefy boy was shocked; so shocked in fact that *he ignored this blatant display of disrespect,* choosing instead to keep his "lesson" going. Must have been a winner.

But it gets better. After being successfully ignored, disrespected, and ignored for about 19½ minutes, Supervisor Stroganoff spent another 9½ minutes telling Mr. Hetfield that he needed to "create a more dynamic environment and differentiate his instruction" Dr. Douchebag also expressed his disappointment that Mr. Hetfield hadn't yet "established written baselines for his students' athletic performance." He left with the words "I'll be back to see if you've taken my suggestions under advisement" hanging in the air as he bolted out of there faster than the 380A out of Shanghai[1] leaving the aforementioned Mr. Hetfield to deal with a disorganized, confused bunch of teenagers with 5 minutes left in a gym class. Oh, and that small matter of the spontaneous "in-house" lavatory trip.

1. The world's fastest high speed train at 380 kilometers per hour. D'iu ne lo mo that's fast!!

I'm getting that pain behind my eyes that usually precedes me waking up bloody in the midst of destroyed property and broken bodies just recalling this, so I'll leave it to you to recount the reasons why certain teachers get frustrated having to answer to their "superiors."

If a supervisor tried to pull that shit at one of my schools, I'd make him publicly apologize to the teacher, clean the piss himself, and *then* fire him. Of course, since my teachers carry those cards we talked about back in the *"It Takes A Lot of Heart"* chapter, I highly doubt any of our students would risk *saying* the word dick, let alone whipping theirs out in class.

Story #2 – [I don't have your] Back in Black

During my first tour of duty at Moorzakunt Academy I endured a plethora of what I will generously call "interesting" situations.[1] I was young and inexperienced, but not so naïve as to get really upset when kids with a whole boatload of physical and emotional baggage acted like a complete ass.

Now when a "professional" administrator, who earned triple my salary (and hid behind my protection when the aforementioned kids tried to kill her) did so…

As Yoda would say: "A bit less forgiving was I."

The first time I met Ms. Écouter, she was two days into her principalship at M.A., and she decided to introduce herself by walking into my class (13 very emotionally disturbed young men in a constant state of its-about-to-get-violent,) interrupting me, and talking about one of the young men's personal information like he wasn't even in the room!

I guess she figured that if she just didn't say his name, and said "excuse the interruption" *after she interrupted*, it was ok.

It wasn't ok, for so many reasons.

Once she left, the young man (let's call him Ang Li) whose business she had ingloriously made public looked at me, took a deep breath and said, in a voice strained by an otherworldly amount of restraint (think the Hulk stuck right in that moment when he's about to change,)

1. Read all about 'em in my first book which, by now, you are sick of hearing about.

"Step…if I didn't respect you and…"

"I know, and thank you, Ang."

"That bitch would be cut wide op—"

"I know, brother, I know. Now calm yourself down and I'll…"

"That shit was BULLshit Step!" chimed in Marcus. *"Who does that bitch think she is?"*

"For the moment, that woman is our principal, and you will treat her as such. Now y'all chill for a minute and I'll go down and speak to her so we can resolve this quickly and move on."

(I said, completely unaware of the impending irony.)

I walked down to the "big" office and was greeted by a look from the secretaries that said "this bitch is getting on our nerves and its only day two." I looked at *them* with a look that said, "I'm going in to talk to Ms. Écouter" and they looked at *me* with a look that said "you can't just go in there like you used to with the other principals, Step, she doesn't know you" and I looked at *them* with a look that said "we'll see about that" and they looked at each other with a look that said "oh, this is gonna be good."

I entered the office of our new principal, who looked like Maya Angelou if Maya Angelou suddenly became a self-important racist bitch that fell out of the ugly tree and hit every branch on the way down.

I was polite, though.

At first.

I was.

Really.

"Excuse me please, Ms. Écouter, but I thought we could…"

"That's DOCtor Écouter to you." (Here, again, we have someone who demands to be called "Doctor." Beware of people that demand to be called by titles, as they are obviously using them to mask authenticity of *character.*)

At this point my blood went from its normal 100.4 degrees to just slightly above hot enough to melt iron, but I tried to remain polite. I did. Really.

"Excuse me, DOCtor Écouter, but I thought…"

> *"You would think,"* she said, interrupting me for a second time, and making a sweeping gesture around her new office, decorated with no less than SIX pictures of herself, in various rehearsed spontaneous acts of accomplishment, *"being somewhat of a leader yourself, that you would recognize the accomplishment behind…"*

She was starting to get on a roll, so it was my turn to interrupt, loudly. I grabbed her door, which was about to be closed shut a bit too forcefully, and looked at the secretaries with a look that said, "This may get messy."

SLAM! "One, MISS Écouter, you're not a doctor, my wife works with doctors, they save people's lives. Two…"

> *"I have never…"*

"TWO! I've got more leadership ability in my little finger than you've got in your whole body, and if I didn't, that student you just embarrassed would have…"

At this point she (clearly flustered) grabbed the phone and prepared to dial, waiting for me to ask. So I did.

"Who ya gonna call? Ghostbusters? Your *boss*?"

Well THAT snapped her out if it.

> *"I have no boss, MISter Stepnowski, I am the principal of this…"*

"Yeah, you do, and call me Step. See that name on the bottom of your check? That's your boss. Call him."

> *"I will, and when I do…"*

"Tell him, Step goes or I go. Then let's see what happens. I'll wait."

> *"You arrogant, incendiary…"*

"I'll WAIT." Folded my arms, smiled just enough to push her over the edge, and refused to unlock eye contact. She blinked. Tried to break the silence.

"This is not going to…"

"Know this," I interrupted, ready to close with the only part of the conversation I had thought out in advance: "See that seat?" (Gesturing to her chair, the only place in the room without a picture of her on it, yet,) "If I wanted it, I would *take* it, but I don't want it, because it gets really, *really* warm. You'll know that soon enough, DAHC-TOUR ."

And with that I excused myself, earning a look from the secretaries that said "we would so jump your bones in a purple kiddie pool filled with rice pudding right now." Actually, that's a lie, they had gone to lunch.

The SECOND time I met Ms. Écouter, she was over two *years* into her principalship at M.A., and she decided to revise my comments on my students' report cards before sending them out, which then led to the discovery that she had "revised" some of my verbiage on some of my students' I.E.P.s.

Yes, you read that right. She altered legal, binding documents, and was caught red-handed.

But it gets better. She accused me of racism when I called her on it.

I'll spare you all the details because A) you've been very patient while I describe the type of behavior I chose not to emulate as leader of T.E.A.M. and B) I'm starting to get that pain behind my eyes again. Soooooooo long story *short*, the board of directors and a few other people in cheap suits drinking expensive coffee had a meeting to address Daaachchchhhhterrr Écouter's federal fuck up.

Wanna know a secret? You do?

Come closer.

Closer. *Shhhh…I didn't want to see Dr. Écouter arrested. I didn't even want her to lose her job. I just wanted to get to the bottom of her agenda against me when I was, by popular opinion, one of the hardest working, and most productive teachers on her staff.*

Until she played the race card and called me disloyal.

Then I wanted her drawn and quartered by four slow walking Clydesdales with no sense of direction.

I'll get right to the good part. After the good "doctor" started the meeting by interrupting the mediator, (not smart) she rhapsodized on about what it was like to be a victimized black woman (at which point two of the black members of the board hid their smiles and looked at me with look that said "what the fuck does that have to do with the price of tea in China?" and I shrugged and gave them a look that said "welcome to my world, folks." Every time somebody that could have fired her tried to speak to the heart of the matter, she would interrupt them with another racial diatribe that had zero to do with the matter at hand. This went on until the tensions and frustration in the room was palpable, at which point, one of the previously mentioned black gentlemen (I'll call him Marion Vortex but he knows who he is and he is the *man*) looked at me and mouthed something along the lines of "you going to speak up or what?"

That's all I needed.

"Hey *doc*," I interrupted, scoring a two-for-one, "you've sold the impoverished, victimized, misunderstood black person thing for going on a half hour now, so let me put this to you straight. You live in a gated community, drive a Jaguar, carry a Coach purse, and you didn't know why Ephraim asked for hot sauce for his food at last week's Spring Fling." (Ready…)

    "What is your point, Mr. Stepnowski?" (Aim…)

(Fire!) "My point is that I'm "blacker," by your definition, than you are, doc, so drop it and let's get down to business."

The big boss dribbled his coffee, some of the board members laughed out loud (although one looked noticeably nauseous) and Marion Vortex high-fived me and regained decorum as we finally got around to the charges against the now deflated doctor.

Even though this is *completely* fictional, the *completely* fictional legal outcome of this conundrum might not be a matter of public record; therefore, I will close by saying that this was one of many incidents that, had they not been *completely* fictional, would have taught me how not to serve as an administrator once I assumed the P.R.I.N.C.I.P.A.L.-ship of the T.E.A.M. Schools.

Which brings us back to the present, and what I expect from myself and the teachers that work for me. I ask my teachers to work hard, harder than the average teacher, and that's saying a *lot*. However, I do so with the promise that I will always, *always* have their back. ALWAYS, do you hear me? **ALWAYS**.

They make mistakes, I forgive them. They correct them, because they don't want to disappoint me; because they love knowing that someone believes in them.

And they carry that into their classrooms, forgiving their students, believing in them and working their asses off to teach them. NOT to pass some state test that's destined to have the results manipulated. NOT to satisfy some state standards that have no bearing on actual learning, and NOT to keep a job. They do it because they get it. They understand that, in the words of Norman Shidle: "A group becomes a team when each member is sure enough of himself and his contribution to praise the skills of the others." My teachers get it. They know that with intelligence comes confidence, and that, in turn, decreases the hostility caused by ignorance. They get it. They know that even though we have that horrible hierarchy of red tape revisionism I talked about back in the *S.C.R.E.W.E.D.* chapter, there is no *them* and there is no *I*. There is only *us*, and we have to get smarter, together, or we're in deep, deep, shit.

They get it.

Do you get it?

You do?

Want a job?

P.A.R.E.N.TS.

Patient, Aware, Realistic, Empathetic, No nonsense, Teacher Support systems
or
Patronizing, Apathetic, Recidivist, Enabling, Non-accountable, Trite Scumbags

"Mommy's alright, daddy's alright, they just seem a little weird."

– Cheap Trick (Surrender)

When I was but a humble servant of our fucked up educational system (read: teacher) I was always stunned at how some of the most obvious reasons for the fuckedupness of said system were so casually ignored. The most obvious example of this blatant example of convenient blindness? Parents. Now this topictopus has many tentacles, and they are all truly sticky and scary, so get comfortable and grab a snack before I make you uncomfortable and give you a smack. Where to begin with a topic so varied and potentially incendiary? How to take the first step in a journey destined to get me fired? Clearly, I should be careful, remain vague, and avoid, at all costs, inflammatory language.

Fuuuuuuuuuuuuuuuuck *that.*

If I may borrow from myself: "Ignorant, lazy, racist, stupid apples often cometh from ignorant, lazy, racist, stupid apple trees."*

---

* Taken from "The 10 ½ Commandments of Teaching" from my first literary opus, *Why Are All the Good Teachers Crazy?* Which I will continue to shamelessly plug in the spirit of capitalism.

You heard me. When I created the very first T.E.A.M. School I knew two things, beyond the shadow of a doubt, must be present for optimal learning to happen: 1. *Everyone* needed to be accountable for their actions every day. 2. *Parents* had to be involved in a positive way. No exceptions, no kidding.

QUESTION: How the hell do you expect to develop intelligent, character-driven students if their parents usurp the system by being deliberately confrontational **because they don't want to face the fact that they didn't do *their* job?**

ANSWER: You can't, most of the time.

So, when you fill out the paperwork to send your kid to *my* school, you agree to be part of the solution. No, you do not have the option to just NOT be part of the problem, that's cheating – you can't just hide away and expect us to raise your children, that attitude is what turned teaching into the high-risk, low-reward clusterfuck that led to the G.E.S. (Great Educator Shortage) of 2011. It *also* led then president Obama to pass the infamous Absentee Parent Act that led to the very first T.E.A.M. school. It also also led to a level of hostility between the two camps (parents and teachers) responsible for winning the war on ignorance that threatened to doom generations of American children to a life of perpetual servitude to anyone smart enough to get over on them with a big, fancy-pants vocabulary. Because I was aware that the issue of mandatory parental involvement was as large and potentially lethal as Kim Kardashian's ass, I called in...

"Ahem!"

Oh, for Christ's sake! *Dawn* called in the prime directors from some of the bigger megapods that expressed interest in the maiden voyage of the T.E.A.M. concept.

What are prime directors and megapods?

Allow me to explain.

During president Schwarzenegger's brief reign as CommANduh in Cheeeef, he established that there should be a small group of people *who started their careers in education as teachers* (those would be the **prime directors**) and each one would rule a triumvirate of three states that were closely related in terms of their education strategies (which would be…you guessed it, the **megapods**.) All those action movies really rubbed off on the old boy huh? Megapods, prime directors, sheesh!

I'll tell you what *didn't* rub off on the Presidentinator, elementary fucking math. Forty Seven states, divided by three, leaves 2 states hanging like a set of shrunken testicles from years of steroid abuse.

I'm just saying.

Obviously, Conan the contrarian knew something about the nation he ruled, albeit temporarily. He made Pennsylvania and New Jersey the two testicle megapod, mainly because they had… yeah, I'll say it… balls. The prime directors were the galactic empire of education, and if we were going to make 8 total lines the legal guardians stand and deliver, we needed to involve them in the conversation. To quote the Greek philosopher Taylorus Corganus: "You need to get everyone to the table before you can carve the turkeys."

Which leads us back to Dawn thinking that it would be a good idea (in the name of *anus protectus legalus*) to invite some of the prime directors from the mighty megapods to offer input as to how we should mandate the voluntary involvement of the parental units. Smart girl, that Dawn Marie, I must remember to stay married to her.

My proposal was fairly straightforward: Parents, if you want your student(s) to attend my T.E.A.M. schools, you're going to pay a substantial price (financially,) you're going to agree with my methods of discipline (socially,) and you – yes YOU – are going to be involved in your child's learning (contractually.)

I, (the P.R.I.N.C.I.P.A.L.,) Dawn (the C.F.O.,) Oprah Winfrey (the President,) the recently defrosted George Carlin (the Secretary of Education,) and six of the megapod prime directors got together to hammer out the details of how much we could *demand* of the parents, and how that would translate into contractual language.

You more astute readers will notice that there were no *lawyers* at this meeting. That's because I agree with ol' Billy Shakespeare on this topic, when he said, in Henry VI part 2, (and I'm paraphrasing here:) "First thing we do is kill all the lawyers 'cause they fuck everything up with their technicalities and hyper sensitive legal gobbledegook."

The prime directors had their say, and we ran it all up the flag pole and waited to see who saluted. Quickly but carefully, with good intentions paving our way, we hammered out a way to ensure that the people who *conceived* our students didn't just drop them at the door and turn their backs. The input we received was, to say the least, diverse. The stories we heard were, to put it mildly, interesting. Would you like to hear some of them?

Your wish is my command.

Now, it might get a bit obfuscated (SAT vocabulary word for confusing) here, so I'll do my best to keep it simple. Each of the prime directors spoke out as to his or her interests and concerns related to the idea of mandatory parental involvement. What follows is my recollection of that spirited debate.

First to speak was **Mr. J. McCarthy (Prime Director of the New York, Massachusetts and Connecticut megapod.)** "One of the main reasons I got out of the classroom was because of the parental apathy. I remember vividly one year a young lady was failing my class, and her mom showed up, livid, with two weeks left in the school year wanting to know "what my girl gotta do to pass this class?" Two Back-to-School nights, three parent-teacher conferences, bi-monthly Emails sent home, four interim reports, three report cards, and several attempted phone calls (all to numbers that were out of order) and this is the first I hear from you?? With 14 days left in the year?!? Absolutely unacceptable; I would strongly suggest that you make it mandatory for parents to attend certain functions in order for their child to graduate; perhaps at least one Back-to-School night, one parent-teacher conference, and one social event, at which they volunteer? The parents must be involved in both the academic *and* social development of their child and reinforce the idea that there is a bigger picture beyond the individual, and by attending certain functions and events, that idea will be made manifest. Simply put, if the parents are involved, they're more likely to stay on top of the kids and less likely to play the 'I didn't know' card when the failure notices come in the mail."

(Mental note to self: That's assuming the address you have is correct this week, or that the kid isn't intercepting the mail before the parent even gets it. All cynicism aside, John's "mandatory attendance" idea was implemented shortly thereafter at all T.E.A.M. Schools.)

Ms. Akima Morgan (Prime Director of the North Carolina, South Carolina, Georgia megapod) was inspired to speak next: "I concur, John. Although I must point out that the term "parents" is somewhat misleading. A lot of these kids are being raised by, at best, one parent. In many cases, uncles, aunts, grandparents, even older siblings…"

(much somber nodding and general agreement.)

"…and some of the guardians are involved, in all the *wrong* ways. When I was teaching, my ICR classes were a study in contrast. Half of the class was comprised of kids that had legitimate learning disabilities, and the other half were kids that had been "pushed through" because their parents taught them how to work the system. I had a mom interrupt me during a phone call home after I told her that her son was late THIRTY-FOUR times in the first 5 months of school. She said, and I quote, *'But he getting there. He very hard to gets out of bed in the day, and so long as he in schools, I get my check so lates to school is not too bad, yes?'* Now I, like others, have heard the rumors that this particular student is the child of illegal immigrants, a fact that the child himself did not deny. While I believe that the young man is entitled to an education, we are entitled to know if our students are actually interested in getting one, or if they're somebody's lottery ticket. We need early and frequent interventions to determine which parents want an education for their kids and which ones want a babysitter. "

(Mental note to self: Might need one of those fork-tongued bastards (read: lawyer) after all; must be sure to include an airtight zero-tolerance policy on tardiness and unexcused absence. I set a reminder to call my brother-in-law (One of the more dignified sharks in the legal ocean) on my Blackberry. We worked it out, and it worked like a charm.

One of my favorite Prime Directors, the distinguished **J. Edgar Lavin (of the Alabama, Arkansas, Tennessee megapod)** commanded the floor next: "Well, now y'all know I don't mince words when it comes to this sorta thing…"

(A few muffled laughs, some mock looks of disbelief.)

"Most of these absentee parents need immediate, no-nonsense, reminders when their offspring are being non-compliant little bast---"

ME: "Point taken, prime director. Your solution to this would be?"

"Shock collars."

ME: "They tried that in Louisiana, didn't work."

"I meant on the parents."

(Silence. Not so much of an "Are-you-kidding?" silence as a "Can we do that 'cause that would be awesome?" silence, broken by Secretary Carlin, who announced with no small amount of fervor: "I LIKE this fuckin' guy!")

"Allow me to E-lab-o-rate!" continued Prime Director Lavin. "Every time one o' the little miscreants cuts class, disrespects a teacher, or something to that effect, ZAP! Just a little shock, nothing even close to lethal, just enough to let the legal guardians know that the fruit of their loins ain't livin' up to expectations. That oughta weed out the 'phone it in/collect a check' parents that the fine prime director of the Carolinas and Georgia spoke of but quick, don'cha think?

ME: "I think we get the point, James. You and I can discuss this in depth a bit later."

"I've been at this long enough to know when I'm being placated, Mr. Stepnowski; and I know that a few of y'all think I'm an extremist. But I've known you a long time, Frank, and I know that if you could find a way to make it work, you'd be on my idea like white on rice in a snowstorm."

(Mental note to self: Whoever made this guy the PD of Alabama knew what they were doing. And for the record, he's right - if I could get away with the "Shock the Monkey" method of parental "supervision," I'd be on it with more vigor than a three legged cat trying to bury shit on a frozen pond.)

Restoring some sanity to the proceedings, **Mr. O. Okay (the Prime Director of megapod Hawaii, California and Arizona)** stood up and spoke, in his often-imitated-never-duplicated Nigerian accent: "Well, I don't tink we need to go as fah as shuck collas fo deh parents, but I do agree dat dey must be involved fah de children to have any hope of dees school of yahs to wahk. You all know mah stance dat small changes are de only way to truly implement a revolution, so I would offer de advice dat you staht with a few basic requiahments, such as de ones Mr. McCarthy spoke of priah. Den, evolve your policies to accommodate what I hope will be a whole new influx of cheeldren. As fah as concrete policy goes, I tink de parents and gahdians should HAVE to meet with you befah de child evah steps tru de dah. To be true, I tink dat you already have a pretty strict admission policy dat will weed out most of de pretenders. I only wish we had sooch a system in place when we were teaching de crazies back at de Academy!

ME: *(laughing and reminiscing simultaneously)* "We wouldn't have had any students left!"

> "Ah know, so eets for de best dat you waited 'till now, yes? I weesh you luck, Step, and you know dat you have owa full support, provided you maintain ya focus."

(Mental note to self: Practical and cautious as always, double O. Playing politics suits you, and the fact that your liberal jabs and my conservative counterpunch are working together on this makes me believe that bipartisan politics isn't just a pipe dream. PS -Love the fact that you showed up for the meeting in a Trybesmen t-shirt and flip flops.)

NOTE: Many of you will remember my ultra-liberal, ultra-intelligent, ultra-hilarious Nigerian brother from the first book. No surprise, given his intellect and charisma, that he rose through the ranks to the realm of the Prime Directors. For those of you that don't know, it's near impossible to talk about him without doing "the voice." He's cool with it, I assure you.

Seemingly ready to burst, the newly appointed **Ms. J. McGovern (Prime Director of the Maryland, Virginia, Delaware megapod)** smacked us back into reality with the type of righteous rage that can only come from someone who still bears the scars from being in the teaching trenches: "With all due respect to Prime Director Okay, I'm a lot closer to the shock collar idea than I am taking baby steps toward a revolution right now! It wasn't the kids that pushed me away from teaching, it was the enabling, blameless assholes that call themselves parents and the spineless, placating puppet administrators that serve up the 'we've got your back' rhetoric and then bend over the minute anything resembling an angry guardian comes through the door."

Secretary Carlin then interrupted :"OK, I really like this guy, (he gestures to Prime Director Lavin) but I wanna MARRY this broad!(Smiles are hidden and gestures of "continue, please" are made; except for President Winfrey, who seems a bit steamed about the use of the word "broad.")

She continued, angrily: "I always made it a point to bend over backwards for my students, but that's never enough for a generation of parents that expect us to raise their kids and then try to beat us down when we fail to do in 45 minutes a day what they couldn't do over a span of years. With your permission, I'll tell you about the straw that broke the camel's back. As you know, I was appointed Prime Director by President Winfrey in November of last year, and I'm the first to be given that title straight from the classroom with no administrative experience which, as I think about it, might be a *good* thing. I was still in the classroom when I volunteered to teach Summer School back in 2017, and I had a student that missed four out the first nine days of Summer School. I had heard all the stories about Warren, but I never listened to that stuff; I figured that with enough effort, any kid could be reached, you know? Now I know that's bullshit. Anyway, I give Warren a textbook, all of his make-up work, clearly marked with Post-its on all the right pages and clear, typed directions for every assignment. I even gave him a composition book and a few pens and pencils that I paid for, of course, and a handmade calendar of the due dates…"

(Mental note to self: I could probably recite the rest of this story verbatim, considering the amount of times I did the same thing, and judging by the looks on the faces of the rest of the people at this table, they know where this is going too.)

"…the next morning I got called to Principal Keef's office and there stands Warren and his mother, who never answered any of my phone calls or E-mails about Warren's absences. I figured at least now we can talk about Warren, until his mom starts screaming at me: *'What the hell you thinkin' sendin' all this work home for ma kid! This kid can't read no Shakespeare by hisself! You Crazy! He ain't got no dictionary for no definitions and now he mad 'cause you give him too much work he don't feel like watchin' his sister while I be at work and he go the hell out and get a new tattoo!'* Other than the *"what work?"* look Warren gave her when she made the remark about being at work, the thing that pissed me off the most was the fact that Mr. Keef sat there typing on his computer while I was getting yelled at, cursed at, and blamed for this kid's new tattoo! Realizing that he didn't have the balls to support me, I grew a set for myself, kept my composure, and said, very deliberately to the mother: 'Your son missed MY class, and he owes me every bit of the work I provided him with on the dates I specified. There are three libraries in this district, take him to one. His grade right now is a *seven*, so I suggest you both get to work *soon*. And as far as the tattoo goes, if I had anything to do with it, it would be *spelled* right.' At least Mr. Keef looked up on that note. Blood is thicker than water, Warren, but the then you want is spelled T-H-A-N, not E-N. The mom looked at me and said: *'his tat is spelled good.* THAT was her response to everything that went down. They both left and I never saw the mom, the kid, the books or materials again. I was, however, visited by Mr. Keef, who interrupted a lesson that was going pretty well by announcing, in front of a class of 16-year-olds, that I was the reason we lost Warren. I was ready to stab him in the eye with a piece of chalk when another student, Warren's friend Clint, spoke up, saying: 'Ms. M. didn't get rid of Warren, that nigga played hisself and he was gonna be out o' here without y'all help, be-LEE dat.' I went home and cried in front of my husband and my kids; it was mortifying. Later that night, I wrote a volcanic, profane letter that I never intended to mail, but one thing led to another, and… apparently the letter I wrote in frustration…

> **President Winfrey**: *"…found its way to my desk. I felt your sense of duty and righteous indignation, but I also felt the passion that I thought would make you a compassionate leader, which is why I was so disheartened to hear you refer to the idea that any kid could be reached as 'bullshit.'"*

(Softly but with a firm dignity) You know I don't really feel that way, Madame President, I was angry and I spoke out of line. It won't happen again.

> **President Winfrey**: *"Yes it will. Such is the price of passion, but I believe in you, and I'd like to hear your suggestion for implementing parental involvement in Mr. Stepnowski's T.E.A.M. Schools."*

(Looking me square in the eye, like she wanted to eat me medium rare with very little seasoning,) Prime Director McGovern admitted: "I don't know how you can *mandate* parental involvement, but some of the ideas I've heard here today sound good. I know *one* thing though."

I raised one medium rare eyebrow inquisitively.

"When the parents try to get involved the *wrong* way, by enabling their children's bad behavior and bullying teachers in the process, you'd better grow a set of balls and back up your teachers."

> I couldn't resist: "My balls are just fine, Prime Director. In fact, that brass clanging noise you heard under the table…"

Cooler heads prevailed and, unless I'm mistaken, Prime Director McGovern offered to polish the brass after a few Bacardi and Cokes at a Christmas Party some years later. The surgical proficiency with which Dawn dissected the lime for my Bombay Sapphire and tonic put a definitive end to *that* conversation.

But I digress…

Finally, as tempers were beginning to flare and exhaustion was becoming palpable, the **Rev. M. Lilley, S.J. (Prime Director of the West Virginia, Nebraska and Colorado megapod)** closed the meeting with some righteous reflection: "I am profoundly disappointed that if any teacher would voice what we clearly define here as a problem of accountability, they would be committing eminent professional suicide. This may come as a surprise to you, given my profession, but I feel that the lack of desire to punish is the greatest crime of all, and this applies to the absentee parents that inflict a life of limited options onto their children, sending them into a society that seems to be designed to incarcerate them once they've exhausted those options."

> *Secretary Carlin (barely audible, but audible) "If THIS guy was around when I was on my first tour I might not-a hated the church so goddamned much."*

(Recovering nicely) "I think it would be entirely practical for you to implement some sort of fiscal and social cost to both parent and student for involvement, or rather lack thereof, which adversely affects the child's academic progress.

For example, young Johnny comes late to class, his parents pay an established, set fine and Johnny must make up double the time he missed. Of course, I am obligated to encourage some sort of reward for continued positive behavior..."

Secretary Carlin "Oh Christ, here it comes...'

"...but that is not what I was asked, nor is this the forum, and I know when to hold my tongue; unlike some people."

Secretary Carlin "Sorry faddah, can't help the ol' comedic instincts since thawin' out, ya know?"

Everyone looked like they needed a break, and rightfully so. We had a lot of ideas to digest, and so do you. We took a break, sat down to a nice lunch catered by *Panera*, and I got to work munching and manifesting.

Here's an idea – why don't you take a break and try to simulate how I felt that afternoon? It'll be fun!

Go grab somebody's Trigonometry homework, drive to the nearest Panera, order a Fuji apple salad (mmmm...) and some soup in a bread bowl. NOW, ask everybody in the place to interrupt you while you try to finish the homework, then hit yourself in the head with a hammer on the drive home.

Never let it be said I didn't offer you the chance to really "feel" my pain.

And so it was with Fuji apple breath and a migraine brewing that I faced the Prime Directors with my response to their input and a preliminary overview of what would become the Parental Realistic Involvement Clause; referred to jokingly (behind my back like I'm not supposed to know) as the PRICk trick.

Just in case you got lost in all that information, or just in case you really hit yourself in the head with a hammer, or just in case you're one of the 7.8 % of Americans that are allergic to Fuji apples, allow me to make sure we're on the same page here. Some of us returned from lunch, some didn't. I faced the Prime Directors and told them what was going to go down as per parental involvement at the T.E.A.M. Schools.

After Lunch…

1. Oprah went back to the White House (seems there was a teensy problem with another one of Mahmoud Ahmadinejad's clones having surfaced at a Barry Manilow (Yep, still going) concert, denying the Holocaust to a small theater full of angry, Pilates-powered yentas.)

2. Secretary of Education Carlin, despite having accrued a plethora of material for what would be his 17th HBO special, "George Carlin, Thawed and Thankless," excused himself to go interview Prime Director Candidates for the Alaska, Oregon, Washington megapod. Apparently, a feisty little assistant Superintendent from Whale Cove, Nunavut named Sam Abbot would get the job. Maybe her Arctic background reminded old George of his time in the deep freeze.

3. Dawn stayed, (despite having her Blackberry go off so many times that if she would have put it on "vibrate" and down the front of her pants…) Apparently, she still wasn't fully convinced that I wouldn't go apeshit and jeopardize the proceedings.

Interesting fact: Spellcheck tried to get me to re-spell apeshit as "apes hit." Apeshit, *still* not an accepted part of the American vernacular, people.

4. The six Prime Directors returned, fresh from carb loading at lunch and their phones still warm from extended "holy shit he's really going to make the parents accountable" conversations with other Prime Directors, who were no doubt on speed dial. (Yeah, we still have speed dial, and iPods, and Dr. Who. It's only 2020 folks, we aren't living on Mars and communicating telepathically *just yet.*)

5. *I* faced the Prime Directors, told 'em what I thought of their suggestions and accusations, and told them just how it was gonna be at the T.E.A.M. Schools for the parents and guardians that thought just handing us their hard-earned money was the end of their responsibility:

"Ladies and gentlemen of the Prime Directive, I appreciate you putting in the time here, and I really do value your input. I can honestly say that none of you were completely full of shit, and that was refreshing. Mr. McCarthy and Reverend Lilley, I think that your suggestions are the most readily implementable, as you will see in the preliminary draft of what I will call the Parental Realistic Involvement Clause; however, I would like to discuss the reward system in greater depth at a time in the very near future as per your mutual conveniences. Ms. Morgan, I feel your pain regarding parents that teach their kids to work the system, and I can assure you that will not happen at any facility that I am putting my name on. The legal teams are currently working out the logistics of how to "auto-drop" a student whose future is compromised by such a situation, and the guardians will be made aware of that during the enrollment process. Prime Director Lavin, while I would be willing to endure a few shocks of my own to get collars on some of these deadbeat motherfuckers masquerading as parents, I think we both know that we'll have to keep that one tucked away in our cathartic revenge fantasy stash for now; this is not to say that we can't hurt 'em in other ways; namely, Reverend Lilley's twofold punishment that will affect…"

Prime Director McGovern interrupted: *"Don't you mean accountability measure?"*

"No." I countered, "I mean punishment. That's another thing that will die a painful death at the door of my T.E.A.M. Schools – the use of soft language and euphemisms.

You will *comply,* or you will be *punished.*

You will *work* hard, or you will *fail.*

You will *obey* our rules or you will

get

the

fuck

out.

I can see the look of consternation from here, Prime Director Okay; rest assured, I will be calling upon your patience and counsel in time, but for right now, we are trying to fix an educational system that has been FUBAR for far too long so, in this case, I'm going to follow the advice of one General George S. Patton, who said: 'A good plan, violently executed now, is better than a perfect plan next week." My plan might not be perfect, but we're going to enforce it with passion and the idea that failure is not an option (I winked) for us, anyway."

Prime Director Okay mock submitted: *"Ah-kay, Capteen America. I undahstand. Ho boy! Eet will be entahtaining to watch you from de comfaht of my office dureeng dose fuhst few weeks when de parents heah dis! Ah don't envy you!"*

"Love you too, my Nigerian nightmare." I cajoled, "It's been a long day, gang, I suggest we adjourn. I'll forward the preliminary draft of the Parental Realistic Involvement Clause, which only now do I realize lends itself to an interesting acronym, to your respective offices. Good day, ladies and gentlemen."

Of course, the shit hit the fan when we dropped the news that parents actually had to be involved in their kids' educations if they wanted them to attend T.E.A.M. School.

News stations, web sites, magazines, and blogs called us everything from "Orwellian control freaks" (well done with the literary allusion, Los Angeles Times) to "Knuckle dragging Nazi Neanderthals" (nice use of alliteration, CNN, sorry you no longer exist,) to "the prototype of invasiveness and corporal punishment," (blow me, Al Gore; when you're done misleading the public and misrepresenting data, of course.)

The results were exactly as you would expect.

"Our phone lines and web sites are jammed," said Dawn, *"it seems like almost everybody with a job in America wants their kid in this school."*

Standardized Testing
Sucks Hot Monkey Ass

"Not everything that can be counted counts, and not everything that counts can be counted."

– Albert Einstein

As I begin this chapter on why we, at the T.E.A.M. Schools, don't give a shit about standardized testing, I cannot help but be acutely aware of the disparity between Einstein's simple but effective eloquence and my profane, emotionally-stunted rambling. That's why he discovered the theory of relativity and I have relatives with theories.

But, of course, I digress…

Back when No Child Left Behind surfaced like the Loch Ness Monster in 2001, I screamed to anyone that would listen that it would affect education the way "Fat Man" affected Nagasaki back in 1945. Many listened, most didn't, we got fucked, all suffered. Thank goodness a tornado of people much smarter than I came out after that and wrote about what a nightmare NCLB was; I refer you to the works of Kohn, Meier, Ravitch, Sizer, Wood, etc., each one simultaneously interesting and infuriating. Unfortunately, it didn't stop President Obama from threatening to totally overhaul it while simultaneously ignoring it during his four year rock star tour of America. Nor did it stop the ill-fated President Schwarzenegger from singing its praises until that fateful day in March of 2014. It didn't even stop the political juggernaut that is Oprah Gail Winfrey, (who was so busy cleaning up the foreign affairs maelstrom and economic quagmire left to her by her predecessors) from being crazy enough to endorse a new breed of independent, extreme methodology schools being run by a spasmodic former teacher who hears voices and drinks far too much caffeine. Suffice it to say, we were still stuck with some version of No Child Left Behind, *and its misguided and dangerous emphasis on test-taking skills and strategies over higher order thinking* in the year 2020.

Well, I wasn't playing that game anymore, folks.

Of course, there was massive opposition from the opposition who, for purposes of clarity, I will call **the coalition of clueless twats who know nothing about what goes on in real classrooms along with the fat cat motherfuckers that are heavily invested in maintaining an ignorant, uneducated population that is grossly unaware of how badly they're being treated.**

> "Your schools are part of the academic framework of the U.S. of A., and they will subscribe to the same testing practices that other schools do" spouted Speaker of the House Pamela Demic.

"Wrong." I retorted, "My schools are the *solution* to what is wrong with the academic framework of the U.S. of A., and I refuse to waste time teaching to tests that have done *nothing* to either raise student achievement or level the academic playing field."

> "Wellllll now," patronized Hemma H. Royd, chairman of the Ways and Means Committee, "that's a prettah vague ah-suh-tion y'all make there, MIS tuh StepAnowski, could ya make ya-self a bit clee-ah?"

Now, as I have told you before, gentle reader, I am a man of the people. You ask me, even in a barely discernable southern drawl, why I don't like standardized testing...

Your wish is my command.

You may want to <u>underline</u> the following passage for future use.

"Certainly, Mr. Chairman. The idea that how kids score on a singular, exhaustive written test, with reading passages that are so deliberately non-offensive that they're borderline unreadable, and math problems so intentionally diverse that they are bound to frustrate even the most ardent left-brainer, the scores of which will be subject to revision and manipulation every year so that they will yield whatever "results" the current regime wants to see is somehow indicative of student and teacher achievement is, to put it mildly, the biggest bunch of bullshit I've ever been unfortunate enough to have been associated with in my lifetime; with the possible exception of this gathering of inbred morons. I won't be part of it, and you can't make me. Now if you'll excuse me, I have children that need to be educated.

They blustered, they hollered, they threatened. President Winfrey called, we talked, I assured, she warned, we agreed. Only now can I make the details of that conversation between me and President Winfrey public to you, the lucky owner of this book.

(But FIRST, you should take a break. I'm concerned that all this dialogue might be too much in one sitting, and your mental health is important to me. So, kinda like when the *Wii* tells you to "go outside for a while," I'm suggesting you take a teensy-weensy break from all this dialogue. Maybe make a sandwich? Catch up on your E-mails? Write a scathing review of this book on Amazon.com? Of course, if your "reading stamina" can take it – read on, soldier. Otherwise, I'll see you in a little bit.)

You're back! Cool. How was that sandwich? Oooooh, PB&J...love it. Now where were we?

Ah, yes – "The *Conversation*" between President Winfrey and myself:

> **The Boss with the hot sauce**: *"You really pissed them off today."*

The indignant entrepreneur: "Fuck 'em, they pretend to care about kids but they don't care about anything but making things easy to grade so even their narrow minds can understand the scores."

> **The Hand that Rocks the International Cradle**: *"Did you forget to whom you are speaking?"*

The suddenly reticent rebel: "My apologies, Madame President; however, you know I'm right. Just give me a chance, give my people a chance, and I'll prove, beyond the shadow of a doubt, that our way is *better*."

The Overlord of the Oval Office: "That's just the point, Frank, how are you going to prove, to bureaucrats and bookworms alike, that the way the T.E.A.M. Schools teach is superior to the status quo?"

The suddenly diplomatic donkey: "What if I could show that we were, if nothing else, as good as the status quo?"

The Black woman in the White House with the red pen that could make my life blue: "Explain."

The white guy in the black suit that can't see things in shades of grey: "What if I agreed, after one full scholastic year, to have all of the students at my T.E.A.M. Schools, take the standardized tests for their area? If we score, based on our numbers, per capita, higher than the average of the other schools in that state, you agree to leave us alone and let us do our thing?"

The Commander in Contemplation: "What if some of your T.E.A.M. Schools exceed expectations and some don't?"

The gambling goofball: "All or nothing. That's how confident I am."

President Winfrey: "I admire your confidence, and I hope you're right, or I'm going to look like a fool for backing you; and if that happens…"

Me (suddenly feeling very alone:) "Message received. Thank you, Madame President, your faith in us will not be taken lightly. I'll let myself out."

Ten seconds after I left that meeting, I had Dawn on the phone:

"Assemble every director of every T.E.A.M. School NOW, I want everyone available for a video conference by 5 pm today. What? I don't give a *damn* how busy their schedules are. Tell them it is good news but that their jobs are on the line and that failure to comply will result in immediate termination. Huh? I know that sounds contradictory but, look, just freakin' *do* it, ok? Yes… I know… I'm sorry, but… yes… ok… I know… love you too."

My ass on the line and my head on a platter and she's worried about me raising my voice, Jesus H. Christ what am I getting myself into?

Well the rest, as they say, is history. Don't ask me how we did it or I'll have to bore you with a long speech about how creating better people supersedes better students and how teaching someone to THINK makes them better prepared for all facets of life, including stupid standardized tests. We rocked, the powers-that-be rolled [over] and the T.E.A.M. Schools were, for the time being at least, exempt from the unrealistic rigors and expectations of high stakes testing. The only drawback I could see was that Ways and Means Committee chairman Hemma H. Royd, (y'all remembuh him, don'cha?) was relieved of his duties and President Winfrey *"strongly suggested"* that I find a place for him in the Department of Education so that he could, in her words, *"atone for his sins."*

"Who am I, lady justice?" I pleaded.

"Just do it." she commanded.

"Fine." I conceded.

"Hey George, remember Chairman Royd, from the Ways and Means…"

"Yeah, I know that fat freakin' asshole," replied Secretary of Education Carlin, upset at having been, as he put it, "disturbed from [my] morning dump. What about him?"

"Big O. wants him to have a job inside the Ed. Department."

"You gotta be shittin' me! Where the fuck am I gonna, no, wait…I got it! Tell the fat fuck to report to me as fast as his fat ass'll carry him. I have just the position for him. He's so concerned about the *children*…"

And so it was that the unfortunately named Hemma H. Royd, former chairman of the Ways and Means Committee, became the Director for Interesting Curriculum for Kids, along with its most unfortunate acronym.

Sucks to be him.

In the meantime, no sucky standardized shit for the triumphant titans of T.E.A.M.!

Immediate result? I poured myself a Bombay Sapphire and tonic, squeezed in a little lime, and sat back to revel in a job well done and the satisfaction of knowing that my faith in my teachers was well rewarded.

Shortly after immediate result? Dawn called to tell me that enrollment applications were increasing by the tens of thousands because parents, now relieved [thanks to the media coverage of the first round of test results] with the way we do things, were suddenly interested in getting their kids in T.E.A.M. Schools. I poured my Bombay Sapphire and tonic into the soil of the plant next to my desk, threw the lime at the garbage can (missed), and contemplated going to the roof of the building, taking a deep, cleansing breath, admiring the sunrise, and jumping off.

What we have here is a
lack of failure to communicate.

"In the age of the modern man; we see the problems but we don't really understand."

– Ratt (Lack of Communication)

Have you ever noticed that when you're trying to spell something with the letters from your alphabet soup, or Alpha-Bits cereal, or those refrigerator magnets, or those punch-out letters you get from the store, etc…that you can NEVR GET ALL OF THE LETERS OR NUMB3RS YOU NED? There's a life lesson in there somewhere. Too many unnecessary letters and numbers leads to confusion.

Almost always, when a new student gets his/her new roster at one of our T.E.A.M. Schools, they ask *which* History class they're in, or what *level* English class they are in, or "am I in Geometry I or II?" The answer here is simple.

You have Math, Reading, and Writing, double periods of each, one period of Character Development, and one lunch period. (Incidentally, we follow the lead of those nice folks in Finland that provide lunch for all of their students.)

2+2+2+1+1= 8 periods. Once you have established yourself in the first three, and your instructors have determined what level your class will be taught at (remedial, basic, advanced) and whose class you belong in, (there are three classes of each subject, and one teacher per level) your basic classes will be reduced to one period each, and you will receive a double period in what we call practical information (everything from how to search the internet safely and efficiently, to how to change your oil in your car, to how to balance a checkbook, etc.) You will remain in Character Development and lunch, and you will be given a period during which you may work on your homework, with teachers around to assist you. Still 8 periods. Start by focusing on the practical basics, both academically and behaviorally. You can *earn* the Arts by proving yourself in the academic realm. No more hiding in pottery class or interpretive dance class because you're afraid of failure. However, the Arts open up a whole new method of higher order thinking, so we make the possibility of earning instruction in them very attractive. (Speaking of *very* attractive, you should see our music theory teacher, Ms. Schmitt.)

But I digress…

So, if you're a student in my school, come mid-October, your schedule would look something like this:

1st period (9:00-9:45) Basic Reading

2nd period (9:45 – 10:30) Remedial Writing

3rd period (10:30 – 11:15) Basic Math

4th period (11:15 – 12:00) Character Development

5th period (12 noon – 12:45) Lunch

6th period (12:45 – 1:30) Practical Information

7th period (1:30 – 2:15) Practical Information

8th period (2:15 – 3:00) Homework

We *tried* deviating from the 8 period system, believe me, but found out pretty early that you can't nuke *everything* these kids have ever known about school and expect great results. Hey, you live and you learn. The main reason we decided to go with general, basic class names is because the alphabet soup of differentiation was becoming clusterfuck stew. Take, if you will, the example of Descaminado High School, the last place I taught prior to T.E.A.M. The Math periods were Imp.1, Imp.2, (what the fuck is Imp? I thought an imp was a bad faerie!) Geometry, Algebra1, Algebra 2 – I could fill half the page with just Math class names! The English classes were either self-contained, Explorations (Exp,) College Prep (CP,) Gifted and Talented (GT,) which became Advanced Placement (AP) *after* 10th grade, etc. I could go on and on and on and on, but by now you're either:

1. Someone outside the educational field; hence, confused.

2. Someone all too familiar with this acronymic Armageddon; hence, frustrated. Funny thing, that's how most students feel when confronted with this bullshit – confused and frustrated. ESPECIALLY when they know what the fancy titles and acronyms *mean*. Trust me; I've consulted a few thousand students over the years and most of 'em know what the pretty titles of their classes *really* mean.

Hey Linh and Courtney! You're in "GT" or "1st track" or "honors" or(insert your school's name for "the smart kids" here.)

Linh and Courtney: "Oh, *the smart kids*. Yes, we assumed as much; we've always been in those classes."

Hey Zach and Alexa! You're in "CP" or "2nd track" or "Pre-collegiate" or (insert your school's name for "the kids that *think* they want to go to college" here.)

Zach and Alexa: "Oh, *the kids that are probably goin' to some kind of college;* yeah, we kinda knew that; we told our counselors that we were thinking about college."

NOTE: I say THINK they're going to college because some of these kids THINK that because they told some counselor that they wanted to go to divishun one kolledge, and got placed [because the counselor is clueless] into a college prep class, that they R goin' to college.

Wrong.

Oh you might *go*, but don't unpack your bags when you get there, 'cause I THINK you won't be staying.

Hey Hector and Tayshawn! You're in "EXP" or "3rd track" or "Foundations" or (insert your school's name for "the behavior problem kids that are lucky if they can spell college" here)

Hector and Tayshawn: "Whatever man."

Before you ask...

"Step, did you realize that the names you gave for the gifted classes were both female, and one was most likely Asian?" Yes, I did that on purpose. "And are you aware that the names you gave for the college prep class were mixed gender and could be from any nationality?" Yep, did that on purpose too. "So, then you're aware that both of the names for the 'lower classes' were both male and decidedly minority in origin?" Correctumundo.

Please send all of your accusations of racism and insensitivity to *The Fans of the Author Frank Stepnowski* on Facebook. Before you do, know that I think you need to get your head out of your sphincter, look around, and check out the unfortunate demographics of the various high school classes in these, our United States.

Please send all of your "thank goodness somebody finally said it" letters to *The Fans of the Author Frank Stepnowski* on Facebook. Before you do, know that I have been listening to you, and that's why I imagine a school of the future where students wind up where they really belong and are engaged at the level that is most conducive to their learning.

Which brings me back to my T.E.A.M. approach; it takes a lot of work in the first few months to determine a kid's comfort level, but my teachers don't mind because they know that, once those few weeks of gut-busting effort are complete, they will be rewarded with a homogeneous group of students on roughly the same academic level that are willing to learn. What's that? You think that's how most classes in high school are *now? HAhhAHHAhhahh... sorry, HAhAHHHahahHhAHAHaHhaHAHAHAAA...no, Hmmph,hmm... no, hmm,* no, sorry –sniff – haha. No, they most certainly are not. Many teachers are teaching classes with such a wide disparity of ability in each class that it is virtually impossible to teach without boring the daylights out of a few students and completely throwing a few others under the bus, usually simultaneously. But we work to avoid that here. Let me explain how a new student is assessed.

New kid comes in, let's call him Lukas, and we put him in to one of three classes for Math, Reading, Writing and Character Development. The teachers of those first three classes have four weeks (basically, the month of September) to determine whether Lukas belongs in a remedial, basic, or advanced class. Once those decisions are made I, along with my advisors, meet with the teachers *and the students* to discuss their placement. Yes, the students have a say in the matter (imagine that!) but very rarely do they dispute the placement. Most kids know what they know and where they belong and MOST KIDS CAN HANDLE THE TRUTH as long as they know:

1. It's being given to them with the intent of improving them,

2. <u>by people that legitimately care about their well-being.</u>

So let's say Lukas is great at math, and we all agree that he belongs in Ms. Semola's advanced math class. Done. Luk, however, doesn't like to read and reading isn't exactly his strong suit. OK, he sucks at reading – into Mr. Jones' remedial reading class, where Lukas knows he'll be given work that he can understand, but that Mr. Jones will push him to work toward his potential. **Notice I didn't say "age-appropriate level." Who decides these levels anyway? If Lukas works toward improving his ability to read the lines (and in between them,) he'll be fine, trust me.**

Finally, Luk loves to write, but his grammar and narrative voice could use some work. Tough call. What do you think, Ms. Runyan, you've had him for a few weeks? Basic class? What about you, Lukas? You think you could make it in an advanced class? I see a look of concern, Ms. Runyan. Tell you what, Luk, you set the world on fire in Miss Runyan's basic class and we'll get together again and talk about you moving into Ms. Dean's advanced class, cool? Cool, but Miss Runyan had better *rave* about you or it's a no go. So, we're all in agreement? Meeting adjourned – your schedule will be finalized in 24 hours, Lukas. Officer Gotchaler will escort you back to lunch.

But doesn't that sort of individualized interaction take a lot of <u>T</u>ime? Sure does. How much <u>E</u>ffort goes into this process and these meetings; this flexibility of scheduling? More than you can imagine. <u>A</u>nd <u>M</u>oney? Surely these teachers aren't willing to put in all this extra time unless they're paid exorbitantly well? Well, most teachers (the good ones, anyway) I know have been putting in levels of effort that FAR exceed their incomes for years, but my teachers are paid closer to what they deserve than those still suffering in the current standard system. We are, after all, a team.

I know money doesn't grow on trees, but you'd be surprised how much people (parents and guardians) are willing to pay for a product they <u>know works</u> and that will <u>help their children</u>. You *wouldn't* be surprised?

Oh, sorry.

Well, you'd be surprised how much money President Winfrey has growing on the money trees in her oval office, and how much of that she's willing to donate to a persistent Polish pain in the ass who's trying to right the wrongs of the educational system. *That* doesn't surprise you either?

Crap.

Well, you'd be surprised to know that pandas have a hard time reproducing because male pandas have very tiny penises. Oh, *that's* a revelation, is it? You guys are hard to surprise.

Pandas of the world, send your hate mail to *The Fans of the Author Frank Stepnowski* on Facebook. But know this – just because you're cute as hell and smell faintly of newly chewed bamboo, my lawyers are sharks and they will be merciless in their litigation.

NOTE: Any sharks that are offended by being compared to lawyers, send your hate mail to… Oh, you know where!

While we're on the subject of keeping things simple, I should point out that the grading system at my T.E.A.M. Schools is much more simplified than the convoluted, compromised clusterfuck that other schools use to "pass" students for simply having a pulse and a pencil [which has been provided for them.][1]

Did that sound a bit judgmental? It did? Sorry. I meant for it to sound a LOT judgmental, so let's try this: Most of the schools in this country are

---

1. The pencil, that is. Although I'm sure with technology moving forward, we'll be able to provide them with a pulse soon, too.

pushing through students that are anti-social, irresponsible, barely literate, weak-willed little urchins with no work ethic, a sense of entitlement, and no foreseeable future other than to contribute to the slow, steady decline of the infrastructure of this country.

They, the school personnel in charge of decisions, do this in a number of ways: Rounding up failing grades to passing grades, (sort of the reverse of what your lawyer and mobile phone company do with your hourly usage!) Overlooking forged notes for tons of excused absences, (don't ask.) Setting up "credit restoration" (which basically involves sitting in a room during off-school hours so Joey can "get credit for" the actual learning time he missed 'cause "gettin' up at 7 a.m. is too fuckin' *hard*, dawg.") Oh, yes, there are so *many* ways the school system you entrust your children to find way to let kids that are dumber than a box of rocks and twice as burdensome graduate next to *your* offspring. One of my favorite tricks is to simply make the expectations so low that a highly motivated panda with a little penis could probably graduate. The passing grade when I was in high school was a 70 (and you'd have gotten your ass kicked for one of those.) Moorzakunt Academy, my first teaching gig, allowed students to pass with a 65. Descaminado High School, my last tour of duty, would round up a 58 to a passing 60. You heard that right – 58 gets you a passing grade.

As one of my teaching assistants used to say: "D" for D-ploma.

More like "F" for farce, if you ask me.

So, in typical crazy (read: common sense compared to the status quo) fashion, I decided to have a simplified curriculum that was graded in equally simple fashion. Wanna hear it? I knew you would. 80-100 = pass. 79 or lower = fail.

You fail; you take that class, at that level, again until you understand the material well enough to warrant a passing grade. No rounding up, no free rides, no exceptions, no kidding. You score in the top 20% of the grading spectrum, you pass – simple.

"But Step," you question with due diligence, "isn't an 80 a bit... low... for a passing grade?" Yes, but we foster a sense of healthy competition that results in veeerrrrry few grades in the 70s.

"But Step," you ask with an impressive amount of concern, "what about a kid that gives you the absolute best he can and his best isn't good enough to earn a passing score?" Then they fail that subject. All men are created equal socially, not academically, and the sooner we admit that the sooner we'll stop trying to fit round pegs into square holes *that they don't want to be in in the first place!*

"But Step," you ask with a warmth and empathy unique to you, "doesn't the word *FAIL* hurt the students' feelings?" Ok... I could write a book just on this subject alone, but you're a busy person, so I'll try to be concise by telling you my feelings, giving you a quiz, then using your answers to tell you the truth about passing and failing, winning and losing, etc.

And the truth will set you free.

First, my response to the word "fail" hurting student's feelings: I DO NOT CARE about hurting student's feelings if that student doesn't care enough to put forth his/her best effort. This country was founded by, and urged into superpower status by, people who could handle their feelings being hurt. The same country is being compromised and weakened by people who use euphemisms and legerdemain to protect their fragile egos and flimsy character. They are weak, and they are bad for this country. My students are hardworking, strong-willed dogs of war that can handle some bruising of the ego in their quest for competence.

Second, I promised you a quiz (oh, quit your crying, this is easy, and done simply to prove a point!) My son Frankie came home with a test a few years ago when he was in 4th grade and, instead of a grade, there was a modified smiley face with two stars instead of eyes.

"What the fuck is this?!?" I *thought*.

"What's this mean, buddy?" I *inquired*.

His answer, which was clearer than most politicians' speeches, made me question, even further, the lengths we'll go to in order to save "feelings," and just how honkin' *stupid* some of those methods are.

1. Take a look at the "grades" on this page.

2. Next to each one, tell me what letter grade it's supposed to represent (A, B,C,D or F)

3. You have one minute. Go.

Alllllrighty then. Let's see how you did (assuming you're not the smart-ass that deliberately messed up the answers- yes, you, the one laughing right over there— you're not helping anyone by being deliberately noncompliant.)

The smiley face with two stars for eyes that looks like Bootsy Collins[1] is an "A"

The smiley face that looks like Paul Stanley[2] from the rock group KISS is a "B."

The standard smiley face that we all know and love is a "C."[3]

The smiley face that looks like he's been spending some time on Prozac, with a straight line for a mouth and a very compliant appearance[4] is a "D."

"Mr. frowny face," the universal icon for *well **this** is certainly a disappointment* is an "F."[5]

So, how did you do? Good for you! I'll be traveling cross country signing books, and I'll bring plenty of gold stars to put in yours 'cause I love you like that. In all fairness, that was pretty easy, right? I mean, *even a 4th grader* could have figured those out right?

Oh, yes, they sure can, AND they can be especially cruel to the kids that get Ritalin smiley or Mr. Grumpy, because they know that SOMEbody is trying to hide the fact that they shit the bed on this particular test.

Bottom line – kids know, they can *handle* it, and they don't need jellyfish "protecting" them from a world they can *deal* with.

1. Great funk bass player, known for his trademark glasses that looked like big stars.

2. Paul's the one with the star, Gene is the uber - capitalist with the tongue, Peter and Ace are …never mind, don't want Gene to sue me.

3. I know; I felt the same way, how did poor smiley get suddenly "average?" Welcome to our super-sized everything world, folks.

4. Ironic that the medicated, compliant (read "easy to control") smiley is a "D" student. But I digress…

5. Ironic that the kid that failed, the one with the best chance of having a fragile ego, gets the most obvious "symbol" dropped on him? I think so!

Which is exactly why we, at the T.E.A.M. Schools, can simplify almost everything: we are not burdened by the colossal, and I mean AWE-INSPIRINGLY COLOSSAL amount of wasted time, paperwork, or logistics thrown away in the name of political correctness, manifestation hearings, or euphemistic verbiage.

We calls it like we sees it, and we knows you can handle it.

If you follow the rules, you will be rewarded and you will earn the perks of being a winner. If you break the rules, you will be punished in a way that fits the crime. If you pass a class, you will move on to bigger and better things. If you fail a class, you will remain there until you "get it." Beautifully simple, right? We think so, and so, apparently, do many…

What?

Yes, students can be required to repeat an entire year if they didn't…

What now?

Oh, Lord. No, dear reader, *No Child Left Behind* does NOT mean that students can't be left back. *No Child Left Behind* is a short, nice-sounding name for a very long, not so nice document designed to improve (or so it says) our students' academic standing, through the use of unrealistic expectations, misappropriated funds, and broken promises. But hey, I'm paraphrasing.

The rocket scientists that created NCLB worked on the premise that if we dump a bunch of money into impoverished districts, thereby "equalizing" the spending per students nationwide, then everybody will be reading at age-appropriate levels within a few years; and unicorns will serve us all free peanut butter and jellies on silver platters that you can keep, and penguins will fly out of my ass and make me a spinach salad with just the right amount of bacon dressing, and Scarlett Johansson will show up with a kiddie pool of warm pudding and…

Oh, but I've said too much.

I always love when I tell [allegedly clueless] teenagers the basic precepts of *No Child Left Behind* and they say – paraphrasing here – "that's the stupidest fucking thing we've ever heard. Oh, you've got a cut on your leg, stick a dollar bill on it! Oh, it's still bleeding? Stick a FIVE dollar bill on it!" (insert uproarious student laughter here.)

And people think teenagers are stupid.

They're smarter than many of our politicians, evidently.

Bottom line: Kids can be left back a grade in any school; although the chances of that happening are pretty rare these days since the cost of keeping a kid for that extra year far exceeds the amount that people give a shit.

Beneath the bottom line bottom line: We'll hold you back here at the T.E.A.M. Schools if we feel you need some further work, because we *care* (and we don't have to worry about the cost of keeping you, thanks to that substantial tuition your legal guardians were willing to pay to save you from schoolus normalus clusterfuckus.)

Easy to understand language, simple scheduling, clearly defined expectations, and an unaesthetic but effective discipline policy in a clean, well-financed, well run school. Think of all the time this saves our students. What, then, to do with all that time?

Oh, I don't know…LEARN, maybe.

Any questions?

Whoa. I didn't expect so many.

You really *have* been paying attention.

O.K., let's start with the intense looking blonde with the "Search and Destroy" cupcake tattooed on her forearm in the front here, and then I'll move along to the left and try to cover all of your questions…

F.A.Q. regarding the previous chapter:

Yes, cupcake cutie in the front row.

Yes, you are correct; there are no "time spaces" between periods for students to get from class to class. Here's the logic: the schedule is much easier to understand in 45 minute increments, and since (in most schools) a HUGE amount of time is wasted getting kids out of the halls and into classes, we figure we still get a lot more leaning done "losing" a minute or two here and there while students move quickly from class to class. Furthermore, since they are ready to work the minute they walk into class, we get (again) more learning done per amount of time than any of our "competitors." Thanks for your question.

Over there, no, *there* – yes, the large fellow with the very black beard and the San Francisco Giants baseball hat.

How can we be sure that the students move quickly from class to class? Excellent question; remember those little riot control devices we talked about back in the "No Left Eye in Team" chapter? Riiight. We have a few other nasty surprises for slackers. Trust me, nobody wants to be caught in the halls when we're testing new ideas. I got caught out there one time and I still can't get the smell out of…never mind. Thanks for your question.

Right over here, the redhead with the librarian glasses and the low cut blouse; *love* that look, by the way, makes me wish I had an overdue copy of *Frog and Toad Together.*

Is it true that students in my old school could actually pass with a 58? Excellent question. <u>For legal reasons, no, that it absolutely untrue</u>, but thanks for asking. Sorry, only one question per…what? Yes, pandas do have very small penises, but they've asked me to clarify that they work them with all the black and white fury of a yin/yang symbol in the dryer on spin cycle.

Young man in the front with the Bad Religion shirt on and the iPod earphones in.

The exact tuition to get into a T.E.A.M. School? Are you interested in an application? The official tuition, as of the time of this publication, is somewhere between "that's not as bad as I thought" and "Mommy and I can't retire early now so you'd better not screw this up you little bastard!" For a more detailed explanation about where the money goes, read the next chapter.

Yes, sir, in the back, with the *"Facebook is Evil"* T-shirt and the fake tan? Speak up, please sir!

Do I think I gratuitously promoted the Friends of the Author Frank Stepnowski on Facebook too much in this chapter? One, it's *The Fans of the*

Author Frank Stepnowski on Facebook. Two, Gene Simmons is iconic to me, so no amount of self –promotion could be, to use your word, excessive. If you take issue with that, send me a message on *The Fans of the Author Frank Stepnowski* on Facebook and tell me so.

Last question, please, I have a meeting with John Heaven from Dell Computers at 3:30. You, the very curvy blonde in the aisle… wait a minute. Scarlett Johansson? Nice to meet you… what's that? You *do* have a kiddie pool and some warm pudding back at your place?

Heaven can wait.

ASCHE ZU ASCHE

Careful what you wish/You may regret it
Careful what you wish/You just might get it

Then it all crashes down/And you break your crown
And you point your finger/But there's no one around

Just want one thing/Just to play the king
But the castle's crumbled/And you're left with just a name

– Metallica (King Nothing)

Hey determined readers! By now you are experts on *exposition*, (background information, gets you up to speed, blah blah blah) so I shan't bore you with an explanation. Let's just get down to it, shall we?

Exposition: Snakes and Arrows

A lot of things happened between the years 2018 and 2020, many of them wonderful. Our students were consistently outperforming students in other schools regardless of how the politicians measured it *this month*. It was becoming like a sad little game, where the powers-that-be tried to design an "assessment instrument" (just call it a test, you fuckwads) on which our kids would underperform. Unfortunately, it seemed that the harder we worked to make the T.E.A.M. Schools the standard by which all other schools were judged, the harder certain forces worked to keep us from the business of becoming better educators. Dawn was putting in marathon sessions trying to keep the books and the enrollments straight, no small feat given how much we donated to charity and how many applications came in every day. The teachers were grinding away with righteous determination, making me proud every day and their students better in every way. The parents, some by force (but, with increasing regularity, by choice) were becoming integral, inspirational members of the T.E.A.M. family.

But, to borrow from Willy Shakes, "Something [was] rotten in the state of Denmark."

It was pathetic; instead of working with us at the T.E.A.M. Schools, and giving us a chance to *learn from each other* about what works and makes our kids better (lord knows, we were still open to advice!) **the people entrenched in the status quo went the traditional route of hating what they didn't understand and tried to vilify us rather than work with us.** Many were the times I thought "no wonder our kids are screwed; look at the people in charge of them." Oh, we were besieged on all sides: "***Where*** does the money go?"

"**What** were you thinking condoning corporal punishment?" "**How** did you let an illegal immigrant get by your enrollment process?" "**Why** do you teach [insert controversial topic]?" The hits just kept on comin'.

I suddenly felt like the guys on the wall during that big fight scene in *Lord of the Rings: The Two Towers*. Here we were trying to do what was right and just, and we were under attack from a rogue's gallery of despicable forces and misshapen creatures. Instead of Orcs, Uruk-hai, Trolls, Nazgul and goblins, we were facing Teachers Unions, The I.R.S., The Moral Majority, Child Advocacy Groups, I.N.S., and my own %$#@! conscience. Come to think of it, those dudes on the wall had it easy.

At least they had weapons.

This was supposed to be a fight for what was right, what was necessary, and what was really needed to fix the current state of education. It was never supposed to be a Civil War of "us" versus "them;" nonetheless, the time between 2020 and early 2022 became more of a battleground than a classroom, and that got me thinking…

Hey, This Isn't Broke – Let's Fix It!

"Broken pipes, broken tools; people bending broken rules... Ain't no use jiving. Ain't no use joking. Everything is broken."

– Bob Dylan (Everything is Broken)

My teachers were thrilled. My students were achieving. The parents were involved, and my books were balanced. We had established a consistent, safe, fiscally responsible learning environment and a simplified curriculum. Everyone was communicating openly, honestly, and simply. I guess it was only a matter of time before the teachers' unions came crawling out of the swamp to tell us why we were doing it wrong.

Apparently, they think that my teachers (all of whom are blissfully happy, mind you) shouldn't be "doing the same thing" year after year and that the students (who were, if you'll remember, outperforming the status quo) needed to "see a greater variety of personnel."

Before I take a deep breath and tell you how I dealt with these nincompoops, let me tell you some stories that provided me with some insight into the things that, with cancer-like insidiousness, wear away at, and eventually destroy, healthy learning environments. These stories are, again, COMPLETELY FICTIONAL but they inspired me nonetheless. Don't you smile at me like that; I'm serious; besides, *they* might be listening...

and we wouldn't want that, would we?

I was enjoying the Summer, in between my fourth and fifth years at Descaminado High School, when the changes came.

In *August.*

Late August.

What kind of changes you ask? Well, I'll tell you, imaginary dialogue partner. It seems that the brain trust that ran the school decided that the English teachers had to teach either 9th and 11th or 10th and 12th grades. Your guess is as good as mine as to the logic there, but I can tell you some of the effects. I, for one, had been given a 10th grade class of gifted students two years prior with the responsibility of restructuring the class from the ground up: order books, design a curriculum, design the tests, etc.

(Mind you, I was given that assignment in late August as well, so I was building the house, getting it inspected, and furnishing it while we all lived in it together "in harmony.") After years of tweaking the material, trimming the fat, and getting the curriculum airtight, effective and universally accepted, I was told that I wasn't teaching it anymore.

Surprise.

This, how shall I put it?

Pissed me off to no end.

It also left enough of a scar that I never asked one of my teachers to put that kind of time and love into something only to take it away from them later. It ain't right, and I won't do it.

But they did, so I was told, *in late August*, that I had to hand all of my materials off to another teacher who, *in late August*, was being told that they now had to inherit the mortgage on a house they never had to pay for before. Thank goodness it was a teacher I respected or all of my materials may have "mysteriously disappeared." NOTE: Just being honest, folks, and underscoring the fact that this shit happens all the time, which may explain [part of] why most Septembers in most schools are a spit-shined, pretty looking, misguidedly optimistic circle jerk.

But it gets better. Many are the times teachers are told, at the last minute, that they're no longer in the same room, or that they'll be sharing a room with one or two or three more people [and all of their stuff!] Did I mention that the class lists that most teachers receive, and plan around, are subject to change? Many times? Throughout the whole year?

I didn't mention that? Well now I did.

Big Willy Shakespeare said: "Shall I compare thee to a Summer's day?"

Little Frank Step says: "Shall I compare this to other professional maelstroms?"

I shall.

Let's say you're like my neighbor, Pete, and you're in the construction business. You've had the plans drawn up for the house you're constructing, you have procured the necessary permits, tools and talent, and you're ready to get started.

Or not.

You receive a call a few weeks prior to breaking ground that you'll be working on a different location, and this job is strictly demolition, and that you have to start on the same date regardless of whether you've got your shit together or not. Oh, and we'll be coming in to inspect your progress early on, and you had better be on schedule and have all of your paperwork in order or else.

Yeah, we'd have a lot of safe buildings and bridges if we did that.

But maybe you're a lawyer like my brother-in-law Richie. You have several cases pending for clients that you have taken a lot of valuable time (and money) building a relationship with, and you've reviewed your materials with due diligence, double checked your sources, contacted your witnesses, and prepared your opening statement.

Whoops! Forgot to tell you, some of your witnesses might be "subject to change," and you won't have the judges we told you would be overseeing some of your cases, and you have to report to a different courtroom, and that other lawyer (you know, the one you can't stand) is taking one of the cases and you're picking up his. Be ready to go on the same date; the futures of these families are in your hands. Oh, and the partners of the firm will be checking in on you personally and you'd better be winning every case, or else.

Yep, the legal system would be running as smooooooth as a glass of Johnny Walker Blue if we did that.

Oh, what the hell – let's say <u>you're a doctor</u> like my wife's friend, Rohit. You have surgeries, along with rounds, along with meetings, scheduled for the next few weeks so tightly that you have to call the secretarial service to schedule a bowel movement. People's lives are in your hands, and the overall excellence of your department will be directly reflected in your performance.

So it will really suck when we change the people you'll be operating on a few weeks prior to the surgeries, and I know you practice bariatric medicine, and that's your area of expertise, but would you mind doing some orthopedics for a few months? And would you mind doing it in the new (unfinished) wing of the hospital? And would you mind if we bring in a few surgeons from out of town, along with the CEO of the hospital, to observe you? You would? Well, as my Polish grand mom used to say: "tough shitskies." You will adapt, excel and be ebullient in doing it... or else.

Yessir, we would be the healthiest nation in the world if we did that.

I could go on, and by now I'm sure you could draw a parallel to your particular profession unless you're a teacher, in which case you're probably yelling at an inanimate object saying: "that's what the $#@!? I'm saying! It's $#@!ridiculous!" Of course, *you* would never use that type of salty language, but I know what you mean.

Which brings us back to how I responded when the guys and gals from the union said that I should change the way I place and direct my teachers;

I said "no."

That was simple. My teachers thought it was hilarious, and they were thankful because the chance to hone your skills teaching the same class year after year is a welcome challenge, and the ability to "freelance" and be spontaneous once you've achieved a certain degree of mastery in that area is a wonderful feeling, and that always translates to the students, who reap the rewards. Trust me on this. Major League baseball managers wouldn't spend millions of dollars bringing a pitching prospect along into a legitimate "ace" and then, when he's hitting his prime, send him out into center field with a pat on the ass and a "good luck." But hey, that's important shit, that's *baseball*. This is only educating the youth of America.

And that, my literate friend, is **verbal irony**.

The curriculum "experts" didn't get it.

They said that they would begin legal proceedings that would result in my compliance.

They said that I should do what was best for everybody.

I agreed.

And so I said, "No."

Again.

"Good luck with your lawsuits and paper pushing," I encouraged, "I have the **President** on speed dial, an angry comedian that happens to be *your* Educational Secretary is having dinner with me tomorrow night, and my students are currently outperforming the ones doing things *your* way. Plus, by the time you get your shit together to proceed against 47 establishments, given your current rate of getting your shit together, I'll be able to just teleport you to Venus and get you out of my hair."

They didn't like that.

Then I told them that Michelle Rhee, my recently unemployed buddy (and secret object of professional and personal lust) was on the T.E.A.M. payroll now.

They REALLY didn't like that.

Now, before you send me hate mail, I understand the point of the teachers' union, and I was glad to be a part of it when I was but a teacher, but I also watched their refusal to negotiate *anything* and bureaucratic nonsense incense the population outside the teaching profession, entrenching long standing biases against teachers. I also remember how the union's inflexibility and arrogance led to that nasty little "police action" back in Jersey in early 2011 (hereafter referred to in the history books as TSx2 or the "Tiananmen Square Tenure Squabble.")

Speaking of tenure, another event from my past that colored my perception of how teachers should be treated involves my take on tenure. Wanna hear it? Your wish is my command.

In my last...what's that? Some of you *don't* want to hear it? Fine, go grab a sandwich or change the wash or something, I'll be done in a few minutes.

Now then, for those of you who are interested and can you believe those other guys? Sheesh! Some people! They buy a book and want to choose what stories they hear. I know, crazy right? Let's get this out of the way before they come back (probably from watching the All-Communist Channel or something.)

In my last book, I spoke with subtlety and panache about what I thought regarding teaching tenure in the chapter *Why Tenure is Bullshit*. I'm going to go out on a limb and guess that, even if you haven't read it, you'll know where I stand. Anyway, we had a situation way back in 2009 when I was still teaching at Descaminado High, and our governor was cutting the educational budget like a wolverine with scissors taped to his paws after drinking a Dunkin Donuts dry. That tornado of trimming made its way to our school in the form of many of our young teachers being asked to *seek employment elsewhere*.

(That's a **euphemism**, folks. They were cut loose.)

I could write an entire book on how and why getting rid of all your young teachers to save money is a violation of all things righteous and intelligent, but my publisher wants this book done before the Apocalypse, so I'll just tell you that after the meeting wherein the young talent (read: non-tenured teachers) were told that they were expendable, one of them – a spirited young lady that was kind enough to have read my first book – approached me in a manner most hostile.

"I guess you don't think tenure is bullshit today, huh?" she asked, brandishing a piece of paper that no doubt was the "thanks for playing, now beat it" notice.

I understood her anger, and I knew it wasn't really aimed at me; however, I felt the need to clarify her insinuation, so I asked: "Why would today be any different?"

"Because [tenure] protected your job today."

I imagine I could have let that slide, given the circumstances, but I felt that this was a "**teachable moment**," so I **teached** her something: "While I understand your frustration, dear, I think we both know two things to be true. One, if any organization wants to get rid of somebody badly enough, they will; for example, if I was the last person hired in my department, tenure wouldn't save me from one of those letters. Two, I don't keep this job because of tenure. I keep this job the same way I've kept any job I ever had, by being really, *really* good at what I do, and by working my ass off, EVERY day, to get better."

She nodded, a little teary eyed, but still proud – and angry. *"Yeah… I know, but this is still bullshit."*

"I never disputed that, kiddo."

I'm going to keep the rest of our conversation private for myriad reasons, but I never forgot how she felt, and I never wanted one of my teachers to feel that way.

I remember that feeling myself, actually. The first year I taught at Descaminado High, I was considered a long term sub, even though I was taking the place of a teacher they knew wasn't coming back. That entire year didn't count toward my tenure, but I didn't care. I was paid like a fourth year teacher even though I had been teaching for 15 years, but I dealt with that, too. What I *didn't* like was the manner in which I was treated at the end of the year.

I was briefed, by the union rep, that *just about everyone would receive a letter saying that due to x, y and z, the school would not be able to maintain your position at this time.* I was also told, by the principal himself, who called me into his office privately right after the letters were released, that it was strictly a formality and that I would, indeed, receive a contract once the board voted on all of the stuff boards vote on; therefore, "chill out, you've been great, so finish the year the same way and we'll laugh about this someday." That made me feel a lot better, especially since the letter itself was an impersonal, poorly worded slap in the face. I would LOVE to reprint the letter here so you could see what I'm talking about, but: A) this is a work of fiction and B) I am not a fan of getting sued or fired. Suffice it to say that the letter made it sound like the powers-that-be were *intentionally* cutting me loose with *no* inclination to hire me back. No mention was made of my service, good or bad, and the possibility of using the school as a reference was left, at best, vague and uncertain.

Thank you, Descaminado High, for teaching me a few things about how NOT to treat my teachers at the T.E.A.M. Schools. I never make a teacher (unless he or she has behaved in a manner that was illegal and/or termination-worthy) feel totally expendable. Furthermore, I don't leave them hanging in uncertainty regarding their professional future. Finally, I see to it that any and all memos/letters/etc. are worded clearly, professionally, and are accompanied by the suggestion that if that person feels uneasy they should seek ME out immediately to discuss their concerns.

I can hear principals and other administrators nationwide whining "I don't have time to meet with or call every teacher that has a concern!" You wouldn't have that many concerns if you took care of the *bigger picture*. **People in any profession are pretty good about working with people that lead by example and consistently have the backs of their subordinates; subsequently, most people in a workplace lack the motivation to do anything beyond their basic job description for people that bullshit them and throw them under the bus at the first sign of trouble.**

Comprende'?

I hope so. I sure did. It isn't easy, but I surrounded myself with people that are brutally honest - and *can* be with no fear of reprisal — so that relieves the burden of leadership a bit, and cuts down on the amount of errors one man will, undoubtedly, make in the course of a day.

Some of those people (my painfully honest entourage, if you will,) told me that I was being as inflexible with the representatives from the teachers' union as I accused them (the union reps) of being, and that just because the T.E.A.M. Schools were private institutions, that was no excuse for not hearing some of their suggestions. Acquiescing to the premise that "none of us is as smart as all of us," I listened, I chastened, and I invited the union reps back for Thai food, American beer, and XXL Polish-Jewish apologies. (Yeah, I'm a "Jewlock." Go ahead, open fire; I've got an Irish father-in-law that *tries* to pretend I'm not the best thing to ever happen to his daughter, so I've heard 'em all…)

We agreed on some issues, agreed to disagree on others, but left with the understanding that we were both sincerely working in the best interest of the students, and I don't believe either of us believed that a few hours prior. I believe there's a lesson in there somewhere, but you'll have to figure that one out on your own, that *Tom yam kung nam khon* is coming back to get me!

(approximately one painful half hour later)

Whew! That was interesting...hey! You're still here! Awesome, I do some of my best thinking on the toil...er, sitting down, and I thought you'd like to hear about the time the I.R.S. came sniffing around the T.E.A.M. Schools looking to know where all the "profits" were going.

Going from *teachers' union to the I.R.S.* was like the opening scene in *Star Wars* – you think the Stormtroopers are bad until Darth Vader[1] comes through the door...

---

1. In the interest of keeping any microscopic profit I may possibly make upon publication of this book, I want it on the record that I think Darth Vader is cool as shit and in no way is my comparison of him and the I.R.S. a slight on what I'm sure is a first class financial organization.

Money is the root of all evil, and yet...

"If I was richer I'd still be with ya, now ain't that some shit?"

– Cee Lo Green (F**k You)

OK, you know that T.E.A.M. stands for Trust in our Extreme Alternative Methodology, and the people that pay us to clean the stain that conventional education has left on their offspring know that it will cost them. Funny thing about guardians and their kids' well-being, money suddenly becomes no object. I remember that feeling all too well the first time I was fortunate enough to take my kids to Disney World when they were little innocent tikes. When I saw the joy in my daughter Sam's eyes, I (metaphorically, of course) bent over, pulled down my pants, handed Mickey my credit card and said, "don't hurt me too bad, mouse."

Anal invasion via iconic rodent mascot aside, I decided right from the beginning...

"Ahem!"

Dawn and I decided right from the beginning that we were going to charge top dollar for the quality of education that our students were going to receive. T.E.A.M. could just as easily have been an acronym of Time Effort And Money because we put a *load* of all three into our vision of education gone horribly *right*. You see, many moons ago, the wife and I co-owned a little club/restaurant at the Jersey Shore and we learned a few valuable, albeit painful, lessons from that near bankrupting experience:

1. There are no "friends" in business; don't trust anybody that isn't looking back at you in the mirror, and question *that* shady looking character from time to time.

2. If you give people something too cheap, or (even worse) for nothing, they will become spoiled, question the quality of your product, and grow increasingly demanding.(Paying attention, politicians?)

3. If you charge people exorbitant amounts, tell people they are not worthy of your time, and make them beg for your time, they'll line up like fucking lemmings and fight each other for the right to jump of the cliff first.

For examples of the **charge them 'till it hurts + call them unworthy = financial windfall** business model, see *Studio 54*, *Lacoste* clothing, VIP seating, and *anything* involving the words Miley Cyrus.[1] This brings us back to where the money goes when you enroll your child at one of my T.E.A.M. Schools.

Of course, our friends at the I.R.S. were curious to know where all of the money was going, despite Dawn's meticulous book-keeping and more-often-than-necessary correspondence from my ridiculously efficient accountant, one Robert Leslie Ellis-Island. I could tell you where the money goes, but I know you guys aren't as distrustful as those bast...ahem, *folks* at the Internal Revenue Service; besides, it would be easier to tell you where it *doesn't* go. It doesn't go to me; I invested everything I had in the crazy idea that people were tired of the way we were "doing school" in this country, so like that Billy Currington song says:" I'm doing well" (of course, most of the cash goes back into the business of making kids smarter...and iTunes.) It sure as hell doesn't go to a veritable daisy chain of useless administrators and ubiquitously titled "staff" that spend the majority of their day trying to create the illusion of being in any way productive. It most assuredly doesn't go to the newest technology that nobody outside the tech. department knows how to use, and it damn sure doesn't go to "professional development" and "motivational" speakers that charge top dollar to come in an bore the living shit out of a room of professionals that have about a million and a half more productive ways to spend their time. And guess what? The cash doesn't get spent equally on each student, either.

1. Miley! Babe! Please no lawsuits. My son Frankie is still in love with you! Can't say I blame the boy, given some of your recent outfits.[2]

2. I felt like that got creepy. Did that get creepy?[3]

3. It did? Don't care. Keeping *Can't Be Tamed* on the iPod.

Yeah, you heard that right. All men are created equal, but they sure as hell don't stay that way, and we [at T.E.A.M.] only plant seeds in fertile soil. Every person that enrolls a child with us does so with the full knowledge that we will appropriate funds in a manner that we see as commensurate with each student's needs. Remember my trip to Disney World? Well, the wife and I didn't keep a little calculator out the whole time: *"let's see, we spent $13.72 more on Sam today so Mason and Frankie can each have a half a lemon slushie each…"*

No, we operated on parental common sense. You remember that antiquated concept, right? The idea that we all might, just might, know what the fuck we're doing when it comes to kids we see every day.

Operating on the same crusty old principle, the powers-that-be at T.E.A.M. (which is to say, me and the brilliant people I've surrounded myself with so as to appear intelligent) move the money around where we think it could be best used at that particular moment of expenditure. Kind of like a big RISK[1] board. Do we make mistakes? Of course we do. Never *could* defend Asia and Europe simultaneously[2]…

But our mistakes are always made with the best interests of our students in mind. Anybody out there think that's the principle currently in operation in our national education budget? Raise your hands if you think so.

Hmmm… not a lot of hands.

Thank you.

Moses needs books with large print? Get 'em for Moses.

---

1. RISK - a strategic board game, produced by Parker Brothers, that we used to play in the 80's. The goal was to conquer the world one continent at a time, using your resources as efficiently as possible. Megalomania and tyranny with dice, awesome!

2. Basic RISK strategy that I refused to adhere to, thus leading to one unsuccessful campaign of World Domination after another, which is why I gravitated toward action figures.[3]

3. Action figures are *not* dolls. No, they're NOT. Captain America was all *about* action, even when he had brunch in the Barbie Dream house. "oooooh, CAPtain, what a big *shield* you have…"

Mollie, Napoleon, and Muriel are tactile learners? Get them the right stuff (and keep that stuff catalogued and in good shape so it can be re-used. See, remarkably similar to parenting with multiple children!)

Benjamin wants to be an auto mechanic, and he's almost 18 years old.

We'll hook him up with an apprenticeship, provide him as much basic skill reinforcement as we can, (Math to manage his money, pay his bills, etc., language skills to read between the lines and be an educated consumer, etc.) but no funds wasted on books that won't get read, supplements that will go unused, etc.

Total financial transparency and REAL, INTENSE, INDIVIDUALIZED educational profiles.

Of course, as any decent teacher will tell you, that requires a big honkin' load of effort, and that's where the rest of the pesos that our parents provide go to – our *teachers*. They drive the curriculum, tell us what each kid needs, and put the majority of the time in with them; hence, they get the lion's share.

Our teachers work twelve months of the year, with a short Summer break, put in extra time, and they freakin' LOVE it, because their students are learning what they need to learn, at the level they can learn it, [more on that later] in an environment where any student that threatens that learning process will wish that he hadn't. Furthermore, every teacher has the ability, under my jurisdiction, to discipline as they see fit, and recommend their peers for merit bonuses based on what they see as exceptional effort or assistance.

We're all in this boat together, and we *act* like it.

My promise.

My guarantee.

And fuck you if you don't like it, I'm sure the local public high school has an opening.

Of course, the politicians, tacticians, economists, lawyers, and educational "experts" nationwide took a break from snorting in the mud and cleaned themselves up long enough to come on television and pass judgment on how we were doing things at T.E.A.M.

(Insert pompous twat accent here) *"Oh, that's a nice little idea in theeeeoory, but you rrreeealllly can't expect that business model to woooork."*

Yeah?

That a fact?

If you are reading this book and you're a teacher, *and* you would be willing to join me in a school like the one I just described, raise your hand, please.

Hmmm, that's a lot of hands.

Thank you.

Back to you, politicians, tacticians, economists, lawyers, and educational "experts."

A question: How's your *current* business model working for you?

Actually, let me re-word that, because I know damn well how it's working for you. How is it working for your student population?

An answer: Not well. The dropout rate has remained pretty constant at about 33% of all high school students (not that you'd know it from your bullshit record keeping,) most states wind up paying over $30,000 for prison inmates that couldn't get ¼ of that spent on them when they were in school, and – I love this one – you spend close to $200,000 **A MINUTE** (!) on the Iraq War while we still have teachers paying out of pocket for learning materials.

Let's review, shall we? **You think that leaving financial appropriation in the hands of the teachers, parents, and students won't work, but *your* system, which creates a "school to prison pipeline"[1] of undereducated, easy to control, consumers who hate school is just fine???**

Wrong.

---

1. I wish I could take credit for that line, but it comes from a book called *Many Children Left Behind* that will simultaneously educate and infuriate you, as all good literature inevitably does. Two thumbs up.

I figured that funds were being so colossally misappropriated at the state and federal level that parents and guardians would literally be willing to spend top dollar as long as they knew *some* of that hard earned cabbage would actually wind up being spent on their child, and that *all* of it would be used as effectively as possible to raise the collective education of the next generation. In short, they trust us to turn tuition into fruition, and that sort of trust is a powerful motivator.

To conclude, let's go back to Disney World with the kids one more time. Do I know the stuffed gorilla (nice product placement from the Tarzan movie, gentlemen, well done) is lasciviously overpriced? Sure. Is it worth the absolute joy on the face of my son as he hugs his new buddy, whom he has named "Monkey"[1] and begins what will be years of loving care?

To quote a certain former governor of Alaska: You betcha.

I suspect that, from an educational standpoint, the T.E.A.M. Schools are the 800 lb. stuffed gorilla. You want the kind of education that can reverse the damage of an aloof, out of touch system that doesn't care about your kid. You gotta pay.

---

1. I know, I know. Gorillas are apes, not monkeys. What can I say? Mason was a master of irony even at the tender age of four.

An afterthought:
Monet is the root of all good.

I was just in the town of Nesquehoning, Pennsylvania visiting my sister (don't ask, even your GPS system will say "where the hell is *that?*") Nonetheless, I couldn't help but notice that one of the things Molly holds near and dear to her heart is a cheap print of a Monet painting that I bought her when we were but crazy kids without mortgages. I *think* just the fact that I knew she liked Monet, and that she needed some art for the walls of her apartment are what counted, not the price. In one of my all too rare moments of lucidity, I sensed a lesson in there somewhere.

Another funny thing (he said with no small trace of irony,) I have NEVER, in my quarter of a century in this business, heard a student say, "you know, I think that the amount of money appropriated to me is helping/hurting me." Students care if the teachers *care* about them, and they want to know what appropriated *means*, even if it's not on your precious *standardized tests* or part of your completely out of touch district *standards.*

Thus endeth our sermon, go in peace, to love and serve one another.

I gotta go, time is Monet.

Some Things Wicked This Way Came.

"The dumbing down of dummies in a shameful, spinning spiral. With puppet masters mastering with plausible denial."

– The Vandals (Dig A Hole)

You are at sea, on a boat, with a full crew of people that are all important to you, family, friends, etc. You have a leak in your fuel tank and, after running afoul of some rocks, a significant hole in the bottom of your boat is taking on water. Now let me ask you a question. Would you rather:

A) *Know* about the leaks because they smelled up the boat, ruined everybody's shoes and socks, made a few people sick and turned a few people off from boating, but allowed you to get the boat back to safe harbor for repairs,

or

B) *Notknow* about the leak, party on, uninterrupted, with your pals, get out to sea far enough to take in some amazing scenery, and remain blissfully ignorant to those inconveniences right up until the boat sank and you all became drowning victims or dinner for sharks?

Show of hands. A? OK...that's pretty much all of you. B? Really? Do you mind me asking you sir, why exactly you prefer B? Ah, playing the devil's advocate and all that. Well, you're a *dead* devil's advocate, you understand that, right? Ah, you're correct, this isn't *real.*

Or is it?

Do you mind if I metaphor?

Thank you, you are too kind.

The boat is the school curriculum; you know, the stuff kids learn. The people on the boat are us, with particular emphasis on the students ('cause they'll be navigating the sea, which is life, soon enough.) The leaks? Those are the *nasty* bits, the things that many people want to omit, repress, or act as though never happened. You know, all those great novels with bad words in them, the parts of our history that we might be ashamed of, or anything that might offend someone's delicate sensibilities.

But Step, you ask, couldn't just about *everything* offend *somebody?*

Yes, my astute reader, the same way a fuel leak could ruin a perfectly good day on the ocean. Oh, well, ignorance is bliss.

Wrong. ***Ignorance is death.***

This, of course, did not stop certain groups, like the ironically named "Moral Majority," from questioning the logic and morality of my T.E.A.M. Schools (because we taught the naughty bits.) To borrow from the infinite wisdom of George Santayana: "Those who forget the past are condemned to repeat it." I'm not in the business of sending students out into the world destined to make the same mistakes as their predecessors; therefore, at the T.E.A.M. Schools we teach *everything*, warts and all.

Yes, empires have risen and fallen because of arrogance and debauchery, and yes, our current "empire" is showing signs of similar potential. Yes, slavery, in one form or another, has been around since the dawn of civilization. Yes, there are tons of dirty words and dirty deeds in the classic literature of every age. Yes, we screwed the Native Americans over something fierce.

And yet, yes, we are still the greatest nation in the world, because we don't repress (yet) the knowledge that these things happened; and if anyone tries to tell me that we have to do so, they're going to have one hell of a fight on their hands because I won't do it, nor will I allow it to be done in my T.E.A.M. Schools. I assume that my teachers can engage in educational dialogue with students and colleagues that differ in opinion with them. As a matter of fact, I encourage it, because that sort of open dialogue leads to mutual empathy, exchange of information, development of argument skills, and it teaches people to THINK, which is what we really need to be teaching these kids anyway.

The ability to think (not plagiarize, memorize, synopsize, or anything else-ize) crosses curricular, ethnic and age boundaries; it is timeless, it is useful, and it is being suffocated by a curriculum that teaches kids not to offend anyone on their way to passing some form of standardized test that will be subject to change and whose scores will be manipulated or changed if they... ready? ...Off*end* anyone.

Oh yeah, that'll work. *That'*ll prepare our kids for the cutthroat, harsh reality of the high-speed working world in our new economy. Sorry, not in *my* schools.

In my classrooms, if you're reading about a person that is mentally retarded, in the sense that that person suffers from a generalized disorder, the word retarded is used and, if need be, discussed for the point of clarification. If, however, you use that term as an adjective, and call someone retarded, you're going to apologize immediately and sincerely (prior to a quick lesson on why that is wrong) OR you're gonna get your *ass whooped*, which foreshadows our next chapter. But I digress...

Just because idiots make the rules doesn't mean I'm going to follow them.

(Hey, I think I just discovered my mantra!)

My teachers are going to educate my students, force them to deal with the unpleasantries of hard work and offensive material. Yes, the word "nigger" is used in *Huckleberry Finn*, and yes, we tried to *burn* books (so they wouldn't offend anyone) at one time. Yes, Hitler engineered the attempted genocide of the Jewish people (and no, Oliver Stone, he didn't get a "raw deal" by the media, you fucking moron.) Yes, we put *our own people* in internment camps *on our own soil* during World War 2. There are so many, many things that we would rather not look at, (isn't that right, Catholic Church?) but only by looking at them, talking about them, agreeing (or agreeing to disagree) about them will we prevent them from happening again.

I've said it before and I will say it again, KIDS CAN HANDLE THE TRUTH.

Their soft-brained "advocates," limp-dicked politicians, weak-willed parents, and ill-advised "advisors?" Not so much.

That's why we, at the T.E.A.M. Schools, make our book selections on what we think the students would like to read, we involve current events in our "practical information" classes, and we don't shy away from hard topics that kids are interested in because we're worried that somebody might get offended. One of the first books I used to teach when I taught High School was George Orwell's *1984*,and students would come in all the time and say *"Step, I heard _____ on the news and that stuff sounded like Big Brother, was it?"* and I would ask *"What do **you** think?"*

Or *"Step, why are they trying to take_____ out of the textbooks in Texas? Isn't that like the whole 'control the past control the future' thing?"* To which I replied, "sounds like it to me, but *why* do *you* say that?"

My teachers teach, but they also let their students figure it (whatever *it* may be,) out for themselves, because they <u>can</u>; and they don't shy away from the ugly truths because the second part of ugly truth is **truth**; the same way the second part of willful ignorance is **ignorance**. Just like a leak in a boat sucks, but knowing about it saves lives, so too does the awareness of terrible things cause discomfort, but learning about them reduces the possibility that they will reoccur; and I'll tell you what else it does. Remember we talked earlier about the poor people on the boat that chose not to know about the leaks? They have a wonderful day on the ocean until they drown or become SHARK BAIT ooh ha-ha!

(How many of you caught the *Finding Nemo* allusion there? Good job!)

 Same thing happens to students that are sheltered from the harsh realities of the world, they just drown in debt because the sharks in their world come in many shapes and sizes, and they all love to feast on stupid people. So, to all of you who want to hide the dirty words and dirty deeds from your student population (yes, YOU, the ones who won't show "R" rated movies in schools even though the kids are watching *far* worse stuff at home, or during study hall on their iPhones!) I've got some news for you; you're raising your kids to be big, tasty bait.

But that's cool, because my students are going to be sharks someday and hey, everybody's gotta eat.

Case in point, I happened to be observing one of my brightest young English teachers, Mr. Daniel Jerome, at the New Jersey T.E.A.M. School one day in late April. He had let me know prior to the class that he was going to "edit" the novel they were reading in class, so he could see how the students reacted to the profanity and potentially offensive material being removed *for their well-being*. I remember the book well; *Third and Indiana*, a phenomenal novel by Steve Lopez, (the guy from *The Soloist*) about a young boy on the streets of inner city Philadelphia. I loved the book as a teacher and almost every kid that ever read it raved about it, talked about it, told other kids about it, and (believe it or not) went out to buy a copy for themselves! There is a lot of what some mentally mushy folks would call "offensive material" in the novel: profanity, drug references, violence, and dysfunctional family issues…*nothing* like what our students deal with, right?

Small wonder students eat this up and don't mind analyzing the metaphors, figurative language, and other literary devices because they get snuck in under the guise of INTERESTING STUFF!

Imagine that.

But let's get back to Mr. Jerome and his "protection" of his students.

Danny (that's Mr. Jerome to you) introduced me and I took my seat in the back of his classroom, opened my laptop and commenced looking impressive. After some brief review of the previous chapter, (done by the students themselves, with a little "filling in" by Mr. Jerome) Danny got down to the business of reading the text. Oh, it was wonderful, he did the voices, he changed his inflection to suit the mood of the story, and he changed every curse word and potentially "harmful" term to something euphemistic. I'm going to trust that Mr. Lopez is a righteous dude and will not begrudge me including a bit of his text for the purposes of elaboration. In the novel, the war on the streets was reaching a fever pitch, and a police officer was chastising a group of young kids caught up in the drug trade for staying quiet about the murder of one of their friends because they didn't want to "snitch."

This **is what the students were reading from the text, as Mr. Jerome was reading out loud:**

"We didn't see anything, Lieutenant Bagno. We don't know anything, Lieutenant Bagno. We're complete fucking idiots, Lieutenant Bagno. Yes, Lalo is our friend and we just watched him get the shit beat out of him by an animal and we didn't lift a hand to help him because we're drug-dealing motherfucking pieces of shit, Lieutenant Bagno, and tomorrow we're going shopping for new sneakers and gold chains." (Lopez, Steve. Third and Indiana. 1st ed. New York, NY: Penguin Group, 1994. 119. Print.)

And *this* is what Mr. Jerome read out loud to the class:

We didn't see anything, Lieutenant Bagno. We don't know anything, Lieutenant Bagno. We're complete morons, Lieutenant Bagno. Yes, Lalo is our friend and we just watched him get beat up by an animal and we didn't lift a hand to help him because we're just kids that make bad decisions, Lieutenant Bagno, and tomorrow we're going shopping for iPods and sunglasses.

The reaction from the class was, as you might expect, interesting. A few of them glanced up after the first or second "edit," but by the time Mr. Jerome had finished, the entire class was looking at him with anticipation, and the minute he stopped to look up, their hands shot up faster than a fat kid after the ice cream truck.[1]

"What the heck was that?!?" inquired a young lady from the front row.

"What was *what?*" responded Mr. Jerome, smooth as buttah.

"Is you changing the book 'cause this guy (gesturing to me) is here?" accused a young man seated right in front of me.

A look from Mr. Jerome, a few seconds, and…

---

1. Yeah, I said it. Fuck you and your political correctness; furthermore, I WAS that fat kid and I would haul some serious ass in pursuit of the patriotic-colored yumminess of a Bomb Pop.

"I'm sorry. *Are* you changing the book *be*cause Mr... *Step?*..."

"Correct."

"...is here?"

A cacophony of inquisitions and accusations followed, all centered around the central theme of *WTF Mr. Jerome? We were totally diggin' on this book and you go and ruin it by taking out the real parts because this asshole in the suit is here?* Of course, they were all much nicer than that – but that's what they meant. And they were *right* to feel that way. Daniel Jerome, Brahma bless him, simply gestured to me as if to say, "the floor is yours, sensei."

"Thank you, Mr. Jerome," I said. "First, you are absolutely right to question why your teacher would change the way he does things just because somebody is watching. I never did it as a teacher, because all that tells the students is that you're not confident in what you do. Isn't that right, Mr. Jerome?"

He smiled, "yessir, it surely is."

"And that's why I did the exact same thing back when I taught your teacher this book back in the age of the dinosaurs, only he didn't even let me finish before he challenged me."

"Really, Mr. Jerome? You called out Mr. Step? What happened? Was there an observer in the room? Did you get in trouble? Mr. Step, did you pick the same section to change? Did your students back then like the book? Did you do this on purpose today Mr. Jerome?"

On and on and on went the questions.

We answered some questions, then I left Danny to a whole new batch of questions, such as why he changed the parts he did, the nature of stereotype, the effective use (versus gratuitous use) of profanity in literature, the reality (and difficulty) of the "no snitching" policy of the streets.

On and on and on went the discussion.

Bottom line. LOTS of questions = LOTS of interest = LOTS of learning.

Imagine that.

By the way, did you notice that nobody was corrupted, offended, or ruined by the intense nature of the text? Au contraire, mon frère. The students could relate to the reality of the text; hence, they could focus more on learning something from it instead of wasting energy trying to engage it. There's a lesson in there somewhere, but there was a real lesson going on in Mr. Jerome's class, so I bid him adieu and left with a warm, fuzzy feeling that a whole new generation of students could not only *handle* the truth, but *embraced* it.

The only thing that bothered me from my time in Mr. Jerome's class was that several of the students didn't know who I was. This was becoming a more common phenomena as I visited various T.E.A.M. Schools, which reawakened a nagging concern that perhaps things were getting too big to effectively control…

I was snapped back into the present by a blast of cold water in the form of an incoming call from Dawn. "Hey babe, I was visiting…"

"CNBC. Right Now. I'm sending you the link, so get to a computer."

"Good enough, what's this ab…"

"And get your battle armor on."

And with that, ever so subtly, I was distracted from a moment of reflection that would come to haunt me later.

So be it.

We had been attacked.

Again.

First the vipers from the I.R.S., then the douchebags from the Moral Majority and the dinosaurs from the union, and now the Child Advocacy groups were lining up. And ever so subtly, I felt my incisors grow, my eyes narrow, and my skin thicken.

Some things change as you get older.

Some don't.

I *do* love a good fight.

On a personal note, I am proud to say that I know for a fact that Steve Lopez (the guy who wrote *Third and Indiana* and a bunch of other books that are ALL better than this one) is a severely righteous dude. I wrote him a letter thanking him for writing such an awesome novel and he sent me back an autographed copy, along with a very personal note, less than a week later. You simply don't see that kind of class every day. You, Mr. Lopez, are a gentlemen and a scholar.

– Step

Captain America makes a Major statement about Corporal punishment in a less than Private setting, and General chaos ensues.

With apologies to Devo:

When a kid is acting wrong / you must whip him.
Now whip him / into shape / shape him up /get straight
Go forward /move ahead /try to detect it / it's not too late
to whip him / whip him good.
DunDunDunDunDUH / DUNdundundadun!

Observation: I don't know if the boys from Devo support corporal punishment (doubt it) but I do know they read Thomas Pynchon novels, so they're smart enough to understand verbal irony.

By now you know that I think that about 23 - 47% of the UNBELIEVABLY GIANT AMOUNT OF TIME we waste in this country on counseling, appeals, manifestation hearings, written discipline referrals, mediation meetings, parental interventions, on-and-on-and-on until I puke could be solved by a swift kick in the ass [or, at the very least, the knowledge that you could, and would, administer one.] That's a lot of time, folks. How much? Like, 18% of infinity big, like 1% of the amount of times politicians lie big, like 100% of the times I tell my mother-in-law, "I'm not picking up your dog's shit in my yard, and then do it anyway" big.

Bottom line: We could save an UNBELIEVABLY GIANT AMOUNT OF TIME that should be dedicated to education by smacking some sense into these arrogant little fuckers.

Now, many of you are cheering as you read this, and I feel you, I do. Some of you are a teensy bit squeamish about the whole corporal punishment thing, but not so much that you haven't contemplated bitch-slapping some obnoxious little bastard at Wal-mart, or "behaviorally modifying" that kid on the 3 hour flight that will not shut the hell up. Of course, there are those of you [how's the weather out there on the fringe?] that will brand me as some sort of knuckle dragging Neanderthal that seeks to resolve all conflict with corporal punishment. For those of you in the latter category, know this:

1. I am not.

2. I have a quarter century dealing with confrontational people, of all ages, multiple times a day, in person. You don't.

3. I have read, literally, thousands of pages of research on both sides of the corporal punishment argument. You haven't.

4. I have always subscribed to the wisdom of Sun Tzu that "*...to win one hundred victories in one hundred battles is not the acme of skill. To subdue the enemy without fighting is the acme of skill.*" So I am in no hurry to put my hands on anyone.

That having been said,

5. I also subscribe to the wisdom of Frank Stepnowski Sr. that "*the best way to keep a wolf from your door is to have a bigger, badder wolf on the other side;*"

Furthermore,

6. The **Bible** says "*He who spareth the rod hateth his son: but he that loveth him correcteth him betimes*" (Proverbs 13:24) So suck on that!

7. This is a work of fiction; therefore, ***taking issue with the T.E.A.M. Schools condoning corporal punishment is like getting mad at polar bears for drinking all your Coca-Cola.***

But I digress…

Dawn had alerted me that the T.E.A.M. Schools were under attack again and, as the "face" of the organization, I had better prepare a response. Notice I didn't say "have my 'team' or 'my people' draft a response." That's because my name is on every contract signed by every person putting every kid in every one of my schools, so when I talk about them, it's me talking. What you see is what you get.

But first, let's hear what the opposition is saying, shall we?

I asked the school's assistant librarian, Ms. Damian, if she would be kind enough to let me use one of the computers in the staff section of the library. She told me that they were all occupied but she was sure someone would gladly vacate their Dell for the founder of the school.

"Nonsense, I'll just use one of these."

As I sat down in the middle of the library and started up one of the student computers, several students and teachers waved, some inquired, most ignored. I connected to the link Dawn had sent me and prepared for the worst.

Percy and Marigold Vulgaire, the co-chairs of S.P.A.N.K. (The Society for the Prevention of Acrimonious Non-verbal Konfrontation) were at it again.

I had encountered this hyper zealous double dose of daftness back when I issued the "Gonzalez addendum" to my discipline code some years back. I politely answered all of their questions while they shouted at me, (konfrontational much, Marigold?) and patiently endured their criticisms while showing hard data that "my way" actually led to significantly less physical confrontations and significantly higher parent and teacher satisfaction. Thank goodness they agreed to go on *The View* with me so I could get a few words in [between their visceral assaults on my character]

Result: more applications to the T.E.A.M schools. So I sent a really nice flower arrangement and a card:

> Thanks Percy, love you Marigold. Give the kids my best.
>
> XOXO - The Antichrist
>
> (PS – the "K" in kommunication? Just acronymic hijinks or secretly Communist? You're secret is safe with me.)

My foremost attorney, Angel A. Skalski, threatened to "make me a woman with a very dull knife" if I did something like that again.

Percy and Marigold were set up, on a fairly impressive grandstand somewhere in Alabama (Oh, Prime Director Lavin is going to love this, I thought,) with representatives from some of the organizations that agreed to disagree with our stand on corporal punishment. Oh, they were all there, EPOCH, The Jefferson County Child Development Council, CHILDHELP USA, The Menninger Foundation, The National Exchange Club Foundation for the Prevention of Child Abuse, Agenda for Children, and Nospankybobby, USA, just to name a few.

"Bloody Hell!" I thought, adopting a British accent in my head for no perceivable reason, "this ought t'be a regular kick in the twig and berries."

Percy, resplendent in pastel colors and elegantly pressed khakis, was going on about how the T.E.A.M. Schools were symptomatic of everything that was wrong about education, that any parent that sent their child to a T.E.A.M. School was, in fact, abusive, *and that my own children were deserving of the nation's pity for having to endure me as a father.*

"Oh **that** was a mistake, Percy!" blurted Ms. Damian, who had apparently (along with everybody else in the library) been listening in. When I looked up, a full library of people of every shape, size, color, age and affect nodded in agreement with the lovely librarian. Being a man of the people, I stood up, buttoned my suit jacket, and addressed the group.

"Does anyone here feel abused or mistreated in any way?"

(Many heads shook in the universal sign for "nope.")

"Does *anyone* know *anybody* from one of our schools that feels abused or mistreated in any way?"

(Many heads turned to each other and shook in the universal sign for "uhhmmm…we don't think so.)

"Does everyone here agree that the Vulgaire's should have refrained from bringing my children into this?"

Approximately 47 people said "Hell yes!" in the universal sign for "Hell yes."

"Thank you. Now, if you'll excuse me, I have surgery to perform."

INCOMING CALL FROM DAWN (spouse)

"Calm down."

"Uh, no." (click)

INCOMING CALL FROM ANGEL A. SKALSKI (attorney)

"You saw it?'

"I did"

"Behave."

"Doubt it." (click)

INCOMING CALL FROM JOSEPH FURANTE (public relation director for T.E.A.M.)

"Commence retaliation?"

"I'm taking this one, myself, Joe."

"Go get 'em, tiger."

"A bit ambiguously sexual there, Joe."

"Really, I was going for suggestively supportive with a dash of bi-curious."

"I'm on it." (click)

INCOMING CALL FROM PRESIDENT WINFREY

"You heard it."

"Heard it, on it."

"Mr. Step…"

"**DON'T** Op…Madame President…don't. They brought up my kids. They will pay."

"Mr. Step. I will support you, but…"

"But **nothing**, I'm going to…"

"BUT you must be diplomatic, and I have a suggestion that came from your appointed Secretary, Mr. Carlin… Mr. Step, are you there?"

"Listening."

"To quote Mr. Carlin, 'dey think his kids are so in need o' proTECtion, they oughta debate them fer Chrissakes.' I think he's on to something."

"(the silence of me contemplating)"

"Mr. Step…Frank?"

"Fine. I think Sam will be more than happy to engage in a little civilized dialogue with these starry-eyed, utopian fuckwads…"

"Frank!"

"Sorry, Madame President; thank you Madame president, fangs temporarily retracted Madame President."

"Remember, Frank, I've seen your work up close and I've got your back, provided you keep this professional and civil. Everyone is entitled to their opinion, correct?"

"Correct. Gotta go, lots of calls, as you might imagine." (click)

INCOMING CALLS FROM JUST ABOUT EVERYONE WITH A PULSE AND A PENCIL.

(phone off)

Need a few minutes to myself while I drive back to ground zero while I think about how I'm going to handle this. Let's go over what my new BFFs, the Vulgaires, said about us:

One, they claimed that the T.E.A.M. Schools were symptomatic of everything that was wrong about education. Since the T.E.A.M. Schools went national, almost a decade ago, there have been 175 incidents of teachers cashing in their cards for retribution. Of those incidents, only twelve resulted in lawsuits alleging unnecessary physical force. Of those twelve lawsuits, only one was deemed viable. 50 schools, over 200,000 students and staff, times 2,250 days, only one documented incident of excessive corporal punishment, and we're everything that's wrong with education? That's the equivalent of saying that koala bears are everything that's mean-spirited about the animal kingdom because one took a eucalyptic shit on a zookeeper *once.*

Secondly, Percy the pussy asserted that, "any parent that sent their child to a T.E.A.M. School was, in fact, abusive." I'm sure the guardians of our nearly 125,000 students, all of whom are paying top dollar to send their children to a school explicitly devoted to the moral and academic progress of their children, would love to have a chat with the Vulgaires about that broad stroke of the judgmental brush. They might not be abusive people *normally...*

Last, but certainly not least, Mr. Vulgaire insinuated, with his wife beaming at his side, that my own children were deserving of the nation's pity for having to endure me as a father. Probably for the best that they're in Alabama and I'm in New Jersey, because if I could get my hands on that Birkenstock wearing little...

INCOMING CALL FROM SAMANTHA

Speak of one of the little devils.

"Hi, Sammie girl."

"Did you hear that asshole on TV today?"

"Miss you too, baby. I'm well, thanks for asking."

"Sorry, dad, but this is tiresome, and the fact that he made it personal…"

"I know, I'm as pissed as you are, believe me. Have you talked to Mason or Frankie?"

"Mason just laughed, you know how he is; and he's so busy he's not going to waste time on idiots like the Vulgaires."

"Yeah, I guess all that pro bono work he's doing building homes for the hurricane victims over in the Gulf Coast doesn't leave him much time to fret about what crappy parents your mother and I were."

(Laughing but still audibly pissed) *"Yeah, right? Speaking of mom, I assume she's ready to bury them in the media?"*

"Your mom is so busy with our enrollment right now that she has to schedule yelling at me, but she did warn me to behave."

"Oh, yeah, that'll happen!" she laughed, "Do they even know that Frankie teaches at the Tennessee facility? Or that he gave up most of the endorsement offers he received to take a teaching gig?"

"Probably not. No need for them to. They probably forgot about his two gold medals the minute the Olympics ended and American Idle started. We live in a sound bite society, hon; you know that. I taught you that much in between the indoctrination videos and extended beatings in the basement."

"I know, dad, I know. But you also taught me to listen to my heart, and my heart tells me not to let this one go."

"Well, it's funny you should mention that, because Oprah and George have an idea on how to repudiate this one."

"I'm in."

"I didn't say what it was yet."

"Geez, dad, I think I can figure it out. I'll get Bob the Builder and Mr.-Olympic-gymnast turned-teacher on the horn and ask them if they want to be there live and in person or via satellite. You want mom there?"

"Ooh, I don't know. She doesn't do cameras, know what I mean?"

"Duly noted. Give me 48 hours. I'll be in touch."

"Hon?"

"Yeah dad?"

"You sure you're OK with this? I mean, the T.E.A.M. Schools are always going to be under fire; in fact, I was starting to consider…"

"Yeah, I'm sure. I'll move all of my meetings back. Believe me, none of the corporations I represent will begrudge me anything, much money as I make them. We're going to take that sanctimonious little turd and make him eat his words."

"Thanks Sam."

"Love you, daddy. Remember, 48 hours and we strike back."

"That's my girl."

As I pulled into the driveway of my house, my two bulldogs, Jefferson and Adams, appeared at the window, and Dawn let them out to greet me, tails wagging, oblivious to the coming storm.

"Cry havoc," I exhaled to myself, "and let slip the bulldogs of war."

(Pssst! No, I *didn't* misspell American IDLE. Think about it.)

– FAST FORWARD TWO DAYS –

Certain that they held the upper hand, the pundits of S.P.A.N.K. agreed to meet with representatives from T.E.A.M. in an acronymal throwdown of epic proportions. News organizations from everywhere were there. Like moths to the flame came Percy and Marigold, joined by a veritable United Nations of "passionate" supporters, all of whom looked handpicked for their diversity, all of whom looked calculatedly middle class, all of whom looked thrilled to be on television.

On the Super Villain side, The Vulgaires were to speak first, followed by Ms. Crédule, a mother whose son (she swore) was abused at one of my T.E.A.M. affiliates. Finally, Miss Sheila Brown-Stone, the mother of Joachim Brown, the kid from that one lawsuit that I told you about where we were found guilty of excessive punishment.

On the sight of Truth, Justice, and the right to put a foot in your ass, I would speak first, albeit briefly, for our side, followed by Samantha, in all her Great White Shark glory; followed by (what Sam referred to as) "our secret weapon."

Lord knows I was excited.

"Whaddya bet none of these people know any of the facts about what they're passionately supporting?" smirked Frankie, who joined us in person, since it was a Saturday, **"I'm going with less than 10 percent of them."**

> *"Less," said Sam, with all the focused intensity of a Carcharodon carcharias homing in on a seal from below, "and I'm going to ram that ignorance back down their throats."*

"She's positively adorable when there's blood in the water, isn't she, Pop?"

Frankie and I laughed for a second, but stopped abruptly when Sam turned her unblinking, don't-make-me-eat-you gaze on us.

Hard to believe that the little girl with whom I used to watch *Bear in the Big Blue House* (while pretending to eat make-believe muffins) had turned into an apex predator.

I almost cried… almost… a little.

Meanwhile, the seals in suit jackets went swimming in Sam infested waters.

NOTE: Hey students! That's called *extending a metaphor*! In this case, I compared my daughter to a Great White shark and then kept the magic going with several other similar references.

The Vulgaires proceeded to wax poetic about why our children are precious, fragile gifts that we, at the T.E.A.M. Schools, were *shattering* with our "clandestine policies of hate."

"Shadooby...shattered shattered, UH!, shadooby..." sang Frankie, under his breath.

"SShhh! This is serious," I hissed, trying not to laugh and/or sing along.

Ms. Crédule then took the podium, and she was less than three minutes into her tale of how her son Claude was routinely punched by teachers for asking simple questions when Frankie suddenly shouted, **"Wait! Claude Crédule?! He's in one of my classes! How come I never heard about this?"**

The S.P.A.N.K. people began protesting that it wasn't our turn to speak yet and chaos *almost* ensued, but Claude himself, who happened to be in the audience, made the mistake of yelling out, "Hi Mr. Stepnowski!" whereupon Frankie invited Claude to come onstage and speak for himself. Caught between a rock (his mother, who was clearly caught lying, and her entourage) and a hard place (his teacher, whom he respected, and a TV audience of millions,) Claude's uncomfortable body language and deafening silence spoke volumes. Mercifully, we let Claude return to his seat and the eventual wrath of his model parent, who apparently thought that it was ok to commit defamation of character in the name of getting on TV.

Undaunted by the instant scandal that was burning up the Blogosphere, (and by the *teeeeeensy tiny* fact that they were caught LYING on national television,) the Vulgaires and their constituency marched out Miss Sheila Brown-Stone, their ace in the hole, who recounted, in graphic detail, how her son Joachim was knocked unconscious by Mr. Martin Chrysler back in February of 2017. She recounted, in graphic detail, with the assistance of the court records, how Mr. Chrysler struck Joachim once, knocking him clean out, an act he later confessed to and for which he was subsequently given a leave of absence. Believe me, I didn't want to do it, but Marty, Odin bless him, took the path of least resistance and agreed to step down for a temporary leave. (I think we sent him for a month of SMARTboard training in Aspen.) Miss Brown-Stone neglected to mention that Joachim was in the act of intimidating another student who, although no angel herself, was a female who had been in special education classes for most of her life. She also conveniently left out the fact that when Mr. Chrysler tried to talk to Joachim, the boy cursed at and threatened him, and when Marty tried to restrain Joachim peacefully, the boy struck and kicked him several times prior to getting his own lights put out.

I guess that wasn't important.

With the crowd in a bit of a quandary as to who or what to believe, Samantha took the podium, ignoring protocol and taking the lead. I swear to God I think I saw her eyes roll over white before she bit down. By the time she was done (elapsed time: 14 minutes and 37 seconds) you would have to have been born with half a brain not to know that the Vulgaires and their paid- for posse were *way* off base with their accusations that we were somehow "abusive." It was amazing; no wonder she got the corporate accounting gig. Sam's facts were airtight, and her presentation was feisty but under control. She smashed the opposition with quantifiable data, buried them under a tsunami of numbers in our favor, and sprinkled a lovely crumbly crust of student and parent testimonials, so that it all came out of the oven warm, delicious and deadly.

And yet she managed to dissect the frogs on the opposition without even mentioning the fact that they just got caught, not 30 minutes prior, manufacturing misinformation, leaving *that* softball hanging in the air for dear old dad. I thought to myself as I took the podium, "Where did that brilliant, beautiful child come from?"

Somewhere, watching at home, my wife was thinking "Three guesses, asshole."

I was determined not to justify the accusations against us with a response or, at the very least, keep the response short, so I stepped up to the podium and said: "I'm not sure what I can add to that very succinct argument, or to the fact that you were exposed as committing libel not less than a half hour ago, other than to say that the woman that just spoke, and the young man who inspired such dedication in his student, young master Crédule over there, are two of the three children that you think need to be saved from my heinous parenting. Obviously, if you're half as wrong about me as a parent as you are about me as director of the T.E.A.M. Schools, and you are, then I really have nothing to add."

"But my brother does," added Samantha, gesturing to a screen she had ensured was set up prior to the "debate." Up until this point, I was wondering what she was planning; then the screen came to life and I saw the bronzed torso and tousled hair of my middle son, Mason, standing in the middle of what appeared to be a construction site. Judging from the fact that he was shirtless and dirty from working, I acquiesced that Mason still had no use for what he called "bullshit fancy gatherings."

"Hi, I'm Mason Stepnowski, and I'd love to tell you how crappy my upbringing was, but I gotta get back to building homes for displaced people."

Yep, Mason was still Mason.

"Look, from what I can see, Miss Corporate Killer and Mr. Olympic Hero already schooled you people."

"Still jealous," whispered Frankie

"Frank!" I chided.

"Sorry."

"HOWever," Mas continued, ***"I figured you would dismiss our "testimony" since we are, after all, the offspring of the defendant. Didn't consider that, did we, little miss big brains?"***

"RRRRRrr…"

"Sam!"

"rrrrr."

"I figured you'd like to hear what my friend, and best worker, has to say about the abusers that work at the T.E.A.M. Schools."

Completely ignoring the fact that Ms. Brown-Stone was tugging at his sleeve with a haste usually reserved for little kids that urgently have to go potty,

Percy Vulgaire inquired, a bit loudly for my taste, "Whyyyyy exactly, should we caaaaare what your best worker has to say about…"

Joachim Brown Stone stepped in front of Mason.

I looked at Sam, Sam smiled at Frankie, Frankie winked at me, Mason rolled his eyes and looked at his watch, and Marigold Vulgaire threw up on Percy's Birkenstocks.

Joachim spoke, eyes down, but with a quiet dignity that he most certainly didn't have a few years back when we faced each other across a courtroom.

"If I had the chance, I would go back to the T.E.A.M. School. When I was there, I didn't want to hear nothin' from nobody and, because of that, a good man almost lost his job. I don't take back any of the things I said in court, and I'm glad my mom got the money she did 'cause it helped out with a lot of things that ain't nobody's business, but if I was going back to school, or if I had kids, I'd send them to Mr. Step's T.E.A.M. Schools, and I'd let Mr. Chrysler teach 'em. That's all I gotta say."

A lot of things happened then.

The Vulgaire's Pubic Relations guy looked, for moment, like he was going to question Joachim about how credible he was, being an employee of my son and all.

(Pssst! No, I *didn't* misspell PUBIC relations. Think about it.)

Sam smiled at the PR guy as if to say, "please, little seal, swim out just a bit deeper," and he [wisely] chose to maintain his silence.

Frankie looked over to Claude and nodded his head in assurance that he had done the right thing, and Claude seemed, for the moment, to believe him.

Mr. Vulgaire stepped gingerly out of his now multicolored Birkenstocks and escorted his wife from the podium.

Mason gave a half-hearted salute, mumbled ***"back to work"*** and the screen went black.

The S.P.A.N.K. people knew they had been… yeah, I'll say it, spanked.

People began to filter out, buzzing about the stuff that went down and the media buzz that was sure to follow. I hugged Samantha, told her to call her mom, and thanked her for defending so vehemently the man who made her teenage years so miserable.

"Anything for you daddy," she smirked, *"and I'm only billing you my standard rate."* She smiled wickedly on her way to her car. Some things never change.

I had to yell at my 22 year old son (the former Olympic gymnast-turned-teacher) to get down from the scaffolding near the podium, as he was doing inverted handstand, in a suit, to entertain the crowd. Some things never change.

I walked to my ride, politely receiving the congratulations of many and the venomous stares of a few, destined to be alone with my thoughts and doubts. Some things never –

INCOMING CALL FROM MASON

"Hey Mayo, thought you'd be back on a roof by now."

"Yeah, I just wanted to make sure you're OK."

"I am now… Mas?'

"Yeah?'

"Thanks, Mason."

"Love you Pop."

I nodded to myself, hung up the phone, and tried to think about nothing for a while; however, those nagging doubts were getting louder in my head. Media circuses like this were going to keep happening, and I was becoming a guy who had to introduce himself to students that went to the schools that he created. But relationships were being forged, kids were learning, and learning a hell of a lot more than just reading and writing. What to do? What to do?

Peter Gabriel sang and his voice resonated through the Bose speakers with eerie clarity:

"When things get so big, I don't trust them at all You want some control -- you've got to keep it small..."

Maybe some things have to change.

INCOMING CALL FROM PRESIDENT WINFREY

But not right now I guess...

The Art Deportment

"So don't tell anybody what I wanna do; If they find out you know that they'll never let me through"

                                   – Genesis (Illegal Alien)

Back in 2010, then Arizona Governor Jan Brewer clashed with then President Obama when she attempted to enact a new immigration law aimed at identifying, prosecuting and deporting illegal immigrants. Of course, this touched off massive debate about whether the borders were secure, (they weren't) whether the violence federal government did everything it could to secure those borders, (they didn't) and whether or not the tensions created by the perfect storm of the vehement adversaries, and the equally passionate supporters of the law, combined with an impending Mexican narco state, would lead to a collision of epic proportions. (It did.)

Rather than have to walk down the blood splattered, incendiary memory lane that recalls the "1070 riots" or, as they became to be known in less sensitive circles, "the immigration immolations," I'd rather just focus on how the sensitive subject of illegal immigration found its way into the halls of our first beloved T.E.A.M. School in New Jersey. This is the story of two young men, Arturo Rodriguez and Guzman Saloza, but before we get to them, let's establish where I stand on the illegal immigration issue (a topic that I will readily admit has more facets than I am prepared to comment on without further research) by paralleling it to another, education-related subject, that I take *very* seriously.

I think I probably said it best during my interview with Fox News personality Bill O'Reilly during the Fall of 2015; Bill was kind enough to have me on his show, *The O'Reilly Factor*, very early in the development of the T.E.A.M.

Schools, and he offered me a forum to defend myself against the backlash of criticism that was aimed at our admittedly "decisive" way of doing things. The interview was a major success; at least, I thought so; I didn't get drawn and quartered by an angry mob, Bill and I exchanged a few laughs, and I got a quick peek at Megyn Kelly getting ready in wardrobe.

We had just finished fielding questions about the T.E.A.M. approach to teaching, and Mr. O'Reilly had, tactfully, dismissed a caller that thought my public hanging would be in the best interest of the nation when he flipped the script on me.

O'Reilly: "Noooww, Mr. Stepnowski, you're a smart guy; obviously, not opposed to speaking your mind?"

Me: "Well, the jury's still out on the smart part, but…"

O'Reilly: "Come onnnn, you're a smart guy."

Me: "Smarter than the average bear, my dad used to say, why?"

O'Reilly: "I was curioussss as to your feelings on the recent reSURgence in hostilities regarding the immigration issue."

Me: "How long have you got?"

O'Reilly: "Tell you what; we have to go to a commercial,"

(to the cameramen and program directors, in a voice that almost made you believe he wouldn't have fired all of their asses if they answered incorrectly) "We can bring Mr. Stepnowski for another segment, right?"

The cameramen and program directors nodded as though they were completely aware that their asses were grass had they answered to the contrary, and I had 3 ½ minutes, while the nation enjoyed commercials for how to buy Gold, Fruity Pebbles, and vacuums with the proper amount of suction, to think of a reasonable statement about illegal immigrants that wouldn't enrage the whole world.

I relied, as I often do in times of trouble, on a trick that has never failed me.

I told the truth.

O'Reilly: (back from commercial, *damn* that was quick) "Welcome back to the *O'Reilly Factor*, joining us is mmmmmaverick school entrepre*neur* Frank Stepnowski, founder of the controversial Trust in Our Extreme Alternative Methodology schools. Now, Mr. Stepnowski…"

Me: "Call me Frank." (I know, lame, but I was stalling for time)

O'Reilly: (knowing this and plowing me over like a poorly constructed sand castle) "Mr. Stepnowski, you are no doubt faMILiar with the unfortunate events surrounding S.B. 1070 some four years ago? Of **course** you are. *WHAT* then, I ask you, are your feeeeeelings on the recent resurgence in hostilities regarding the immigration issue?"

Me: "You've thrown me into some deep water here Bill so, if you don't mind, I'm going to swim toward the shallows and speak on this from a perspective I can relate to."

O'Reilly: "By all means."

Me: "Well, the last place I taught at, prior to starting the T.E.A.M. Schools…"

O'Reilly: (checking his notes) "Descaminado High School?"

Me: "Correct. It was well known that we had quite a few students from a nearby school district that was, to put it mildly, a war zone. Many of the kids from that district were trouble makers who did nothing but diminish the quality of our school, lower the average of our state test scores, and disrupt the learning process; however, many of them were good kids whose parents, out of desperation, claimed that the kid lived with an 'uncle' or something in Descaminado so their son or daughter could attend our High School. Now, I know this is a slippery slope but I'm going to head up anyway. I have no problem with parents, or children, or *anybody* trying to escape a terrible situation in favor of a better one, provided the person that comes to our school *tries their best, follows the* *rules* of the school, and *respects the valuable opportunity that they have been given,* rather than exploit and defile it. I'm sure you can see the parallel with the immigration issue?"

O'Reilly: "So you're saying thaaaaat, as long as they follow the rules, people can sneak into this country?"

Me: "I believe what I *said* was that if a student from another district found a way to get into my school, and he treated that opportunity as a gift and behaved as such, that I'd rather have him than some little punk that doesn't give a(BLEEP)about us."

O'Reilly: (smiling but still winning) "Well played, *Frank,* but what about the kid that sneaks in and breaks the rules?"

Me: "Out. Immediately."

O'Reilly: "Out? As in *deportment* out?"

Me: "Is there another kind?"

O'Reilly: "Thank you Mr. Stepnowski, I wish you all the best with the T.E.A.M. Schools; thank you for the book, and we'll be watching your progress. Next on *The O'Reilly Factor,* the culture warriors debate the merits of orangutan adoption…"

And now back to our story.

"Hey Step," introduced Mr. Psicopata, *"this is Arturo Rodriguez…"*

"Call me Art."

"Art is finishing up his first year with us here at T.E.A.M. New Jersey"

"I've heard about Art," I admitted, "word has it you're one hell of a student, and that you've been mentoring some of our newer kids. I believe I talked to your parents at the last parent-teacher social, Kate and Jen, was it? Extremely nice people."

"Yes, sir. Thank you. I'll tell them you asked about them."

"You're very lucky to have Mr. Psicopata as one of your instructors Art, he's a great guy and fantastic in conversational Spanish."

"I don't think he needs my help with that," Mr. Psicopata lied, *"Arturo's fluent in Spanish; he even speaks a little bit of Nahuatl!"*

"Wow. That's pretty impressive," I admitted.

"Hey Art, why don't you go on ahead to the library while I talk to Mr. Step. I'll be right behind you. Ms. Zeeno should have everything set up for us, so ask her if you can start making the Wiki and I'll be right there."

"OK," said Art, "nice talking to you, Mr. Step."

And off went Arturo "Art" Rodriguez.

"Seems like a nice kid," I observed. "I would say maybe we should pair him up with Guzman to show him around, since they're both fluent in Spanish, except..."

"Except for the fact that Guzman Saloza is an ignorant little prick," said Mr. Psicopata.

"Yeah, that." I smiled. "Go ahead to the library, and let me know if Ms. Zeeno got her people acclimated to the new server."

And off went Joshua Psicopata.

At almost that precise moment Darlyn Media, one of my favorite young ladies, came around the corner, walking with intense purpose, so much so that she almost walked right into me.

"Oh, I'm sorry Mr. Step."

"What happened to your shirt, kid?"

"Guzman Saloza happened."

"Speak of the devil."

"Yeah," she fumed, *"he **accidentally** dropped his lunch tray on me, no doubt because I pointed out that he was trying to steal from the lunch line last week, then didn't back down when he threatened to crack me in the jaw for doing it."*

"As I recall, Ms. Gonzalez cashed in one of her cards because of that."

"Yeah, well, she didn't get a good shot in, 'cause officer DeChiefs had to grab Guzman for threatening the lunch lady. He really is an assh-... jerk, Mr. Step. I didn't think you let kids like that stay at the T.E.A.M. Schools. I'm sorry, I gotta go before these stains sink in and..."

"Of course, sorry for holding you up, Darlyn."

And off went Darlyn Media.

I needed a minute to think, and calm down. As I sat at my desk, I noticed the dust and piles of papers that exemplify an office that doesn't see its inhabitant very much. I thought, for about the millionth time that week, about whether the T.E.A.M. School idea had grown too big, and whether I had lost the ability to stay "hands on" the way I had promised I would. I absentmindedly fingered the modified Ace of Spades card I kept in my suit jacket pocket, a card I had threatened to cash in several times. Fortunately, *that* kind of "hands on" activity becomes unnecessary once you've done it once *the right way.*

"Ah well, since I'm here, maybe I'll clean house a bit."

 Little did I know, truer words had never been spoken.

I was about ten minutes into straightening up the office, singing, against my better judgment, the Barney "clean up" song to myself, when my Komm-1 (new term, although I still call 'em walkie talkies) came to life.

"Mr. Stepnowski, we have a situation in the rear hallway, are you available?"

"On my way," I sighed, "care to brief me on what I'm coming down for?"

"Yes sir, we have a Guzman Saloza here, and he..."

"I'll be right there." I spat, cutting of the connection. I must remember to apologize to Mr. Yourison for being so rude and cutting him off in mid-sentence, but right now I can feel the hostility I was trying to forget rising like acid in my mouth. The nagging doubts I've had about whether I'm losing control of the T.E.A.M. Schools, combined with a major lack of sleep, combined with Darlyn's earlier comment, combined with... arrrrggh, this little bastard is catching me at the *wrongest* time imaginable. Breathe, remain calm, and stop thinking about that card in your pocket."

I heard Guzman before I saw him...

And I saw him before I knocked him on his ass, but I'm getting ahead of myself.

"Yo! I told y'all...DON'T touch me!"

"Young man, walk where we ask you to and..."

"I TOLD y'all I'm going to lunch, and ain't nobody gonna stop..."

"ACTUALLY," I interrupted in a voice much louder than I probably needed to use, somebody *can*, and *will* stop you."

Turning the corner and standing in front of a posturing Guzman, I ignored him for a few seconds, looking into the eyes of a simmering Officer Gotchaler, a frustrated Mr. Yourison, and an irate Ms. Zeeno. The voices in my head told me to excuse myself and avoid the oncoming storm. I really must learn to listen to those voices in my head more often.

All of the real voices started talking at once, but I only heard bits and pieces, interrupted by spasmodic bursts from the voices in my head that had been bothering me for so long. God, it was like one of those action movies when quick clips of things that happened in the past shoot by, and the music starts building so that you know the shit is about to hit the...

"Young man struck another student..."

"Cursed me out..."

IT'S GETTING TOO BIG

"Man, fuck all y'all…"

"Watch your language"

"Man, fuck you too…"

I DIDN'T THINK YOU LET KIDS LIKE THAT STAY AT THE T.E.A.M SCHOOLS

"…came in the library for no reason…"

"Do not bump me again, Mr. Saloza…"

"…about to go the fuck off, dawg!"

CHILDREN DESERVING OF THE NATION'S PITY FOR HAVING TO ENDURE ME…

"Mr. Rodriguez has been taken to the nurse for examin…"

"Wait, what?" I snapped back into real time.

The angry mob, with the exception of Guzman Saloza, looked at me quizzically, like maybe I looked like I felt, like I was emerging from a fog; an angry, internally-conflicted-about to- snap-and-release-a-nuclear-amount-of-stored-up-frustration fog.

Yourison spoke: "Arturo Rodriguez?"

"I know him."

"Right. Like we said, Mr. Saloza here hit him over the head when he went into the library and then cursed out Ms. Zeeno when she…"

"Man! you ain't gonna talk about me when I right here and…"

LOSING CONTROL

PEOPLE DON'T EVEN KNOW YOU IN YOUR OWN SCHOOLS

INCOMING CALL FROM PRESIDENT WINFREY

I didn't think you let kids like that stay at the T.E.A.M. Schools

INCOMING CALL FROM YOUR CONSCIENCE

TOO BIG

> *"Fuck dis shit, I'm goin' to lunch, and none o y'all better touch me when..."*

That was the last thing Guzman Saloza said for quite some time.

Unfortunately for *me*, he bumped me (intentionally) on his way to lunch and, before I knew what I had done, the voices, the frustration, the indignation, and old instincts [that never really die] collided.

Unfortunately for *him*, they collided in the form of one singularly vicious straight right hand that, fortunately for him, I managed to catch myself at the last second and pull. Otherwise...

Best not to think about that.

The hall was silent, except for the sounds of Officer Gotchler and Mr. Yourison carrying an inert young man to the nurse's office for examination. Before they left, I had to do something, something to let these people know that the person they had placed their faith in hadn't made a mistake, something to let them know that I still had their backs.

I threw the modified Ace of Spades, with disgust, onto Guzman's chest. He was starting to come to, so I looked him intently in the eyes and spoke in a quiet monotone: "You, Mr. Saloza, are an ignorant little piece of shit. You made *me* cash in a card...ME! You will, starting tomorrow, become the model student, or I will kick your ass out into a world filled with people who hit harder than me, care less than you, and *finish* what they start. Do you understand me, boy?"

He just closed his eyes, pursed his lips and turned his head as they carried him away.

I returned to my half dusty office, shut the door and sat down.

It didn't take long.

I picked up the phone, and was in the process of calling Dawn when my cell phone rang.

It was Dawn. "Hmmmm, *that's* serendipitous," I thought, my mood beginning to brighten now that I had finally made the decision that had been coming for a while. "Hi, babe, listen I've come to a dec…"

"You need to come to Central Administration right now."

Her tone removed whatever relief I was feeling. "I'm right down the street at the school building, give me five minutes. What's this about, Dawn? Quick and to the point, please."

"Arturo Rodriguez's family members are here to claim him."

"Jesus, how do they know about the incident? It just happened a few minutes…"

*"Frank, his family is being deported, and you need to get down here **now**."*

I'll save you all of the details. Actually, that's a cop out – *I* don't *want* to go over the details; I've got a headache and every time I think about it… Suffice it to say that I was the P.R.I.N.C.I.P.A.L. of a group of schools that allowed a malcontent like Guzman Saloza to behave, continually, in a manner that was expressly forbidden in my vision but, at the same time, had to sit on our hands while a model student and citizen was taken from us.

The bottom line is that this was the final straw, the realization made manifest my fear that the T.E.A.M. Schools had grown too big, and that I could no longer guarantee the type of extreme alternative methodology that I promised those who enrolled with us.

And I wasn't going to stand for that any longer.

And off went Frank Stepnowski.

47 – 45 = 98.6 + (120/70)

"When it's all been said and done, I did alright, had my fun; And I will walk, before they make me run."

– Keith Richards (Before They Make Me Run)

In my little office at home, I have a signed plaque from the members of the notorious "Soul Patrol," the legendary secondary of my beloved 1970s Oakland Raiders. I loved the Soul Patrol for a variety of reasons, and I like them even more now for reasons that have matured along with me.

"Old Man" Willie Brown, Jack "the Assassin" Tatum, George "the Hitman" Atkinson, and Skip" Dr. Death" Thomas were, to my 10-year old eyes and ears, the baddest mothers on the planet: dressed in black, talking and acting with confidence that came from *knowing* they were good – good enough to be feared by other men who earned a living being badasses. Plus, they had the coolest individual nicknames ever. (Come on, The Assassin? That's BAD.)

As I got older and watched my beloved Silver and Black attack continue to win while playing by their own rules, I've kept up on the guys from those 70s teams, enthralled by a group of men that defied convention, laughed at political correctness (the "Soul Patrol?!?" Yeah, you *might* get away with that today,) yet treated their profession like it was the very essence of their existence. Their demeanor virtually screamed, "don't worry about what I do *off* the field, just know that I'll give you 101% when I'm *on* it." They had swagger before it became a household term.

Now that I'm a bit older and the Oakland bad boys have had some of their legacy and luster knocked off of 'em, I stay loyal, but I remain semi-infatuated with those Soul Patrol rebels from the early days (R.I.P. Jack,) who have now (according to the interviews I've read) learned to see life for the beautiful gift it is; they don't apologize for their ruthless approach to their business while they were at it, but they don't allow the past to define them, either.

You might say that I can relate.

I made a pretty good career, and earned a pretty decent reputation, off of doing things the way I thought were in the best interest of the kids I was raising, coaching or teaching; secure in the knowledge that I was [*very* often] doing the aforementioned things in a manner that most of the "experts" would say was "wrong."

Fuck 'em.

My kids turned out okay, my players were good, and happy to be playing, and my students… well, you can ask 'em, they're all over the place. Look for well-adjusted, responsible people, between the ages of 14 and 44, that are altruistic and can think for themselves and you'll find one sooner than later.

To continue, I got cocky because I knew how much work I put into my job(s,) and how much I loved my kids; my arrogance came from results, the kind you could measure and the kind you couldn't. Along the way, I earned a cool nickname (Captain America) that was, if you can believe it, frowned upon by many during our government's "we apologize for America" campaign. Fuuuuuck that. Of course, my mother was right when she told me that "[my] big mouth would get [me] in trouble someday." (Good call, Mom.) And I, along with my endeavors, were besieged and vilified, from my books to my schools to [in the case of the S.P.A.N.K. debacle] my own children.

I stared at that plaque in my office while I contemplated what to do with the 47 T.E.A.M. Schools that were, by my own admission, becoming too big a venture to maintain without compromising their "swagger." I wondered what the guys from the Soul Patrol would do. To a man, they played the game as hard as they could until they felt they couldn't maintain their level of excellence; then they moved on, thankful for the opportunity to have done it right when they had the chance.

You might say that I could relate.

I had made a promise to all of the people that hitched their wagons to my version of the revolution, and I felt that, being unable to keep my finger *actively* on the pulse of every school, I was becoming remiss in keeping that promise.

I don't break promises.

Ever.

So I said to myself: "you're a smart guy, you're business savvy, and you know the right thing to do in most situations, so do what you know is right."

So I did.

I called Dawn.

What followed were a titanic amount of conversations, conference calls and video conferences, along with enough Blackberry texts and paper signings to create a virtual or origami Great Wall of China, whichever you prefer.

The end result was that we sold off the facilities to all but two of our T.E.A.M. Schools. We decided to keep the original two in Pennsylvania and New Jersey so we could be close by. (Dawn was going to keep her main office in the PA school and I was actually going to teach a few classes at the NJ school.) Many of the people that "inherited" our former properties said that they were going to maintain our "business model," (which, in most cases, involved keeping the staff in place,) which was pretty cool. As of the writing of this book, many of them have kept that promise, which is really cool, and a bit surprising. We closed down the "Two Towers" (thanks for the nickname NJEA magazine) for some sprucing up and renovations, and scheduled our grand re-opening for September, 2022.

Can I tell you something? Without my wife and daughter, I wouldn't have had a clue how to make all that happen. I would've probably just given everything away; in hindsight, seeing the amount of money we made (and subsequently gave to charity,) I know that behind every good man is a woman.

"Ahem!"

Or women. Sheesh, are they ever not listening?

At any rate, we were going back to where we started, secure in the knowledge that it wasn't the size of the dog in the fight; it was the size of the fight in the dog that mattered.

I CAN SEE
CLEARLY NOW

"My mind is clearer now. At last, all too well, I can see where we all soon will be."
– Andrew Lloyd Webber (Heaven on Their Minds)

Hi everybody. Now it's *your* turn. I wouldn't be much of a teacher if I failed to teach you *something* throughout the course of this book, right? So, you tell me – what is an exposition?

Riiiiight, what else? Gooood. Well done! (Except for *you*. Yes, *you*, in the back, in the Hollister shirt. Look at me, please. LOOK at me. Thank you, now - go back and review the definition for exposition and check in with me by the end of the book; you still have a few pages left and I know you can do it.)

Exposition:
How Can You Come Out of the Woodwork if the House is Made of Glass?

Well, friends, the great garage sale was finally complete and the T.E.A.M. Schools' entire operation was now back to the original two locations in Pennsylvania and New Jersey. We took some time to spruce up the buildings themselves and ensure that they would open in a smooth transition legally, emotionally, and academically.

The phrase "come out of the woodwork" usually applies to cowardly people who, after being hidden, suddenly appear in order to do something unpleasant. The etymology of this idiom is based on the idea of insects that suddenly come out from under boards in a house where they have been hidden.

Some of those insects came out of the woodwork when we tucked our tails and admitted that we had simply gotten too big to maintain our vision. Funny thing about insects that come out of the woodwork, though, they scatter when the lights get bright. We were determined to make our schools the proverbial Glass Houses, and the bugs didn't like that degree of illumination. Another funny thing about insects that sneak around looking for opportunities to be nasty – it takes very little effort to smash the little buggers.

And Then There Were Two

"Have you heard the news? Bad things come in twos."

– Danny Elfman (The Little Things)

Well, some of the little doggies in the media couldn't wait to sink their artificially whitened teeth into this one. The "downsizing" (hate that word) of the T.E.A.M. Schools brought the cowards (that didn't have the balls to go after us when we were at our zenith) out of the woodwork ,and they wasted no time telling the whole country how they always knew we would fail. The headlines were hilarious.

Some of my personal favorites?

"NO LONGEVITEAM" (Fuck you, *Rolling Stone.*)

"HANDS ON LOSES, HANDS DOWN" (suck me sideways, *New York Times.*)

"ONE STEP FORWARD, 48 STEPS BACK," (a *personal* attack, stay classy *Newsweek.*)

Of course, some actually shed some metaphorical tears for the bad guys:

YOU CAN'T HANDLE THE TRUTH! The Rise and Fall of the T.E.A.M. Schools (Thanks for the nod, *Playboy*)

PROOF THAT WE *WANT* TO BE PUSSIES: What the Failure of the T.E.A.M. Schools Says About Us as a Country. (A bit hyperbolic there, *Maxim*, but I framed it anyway.)

"Are they fucking kidding?!?" inquired, loudly, my normally non-profane significant other, Dawn. *"Fall? What fall? We went international, downsized intentionally, and **changed the landscape of education** in this country along the way! How, exactly, is that a fall?!?"*

"Hon," I placated, "relax. First of all, I have no idea how I'm going to punctuate that outburst when I finally write my memoirs; second, like Gene says, no publicity is bad publicity."

> *"Gene my ass!"* She fired back, *"how many times has your 'buddy' called since we sold the affiliates and put his investment back in his pocket and then some? Tell him to stick to 'retirement' tours and breathing fire."*

"Not nice, Dawn Marie, not nice. Mr. Simmons was nice enough to invest heavily in our venture when we were having trouble raising capital and, for your information, he sent a sizeable contribution to Mason's relief effort when he was out in the Gulf building houses. So apologize."

> *"RRRrrrr…"*

"Apolooooooggiiiiizzzee," I laughed, as I tickled her feet, against which she still has no defense.

> *"I know, I know,"* she admitted, exhausted from laughing, *"I'm just venting. Gene and Shannon are great people; we had a lot of great people help us. We still do. But I can't help but want to slap the crap out of these cowards that label us failures because…"*

"Because the people on the sidelines always have something to say about the players on the field. They hate us because they don't have the stones to be us."

> *"I know,"* she confessed, snuggling up to me on the floor, *"but can't we kill just a few of them?"*

"I've got a better way you can exert all that energy. I'll help; because that's the kind of helpful guy I am…"

> *"Asshole,"* she purred, moving closer.

I wanted to thank her for sticking by me, and for running the operation behind the scenes, but I wasn't going to ruin the moment by going all serious. Besides, I could tell her all of that in about an hour…

FOR THE RECORD: I wrote an awesome sex scene here, full of metaphorical imposition of will and lots of exotic positions, but Dawn read the rough draft and threatened to turn me into a eunuch with a dull pizza cutter if I published it. Your loss, gentle reader, your loss.

13 ½ minutes later:

Vitriolic literature and the homicidal urges of my wife aside, I was happy. I felt more relieved than I had in years, and now that we were down to the original two schools in Philadelphia, PA and Cinnaminson, NJ, I was much better able to monitor the daily goings on at both facilities.

I could now ensure that the vision I first had when I created T.E.A.M. kept from getting blurry. Quite the contrary, as the best of the best teachers from the other T.E.A.M. Schools earned spots in our two remaining schools, and the enrollment process was scrutinized more intensely than ever, things were as locked in as they were when we first started, *plus* we had all of the experience of the past decade to guide us. In short, we were a lean, mean learning machine again. So put that on the cover of your magazine and read it!

Speaking of "read it," Sam was sitting at the kitchen table reading a rather non-flattering article on T.E.A.M. (blow me, *Harper's*) when I came downstairs a few days later. Samantha had very generously taken a few days off to help make sure the two remaining schools' "grand re-openings" went smoothly, from a legal standpoint.

> "I think mom's right," observed Sam, "we could probably arrange for a few of these people to accidentally 'disappear'."

> *"See,"* echoed my egg frying wife.

"Jesus, you two are amazing," I said, between gulps of Blue Mountain coffee,(goooood stuff folks, worth the extra coin, trust me) "when I was going all John Rambo on people back in the day you were both in my ear constantly! Now…"

"Don't play righteous with us." countered my darling wife, *"You already said you weren't going to re-open T.E.A.M. without firing back at the critics."*

"Really?" asked Sam, looking up from her scrambled egg whites and yellow journalism.

"Really really" I answered, "but, to borrow a metonymic adage from Edward Bulwer-Lytton, the pen is mightier than the sword."

"I have no freaking idea what a metabolic algae is," mumbled Sam, "but I think I'm gonna like this."

"Metonymic adage, Sam"

"Whatever."

NOTE: The brilliant and painfully helpful Mr. Trautz, in his proofreading comments, suggested that I teach you what metonymy is. To which I reply: "No, they've got to learn to look some of this shit up on their own." If you *already knew* what metonymy was, to paraphrase Samuel L. Jackson in *Pulp Fiction*: "Check out the big brain on YOU!"

The day before the N.J. and P.A. T.E.A.M. Schools reopened, my dear friend Matt Brannon, who was now the editor in chief at TIME, got me a full page to print my "open letter to the critics" in the first September issue and, thanks to his connections at Viacom, a chance to *read* it on national television the day before the issue hit the stands.

I am not ashamed to admit that I was going to enjoy this.

The day of THE BIG READ the news lines were buzzing. Apparently, the debate over whether the T.E.A.M. Schools were divine or demonic was still white hot and a whole host of radio, TV, and internet sources were going to cut in to live broadcasts during our "story hour from hell."

For a few seconds I considered revising my words, but then I thought, "written with passion, authentic if not erudite – it stays as is."

(Much the same way I feel about this book you're holding!)

Good thing, too, because by the time everybody took their places, and the cameramen and set supervisors were happy, I didn't have time to fart let alone revise a letter. I thought it would be cool to have a bunch of the T.E.A.M. students standing around me while I read, but I rejected the director's idea that "we needed to have a balanced demographic of kids so as to promote equality."

"No way;" I rejected, "that kind of politically correct bullshit goes against everything we stand for. Whatever kids want to show up and be on with us can be on with us, and I don't care if we have 3 Africa-American girls, 7 homosexual Pakistanis in skinny jeans, 12 fat Chinese guys and a white kid with freckles in a wheel chair."

Little did I know how many kids would show up. The producers were having a conniption. "What are we going to do with hundreds of people?! We can't fit them all in the studio?! This isn't a soy latte'! I specifically said soy latte'!"

I thought it best to step in and offer a suggestion.

"That might work" acquiesced Mr. Soy freakin' latte'.

Dawn and the kids were watching ESPN when they cut away from some special about the new stadium being built for the Arizona Raiders (don't ask) into what they were calling our "press conference." Oh, yeah, ESPN has been interested ever since DeMarcus Nurse turned his life around, broke all the receiving records at Florida State University, and went on to become rookie of the year for the Los Angeles Bengals (don't ask) and told everybody that would listen that "[he] owe[d] it all to the T.E.A.M. schools."

SHOWTIME:

"Thanks Dan," intoned veteran announcer Scott Van Pelt, "but we're cutting in to the much anticipated press conference from Frank Stepnowski, the controversial founder and the man behind the two fisted approach to academics that is the T.E.A.M. Schools. The T.E.A.M. Schools have recently downsized (yep, still hate it) to their original two locations in New Jersey and Pennsylvania, and some people see that as an admission of defeat, although Stepnowski, and his people, adamantly deny that. They claim that this is a chance to reclaim the initial vision of the schools. Stepnowski has taken a full page out in this weeks' TIME magazine, and several other publications, both in print and online, responding to his critics that claim that the T.E.A.M. Schools remain an academic anomaly destined to fail. We go now live to New Jersey, Hannah?"

"Yes, Scott," responded awesome announcer with awesomer name Hannah Storm.

"Mr. Stepnowski is set to broadcast from this podium here and... oh, it's starting, back at the conclusion, Scott."

The camera shot opened with a wide shot of the hundreds of T.E.A.M. students (and staff, Zeus bless 'em!) that converged in the studio parking lot around the podium (which we had moved to be out in the middle of the throng,) announcing immediately that we were a force to be reckoned with and not going away any time soon.

As I spoke, the camera angle narrowed slowly, picking up the determination and emotion on the faces of those that still believed in what we were trying to do. By the end of the "reading" my face would be framed by the camera, allowing me to "look" directly into the eyes of the TV audience and, hopefully, some of my detractors. I jumped right in, fast and furious, all killer, no filler.

"Dear critics,

I Hear you.

We all hear you.

Your criticisms, frequent and loud reveal you;

but the people in the stands have always criticized the fighters in the arena.

I know why.

I am a fighter

and I hate the mob

because you are fickle,

because you are weak;

and you hate me

because you lack the strength,

the stamina

and the guts

to *be* me.

You think it, but I *say* it

then you say it, but I *do* it,

then you do it, but I *live* it.

When you're chaining yourself to the safety of stereotypes,

I'm destroying the limitations people put upon me,

When you're hiding behind your busy schedule full of nothing new

I'm throwing myself into the arena and fighting

and getting hurt

and making mistakes

and failing but enduring.

So sit back, relax, and think you're getting over by undermining me

Enjoy the fat belly, small mind, and weak will that come from a life on the *sidelines*

Someday push will come to shove

and it will be just you, me

and the legions of kids that I teach *my way…*"

(And then, in a rare moment of melodrama, I looked right into the camera, paused, and smiled, like a wolf about to dine on a fat, sanctimonious sheep.)

"And that thought will keep me warm tonight."

Needless to say, reactions to the speech, if you want to call it that, were immediate and diverse. Many claimed that the implied violence behind the words gave ample evidence to the fact that I was, as they had always claimed, a "thug claiming to be a messiah." Many championed the speech as an unapologetic statement that what we were doing at T.E.A.M. was still a righteous response made necessary by a broken educational system.

I didn't care. I didn't care that my face was on TV more than Baby Gaga (don't ask) for the next few weeks. I didn't care that I was getting Emails by the hundreds from administrators (including most of those that took over our affiliate sites when we sold them off) claiming that they were adopting many of the principles that we used at the T.E.A.M. Schools, with amazing results. I didn't care that the Tea Party (no, they didn't go away) was starting to kick my name around as a possible third party candidate to run against my dear friend (and very vocal supporter, God bless her) Oprah Gail Winfrey, who was going to be elected to a third term in a landslide unimpeded by my dumb ass. I didn't even care that Olivia Munn finally got around to asking me to be on her show. (Actually, I had a little bit of a nerdgasm about *that* one.)

I didn't have time to care, folks.

School was in session.

Kill or be Kilt:
Wherein a Tea Party Teacher Attempts to Abduct a New Comedian.

"There never came ill of good advisement."

– Scottish Proverb

OK, school is back in session, things are running like a finely oiled machine, and we are balancing the sweet and sour of education and discipline with efficiency and panache. George Carlin, tired from the rigors of being Educational Secretary and worn out from his *"I'm 86, Unfrozen and Unhinged"* HBO special, decided to go back into the deep freeze. He gave me explicit instructions not to wake him up unless Richard Pryor de-thawed first or he was gonna kick me in the nuts.

"Thanks, George."

"Ah, it was fun."

"Any suggestions about who I should get to oversee the Two Towers while I get back into the classrooms? I kind of like the intelligent-comedian-in-charge thing."

"What about Colbert or Stewart?"

"Getting set to run against Oprah and Ellen on the independent ticket."

"Ah, yeah. See? I forget this shit! Gettin' old. What about the Scottish guy that that won the Peabody Award?"

"Craig Ferguson? But he's had a gig with CBS for an eternity now."

"Oh... yeah... he probably wouldn't wanna give that up. See ya kid."

And off went George Carlin, managing to zing me even as he became a frozen genius McNugget… again.

So I had my people call Craig's people (I know, pompous much? But that's how things get done in certain circles, so piss off) and, on a miserable, rainy Sunday morning the phone rang.

"Will somebody answer the freakin' phone?!?" I yelled. "AAArrgghh! I'm in the MIDDLE of something here…freakin' rainy Sunday, hate rainy Sundays, I'm COMING! Hello?"

> *"Are ya curazy, yah bahstahd?!? What're ya dyooin? Tryin ta cut yerr noots off befurr ya even even get started?"*

"Craig Ferguson?"

> *"Yeah. Craig Ferguson. Tee VEEs Craig Ferguson! What're yah thinkun, offerin' me a educational pasishun?"*

"Now, Craig, you're judging me before you understand the significance of the title."

> *"Noobody's judgin' ya heah Frrahnkie, Ahm simply looookin' out fer yer best interust, fahnancially speakin'. Yooo know damn well the conterraversy this'll cause."*

"Listen, if people are going to make the age old mistake of joodging a boook by ats cover, then I don't want them reading it."

> *"Nah need tya mock the accent, lad. Ahm jes looookin' out fer ya."*

"You're right, Glenn Beck might be available"

> *"Ach! That fookin noot jab. Dya really wan be on his speed dial?"*

"You sound pretty defensive for a guy that doesn't want the job, and your Scottish really comes out when you're pissed, did you know that?"

> *"Nah, I'm almos sehxty and I haven't figured out mah accent yet. Tell ya what, come on the show, we'll chat, and I'll decide wherenot I want the gig."*

"Deal."

The appearance on **The Late Late Show** was everything I always dreamed it would be: funny, irreverent, and spontaneous. We hardly talked about anything serious, let alone educational, until he fired off what I immediately recognized as his "test" question.

"Soooo, whaddya thin about the Tea Party folks throwin yer name out there? You OK wi thot?"

"Flattering as it is, Craig, I do not belong to any particular political party, nor do I define, and thereby limit, myself by blindly accepting all of the precepts of any organization, religion or affiliation. I am a Stepnowski, and I am an American. American *on purpose.*

I thought the allusion to *his* autobiography would get me out of this and give him a nice segue into another topic.

Wrong.

"So, ya don't like the Tea Party People, eh?"

"I didn't say that, Craig, I don't mind the connection to the "Tea Party" movement in this country; I am intrigued by it, as I am with anything that grew organically out of the will of the people. Let's face it, without the will of the people, the T.E.A.M. Schools wouldn't exist."

"Then why ... "

"I've met a LOT of the Tea Party people" I cut him off, deliberately, "and they've all been very cordial and sincere, even when we agree to disagree on certain things. I am also fascinated, and more than a bit concerned, when I see certain media outlets immediately vilify any group that doesn't follow the herd the way they did the Tea Party folks; always smacks of Big Brother to me. Throw in the average person's misconceptions about the *actual* Boston Tea Party of 1773, and there are many, as you know, and you've got yourself a *pretty freakin' good metaphor* for something that people seem to continually judge quickly without knowing anything beyond their initial perception. I can relate."

"Really? How so?"

CraigyFerg looked sincerely interested at this point, and I figured that what I said next would determine whether I had myself a Scottish-born-American-made administrator in alliance or not. Oh well, kill or get kilt.

"A whole honkin' lot of people read stuff and perceive me as some sort of monosyllabic bully that gets his rocks off on imposing his will on troubled teens and thinks every problem can be solved with a swift kick in the ass. They're wrong. They are so very, very wrong.

"What if I was one o' them?"

I leaned across his desk and shouted, in the worst Scottish accent I could muster: "Then pees ahf, ya foookin' joodgmental bahstarrd!"

We both laughed out loud, my curses got BLEEPed, and we went to a commercial for McWendy's (don't ask.)

...oh, and I got myself the funniest educational assistant since I pulled Carlin out of cryostasis. Rock on! First order of business, have Craig work the "shock collars for parents" thing in to his farewell monologue..."

Astute reader QUIZ!

I included this chapter because:

A) I wanted to "write in a Scottish accent."

B) I had to let George rest in peace.

C) I wanted to annoy the hyper-liberals with a Tea Party reference.

D) I plan on sending a copy of this book to Craig Ferguson to try to get on his show.

E) All of the above.

Did you say "E?" *You* are one *smart cookie*, but we already knew that, didn't we?

The Monster at the End of the Book

"Now I'm calling on citizens from all over the world, this is Captain America calling I helped you up when you were down on your knees, so won't you catch me now I'm falling."

– The Kinks (Catch Me Now I'm Falling.)

I *remember* one of my favorite books as a kid was a *Sesame Street* book called *The Monster at the End of This Book* (by Jon Stone and Michael Smollin.) In the book, lovable blue monster Grover is told that there is a monster at the end of the book, and he's more than a little nervous that, as he moves through the book, he is getting closer to this horrible creature. I don't want to spoil it for you, but when he gets to the end it turns out that there is a monster at the end of the book, and it's him. Silly old Grover teaches us a valuable lesson about letting fear paralyze us, and that what we imagine is very often worse than the reality that we turn out to be strong enough to endure.

Guess what? There's a monster at the end of this book, too. It's the idea that the T.E.A.M. Schools could happen. Maybe not exactly the way I described them in my little fantasy novel here, but I think we can both agree that it would take some sort of "extreme alternative" to shake the rust off the default system of education that has outgrown its agrarian roots.

So, just for the sake of argument, let's say this little work of fiction gets me fired and I get cranked up enough to actually start something resembling the T.E.A.M. Schools, *after* I review my **extensive** notes and write a **scathing** expose' on the people who fired me, of course.(Not kidding, AT ALL.) What would be the chance that people would be afraid of the little monster? I wonder.

Now, you could rightfully ask, "What are you afraid of, Step? How come you haven't tried an entrepreneurial venture like a T.E.A.M. School yet?"

Good question.

Easy answer – I am a teacher. I *like* being a teacher and, if I may be honest, I think I'm getting pretty good at it. I also happen to be the parent of (as of this writing) 14, 13 and 12 year- old children that need my time and energy; therefore, following my own advice, I'm going to make sure my yard is clean before I go landscaping the nation. Know what I mean? I'm sure that you do. But, just for the sake of curiosity, let me ask you something:

There's this school, let's call it a T.E.A.M. School. You are asked, upon arrival, to trust that our methods, which will appear extreme compared to the current status quo, will work. If you want out at any time, you need only ask and you will be refunded a portion of your tuition payment.

The *building* looks nice, is kept ultra clean, and has plenty of parking.

The *tuition* is in keeping with the top private school in your area, although financial aid is available.

The *staff* is assembled from a waiting list of highly motivated, well compensated men and women who agree, contractually, to improve their craft continually; but will not be judged in the traditional manner. Rather, they themselves, their students, the students' guardians, and their peers will decide whether they're performing in a manner commensurate with our standards.

As a *parent/guardian,* you agree, in writing, to be involved in both the academic *and* social development of your child by attending (every year) one Back-to-School night, one parent-teacher conference, and one social event, at which you'll volunteer. Failure to do *your* job will result in your tuition forfeit and your child being removed from the program.

The *administration,* under my direct guidance, will support the teachers and trust them in the event of a conflict. Your job is to be an educational leader, not a paper pusher; we have people for that. No staff member is to be threatened or made to feel inadequate by any student, parent, administrator, or peer. Any person in violation of that will answer to me directly, and I am happy to put the "dic" in dictatorship.

The *students* will be expected to behave appropriately. (We will let you know what is "appropriate," and you *will* listen.) From an academic standpoint, each student will be allowed to progress to the next level of instruction once they have:

1. Demonstrated mastery of a certain concept,

2. overcome their most glaring weakness in that area of instruction, and

3. conferenced, and agreed with, their instructor and guardian.

The *counselors* will be realistic and painfully honest. No more lying to the chronically average kid that he could survive academically at a Division 1 school *and* play football there.

The *curriculum* will be simplified [initially] into reading, writing and mathematical skills, later evolving into a course of study that is geared toward the student's legitimate area of interest. No more Hemingway for John if he wants to be a mechanic, but his ass will be in auto shop every day and he'd better be an "A" student there! Stacey can forego World History since she wants to study nursing, but she'll be up to her neck in sciences, and she had best be doing well, or we may have to have a talk about the level of her commitment.

The *discipline* will be swift and uncompromising.

Nobody hides in their rooms or offices; open door policy, school-wide, at all times.

Starting from the top, with me, all the way down to the most recently enrolled student:

You *will* comply, or you will be *punished.*

You will *work* hard, or you will *fail.*

You will *obey* our rules or you will

get

the

fuck

out.

You probably wouldn't be interested in a school like *that…*

would you?

Still Screwed

"All animals are equal, but some animals are more equal than others."

– George Orwell (Animal Farm)

As with any lesson, I try to talk with my students before they leave for the day and see if, despite my inadequacy, we actually learned anything today. I say we, of course, because I learn as much from you as you do from me (probably more, come to think of it.) Very often, when my students tell me what they *learned* it has nothing to do with what I intended to *teach* that day.

Such was the case, to some degree, with this here book y'all just read. I used to read interviews with authors (real authors, not assholes like me,) musicians, and other artists where they said "the [insert piece of art] took on a life of its own" I always thought, "what a load of shit, *you're* composing the thing, you control whatever *life* it has!" I was wrong, and I apologize to all the brilliant artists who had no idea, nor care now that they know, that some tool from New Jersey thought you were inauthentic.

I thought that this book would be *Why Are All the Good Teachers Crazy* **Continued**, you know? Still funny, still irreverent, but maybe a bit more cathartic and serious.

Didn't happen that way.

What started as a "fantasy school of the future where teachers could do whatever they wanted to get the job done" novel became a story fraught with the same issues and problems that keep our educational system from evolving. Most of this book was written in the 76 days I had "off" for Summer vacation in 2010, and many, *many* times did I consider deleting the whole freakin' thing because my brain was arguing with my heart and my body was too tired to referee. I could have taken months and months to edit and rewrite, omit and refine, but while I wanted this book to be a bit more polished than the last one, I wanted the passion and spontaneity that only comes from working without a net, know what I mean? I hope I came close, and please don't hesitate to let me know what you think. That way I can learn, like I said in the beginning, from *you*.

But for now, I'm the teacher here, and I started our lesson some few hundred pages ago by telling you that we were screwed. So, what do I have to teach you here at the end? Let me check my notes... here *somewhere*... ah! No, that's not it... here we go... yes... what's the state of education now? Say it with me: still SCA-ROOOOOOOD.

Why, you ask, are we still screwed tighter than a lighting fixture your father installed twenty years ago? Well, maybe you didn't ask it just like that, but I know what you mean. Allow me to explain.

Students (my real students, that is,) I started this book in top down fashion, BIG politicians, Senators, local politicians, superintendents, principals, vice principals, supervisors, teachers and students. Watch how adroitly (SAT vocab word!) I come full circle by closing in *reverse* fashion!

The <u>students</u> remain at the bottom of the totem pole, subjected to all the bullshit that slides downhill upon them. The average kid is a study in dichotomy, perfectly ready to ride the scariest roller coaster ten times with a belly full of treats, but hijacked by a prefrontal cortex that paralyzes them with fear of being embarrassed that they can't read all those words in that poem you want them to read in front of the class; these people will never be "normal," and they need the people in charge of them to be focused and have their best interest in mind.

Riiiiiighhhht.

The <u>teachers</u> are still stuck between a rock – wanting to teach meaningful stuff to kids that need help, and a hard place – the need to write lesson plans that satisfy state standards and have our kids pass state tests so as to appease our "bosses," many of whom we have lost *all* respect for becaaaauuuuuussse

the <u>supervisors</u> are under pressure to provide the administrators with some sort of tangible proof that the teachers are teaching. The problem? YOU CAN'T MEASURE REAL TEACHING. They know it, but they have to ask us for it anyway

becaaaauuuuuussse

the <u>vice principals</u>, and <u>principals</u> (thanks to *No Child Left Behind* and other such cataclysmic bullshit) spend more of their time analyzing data, overseeing committees, and trying not to get fired by proving [with data, hah!] that they're doing *their* job than they do providing educational leadership.

The <u>Superintendents</u> and the <u>local politicians</u> are too focused on two bottom lines to worry about minor details like whether the children they pledged to be responsible for are actually learning. The two bottom lines? The one they *spend*, because money is the root of all evil, and the one they *sit on*, because their asses will be out of a job if they can't appease

The <u>Senators</u>, who are busy trying to get re-elected and "pay back" the small handful of people that funded their $100,000,000.00 campaign for their Senate position. Sorry, nothing's changed here, kids.

There's an old Greek saying that "the fish stinks from the head" and the head of this stinky fish remains the <u>BIG politicians</u>. Pick a news station (TV or radio,) or *any* news magazine, periodical, or website – check out how much time the big guns spend talking about education in this country. Good luck with that, but I think Joe Jackson summarized it best in *The Obvious Song*: "So we starve all the teachers, and recruit more marines / how come we don't even know what that means/ it's obvious."

That's a lot to digest, and I haven't even *mentioned* the parents (that's a whole book in itself) or the teachers that *don't* care. (I think I went after them enough in the last book.) But I have a message of hope, which is against my cynical nature, so LISTEN UP!

We can fix this. You can fix this. If *you* do the right thing, then that becomes *us* doing the right thing, and eventually *all* of us are doing things right, and the ship, though massive and entrenched in the metaphorical ice, turns around and starts sailing for better waters like the one in *Frankenstein*. Whatever role you play in the education process, (and if you're breathing, you play a role, whether you know it or not) you need to do a few simple things:

Find out what our kids need to know

Understand that they all won't learn the same way, (nor should they)

Care about each other enough to be honest,

Know that real learning *can't* always be measured by data and tests, but

Embrace the idea that real teaching and learning *do* require hard work, so

Don't quit.

If we can do that, we're on our way; if we can't, we're...

Screwed.

But there's HOPE!

"I search for connection in some new eyes
But they're hard for protection from too many dreams passed by."

— Bruce Springsteen (My Love Will Not Let You Down.)

I know it seems like I'm leaving you in a cynical place, and to some degree I am, because the problems I talked about in this book are very real, and it's getting harder every day to extricate ourselves from them; however, I wouldn't be worth much as a teacher if I didn't believe that there is a way to overcome all obstacles, so I'm going to tell you something kind of sad so I can leave you with something very encouraging.

I used to have all kinds of dreams. I used to think I was going to change the world in some way, maybe save some people's lives, become super rich and well known just so I could become the anomaly that gave most of his money to charity and stayed nice and accessible despite fame and fortune. Life has a way of smashing those bigger dreams into pieces so small that you barely recognize them.

So my dreams became smaller, more within the realm of possibility, if you will – perhaps win Teacher of the Year, get a radio interview or two, win some sort of literary award, maybe see my abs again. People (even those close to you) sometimes have a way of draining your ability to dream even little things after a while.

I don't really have dreams of my own anymore, and only now, as I finally put this confession on paper, do I realize how pathetic that is. Maybe that explains why I feel so terribly alone, even in crowded places, as I'm not in the habit of sinking other peoples' ships with bullshit that I alone can, and need to, fix. But I promised you a happy ending and you shall have one.

I live, for all intents and purposes, for the dreams of my kids.

I think that makes me a very effective teacher.

I think I'm not alone in that respect.

Allow me to explain. I desperately need to know that dreams are alive and worthy of pursuit, and I see them in the eyes and feel them in the hearts of my children and my students; therefore; as both a parent and a teacher (and aren't they really the same thing?) I work with my kids like my life depends on it - because it *does*. I would be lying if I denied the fact that the chance to help my kids realize their dreams is the only thing that gets me out of bed most days. I'm like any other teacher. I get tired of the apathy, the bureaucracy, and the bullshit, and I am secretly terrified that nothing I do makes a damn bit of difference.

I'm like every other parent. I get exhausted walking the thin line between discipline and destruction, between creating spoiled brats and kids with opportunities, and I am secretly terrified that nothing I do makes a damn bit of difference.

But all it takes is that spark, that light, however fleeting, in the eyes of my kids to bring me to life, and I am ***dangerous*** when I am brought to life. Think of me as a transitive vampire – nourished by the hopes and aspirations of others, so much so that my existence depends on keeping their hopes alive. It ain't about the legacy, it ain't about the summers off, and it sure as hell ain't about the money, I need to make the dreams of your kids [and mine] come true because I don't have any of my own left.

You want me teaching your kids, you *really* do.

And now for the good news: I think that thousands, if not tens of thousands, of teachers and educational staff feel the same way. I think that we have sold our own futures in the hopes that the dreams of the next generation will pay the mortgage once their dreams are realized, and we teach like our lives depend on it because they *do*.

And that's gotta make you sleep a little better, right?

Acknowledgements:

Because my first ever book, *Why Are All the Good Teachers Crazy*, actually sold more than four copies to my immediate family, I need to thank a bunch of people before I offend a bunch of other people. So here goes – in no particular order:

Why Are All These Good People Crazy?

• My kids, Samantha, Mason and Frankie, who generously donated money from their savings accounts so that their dad could get his first book published. You guys are the only things that I'm *sure* that I did right in my life; you simply cannot know how much I love you. I'm sorry I yell so much. Everything I do, I do to make this world a better place for you.

• My sister Molly and my cousin Colleen, for starting the *"Fans of The Author Frank Stepnowski"* page on Facebook, which gave me a chance to interact with some ridiculously cool people from all over the country who were unfortunate enough to have read my first book.

• Kathy Westfield, the Milligans, and Matt Brannon of *The Spirit* for giving a local boy from Fishtown his first interview as an author, an honor I won't soon forget.

• Bridget Zino, for having the balls to put a potentially incendiary book with lots of profanity and grammatical errors on a library shelf, moving me one step closer to legitimacy. Thanks, Big Z, may your world be free of zombies.

• Erin Dowd, Samantha Abbott, Steve Jones, April Estep, Stacey Schwab, Carolyn Martino, Tim Miller, and the legions of people that sent me messages, Emails and letters telling me that my book inspired them in some way. You all inspire me to keep it real, even if it hurts. Ladies and gentlemen, I remain your instrument of righteous cruelty.

The Avengers:

- (Black Widow) My wife, Dr. Dawn Marie, the brains behind the operation; you're once… twice… three timmmmmes a lady, and I low-oo-uuuuvvvvvv youuuuu.

- (Iron Man) Ed Trautz, wrote a stunning foreword for the last book, and helped immeasurably with input for this one, never once claiming any connection to them, even at the height of the hoopla. Ed is the best thing to happen to English teachers since the printing press, and I am painfully jealous of how good he is at such a tender age. Ed and his wife Emily are currently hard at work conceiving the next wave of the revolution.

- (The Hulk) Peter Nardello, still gets high blood pressure thinking of how I thanked him for him "proofreading prowess" in the last book, yet went to print in haste before he had a chance to edit the final copy. You and Kristin *must* teach the future generations of Nardellos not to be as impulsive as their uncle Step. Pete is a mountain of a man with a heart big enough to make a difference, and I love him for it.

- (Nick Fury) Fred Roth is always there when I reach out from planet domestic and require Rock and Roll. A true friend, always giving and never asking in return. You remain an angry, authentic, unapologetic wolf in a world of stupid sheep, and I am proud to call you and Kim my friends.

- (Thor) Billy Staab, always knows when to talk, and when to listen (rare wisdom in this day and age,) and when to show up at the beach with Coronas and limes. He also keeps an eye on mom and dad across the bridge. I love you, brother.

- (Hawkeye) Marc Granieri, [almost convincingly] lies to me every day about how our teaching ability is frighteningly similar. Incorrect; he's twice the teacher in half the package. Marc's wealth of knowledge is a hidden stash of candy that I will continue to steal from without remorse.

The Mind, the Body, the Spirit

I read a *lot* while I was writing this book, and maybe only trace amounts of that copious consumption made it in here but sometimes, a little bit of a great seasoning can make an ordinary dish extraordinary. (If you don't believe me, add a tiny bit of truffle oil to plain macaroni and cheese... wow.) A few of the books that turned my mac n' cheese into something better were:

NurtureShock – Bronson & Merryman

Doing School – Pope

Class and School – Rothstein

Many Children Left Behind – Meier & Wood

The Struggle for the American Curriculum – Kliebard

Dismantling America - Thomas Sowell.

Myths, Lies and Downright Stupidity – Stossel

Why Are All The Black Kids Sitting Together in the Cafeteria? – Tatum

Readicide: How Schools Are Killing Reading and What You Can Do About It. - Gallagher

There's A Monster at the End of This Book – Smollin

- Thanks, mom, for buying books as fast as I could read 'em.

- I have to give thanks to the folks at **Crossfit**. Three years ago, I was big, strong, and *completely clueless* regarding *total* fitness and longevity. Now I fear my workouts, love my workouts, and feel better at 42 than I did at 22.

- As always, thanks to my students; for keeping me sharp, keeping me angry, telling me when I'm full of shit, and reminding me that none of us is as smart as all of us.

- Almost last but certainly not least, thanks to my fellow teachers, all of whom are better than me but let me hang around because I promise to use their names in my novels.

- And, of course, my late son, Cain, for reminding me to live every moment with intense purpose; driven by love of life but undaunted by fear of death.

Donations to the Wounded Warrior Project

One does not accept the nickname "Captain America" from his friends and take it lightly. Freedom is not free, and I am happy to fight for, pay for, and protect it. With that in mind, I am proud to say that a portion of the proceeds from this book will be donated to the **Wounded Warrior Project**, a non-profit organization that provides tangible support for wounded service men and women and helps them on the road to healing, both physically and mentally.

For more information, check out **www.woundedwarriorproject.org**

About the Voice

Step is a product of the educational system he thinks is in the toilet; ironically, this proves him right. He reads Playboy for the articles and Food Network magazine for the pictures (although the pages of both are mysteriously sticky at any given time.) He likes his in-laws, loves his country, exercises regularly, and reads for *enjoyment.* He says "please" and "thank you" and takes account-ability[1] for his actions.

Clearly, he belongs locked away somewhere.

Until they catch him, you can send him your compliments, criticisms, peanut butter cookies, gratuitous sexual advances and/or death threats by contacting him @ *Fans of the Author Frank Stepnowski* on **Facebook.**

1. **ac·count·abil·i·ty** *noun*

    A. the quality or state of being accountable; *especially* an obligation or willingness to accept responsibility or to account for one's actions

    B. **COMPLETELY** outdated concept often overshadowed by people who claim they're being targeted due to some element of their person that they only thump their chest about in times of trouble (read: when they get *caught.*)

    Example: *Most public officials lack accountability.*

About the Cover

The cover, which was created by Tommy Castagna, graphic designer extraordinaire and all around good guy, has a lot of meaning behind it. It should be noted that without his formatting expertise and dedication to quality, this book may have never made it to print. I owe him BIGTIME.

The black and silver layout is a nod to the Oakland Raiders, a team whose image resonates with me for numerous reasons, some of which are mentioned in these pages.

The singular apple, along with being an iconic image for education, is an homage to the cover of a book that was given to me by a former professor who, evidently, saw potential for educational disruption in a young, stupid, kid from Fishtown. The book, *Teaching As a Subversive Activity*, and it's "apple as a bomb" cover, remains as pertinent to me now as it did when I first received it. I love that.

The subheading, "An Educational Fairytale," is a nod to one of my favorite books by one of my favorite authors: *Animal Farm*, by George Orwell. Orwell, no stranger to irony, called his little novel "A fairy story," while scholar Russell Baker called it, "one of the century's most devastating literary acts of political destruction." I *really* love that.

The picture on the back is another homage to another writer that died with more talent in his pinky toe than I have in my entire body – Shel Silverstein. I don't think I've ever read ANYthing by Silverstein that wasn't great, and his author photos were always very cool. His picture on the back of *Runny Babbit*, which was published posthumously in 2005, is a study in calculated coolness from an erudite, compassionate guy who respected his readers enough to know they could handle whatever he dished out. I *really*, **really** love that.

Some recent observations, a request, and a few words for you.

"Begin at the beginning…and go on till you come to the end: then stop"

-Lewis Carroll (Alice in Wonderland)

Some recent observations

A lot of things have happened since I scribbled the first words that would become chapter one of this book into a marble composition book decorated with a "thank you" note for writing book one. (Thanks, Emily.)

Many of the aforementioned things convinced me that I'm not completely bat-shit crazy in my assessment of things educational and otherwise. Here are a few of them, in no particular order:

- I've recently read about how Finland went from the outhouse to the penthouse in terms of their educational system by doing things pretty much the *opposite* of how we're doing 'em here in the U.S. of A. Okay, so I'm not too far off with the whole "nuke the current system and start over" idea.

- I've also been inundated with a ton of literature (written by people with a lot more time to do research than I,) that supports my theory that we are creating a generation of test taking automatons that can't *think* and, therefore, are ill-prepared for the hyper-competitive global economy that awaits them. Okay, so people who actually know what they're talking about agree with me, that's gotta be good, right?

- Oh yeah, the movie *Waiting For Superman* came out, and a virtual army of people (that didn't need much of a push) projected their own self-loathing (at the inadequacy of their leadership skills) onto schools and teachers. However, Geoffrey Canada, the film's primary "voice," shares my assertion that the current system is "broken" and needs to be rethought intensely and immediately. While I take issue with the limited scope of the film, I'm glad to see that common ground exists in our desperate desire to save future generations of American kids.

- Interestingly, my daughter Sam started her freshman year in September, and she has to take a class called "Practical Skills" *and it teaches much of the same stuff I imagined our T.E.A.M. School class of the same name would teach.* How about ***that***?! I felt pretty smart for a minute when I heard that.

- In the non-academic realm, Alice Cooper FINALLY got nominated to get in the Rock and Roll Hall of Fame and Scarlett Johansson was elected GQ's "Babe of the Year" so, clearly, I know quality when it comes to ear candy and eye candy.

A request

At the risk of sounding like a capitalistic whore, I'd like to make a request of you, gentle reader. I'm a self-publishing author. (That means I pay for everything and the only promotion for my books comes from *my* hard work and *your* word of mouth.) Having said that, I'd humbly request that if you loved, hated, or anything-in-betweened this book, tell somebody, go online and write a review, talk about it on Facebook, etc. That way I can keep my little book in the public eye. Do NOT underestimate the power of the people!! Online reviews and internet chatter got my last book to #1 out of over 200,000 books about teachers on Amazon.com! Can you dig it? I knew that you could. Everything but the cost to publish another book (and maybe one spending splurge on iTunes) is going to charity anyway.

Unless Oprah calls, then the party's at my house and everybody holding a book is invited.

A few words for you.

Much as I love to read and write, I always maintain a sense of disbelief that anyone would actually take the time to read a book *I* wrote. Apparently, you did.

That promotes literacy, that helps out the Wounded Warrior project, and that makes my kids [secretly] proud of their dad. So thank you.

Really,

sincerely,

thank you.

CPSIA information can be obtained at www.ICGtesting.com
Printed in the USA
238391LV00002B/33/P